the superlatives

Also by Jennifer Echols

Endless Summer

The One That I Want

The Ex Games

Major Crush

Going Too Far

Forget You

Love Story

Such a Rush

Dirty Little Secret

the superlatives

biggest flirts

JENNIFER ECHOLS

Simon Pulse

New York   London   Toronto   Sydney   New Delhi

SIMON PULSE

An imprint of Simon & Schuster Children's Publishing Division

1230 Avenue of the Americas, New York, NY 10020

This Simon Pulse edition May 2014

Text copyright © 2014 by Jennifer Echols

Cover photographs copyright © 2014 by Michael Frost

All rights reserved, including the right of reproduction

in whole or in part in any form.

SIMON PULSE and colophon are registered trademarks of Simon & Schuster, Inc.

For information about special discounts for bulk purchases, please contact

Simon & Schuster Special Sales at 1-866-506-1949 or business@simonandschuster.com.

The Simon & Schuster Speakers Bureau can bring authors to your live event. For more information

or to book an event contact the Simon & Schuster Speakers Bureau at 1-866-248-3049

or visit our website at www.simonspeakers.com.

Cover design by Regina Flath

Interior design by Mike Rosamilia

The text of this book was set in Adobe Caslon Pro.

Manufactured in the United States of America

2 4 6 8 10 9 7 5 3 1

Library of Congress Cataloging-in-Publication Data

Echols, Jennifer.

Biggest flirts / Jennifer Echols. — First Simon Pulse edition.

p. cm. — (The Superlatives)

Summary: Tia likes to flirt, but she isn't looking for a serious relationship. Will is the same way—

at least, that's what Tia thinks. But Will wants a real girlfriend, so despite their chemistry,

he starts dating someone else. Then Tia and Will are elected their yearbook's

Biggest Flirts, and things get really complicated.

[1. Dating (Social customs)—Fiction. 2. Flirting—Fiction. 3. Self-perception—Fiction.

4. High schools—Fiction. 5. Schools—Fiction. 6. Florida—Fiction.] I. Title.

PZ7.E1967Bi 2014

[Fic]—dc23

2013027781

ISBN 978-1-4424-7446-8 (hc)

ISBN 978-1-4424-7445-1 (pbk)

ISBN 978-1-4424-7447-5 (eBook)

For my son,
an awesome drummer

1

"YOU MUST BE TIA CRUZ."

I glanced up at the guy who'd sat next to me and said this quietly in my ear, in an accent from elsewhere. We were on the crowded back porch with the lights off, but beyond the porch ceiling, the summer night sky was bright with a full moon and a glow from the neon signs at the tourist-trap beaches a few miles south.

The diffuse light made everybody look better: smoothed out acne, canceled a bad hair day. And I definitely had on my beer goggles. Boys grew more attractive when I was working on my second brew. This guy was the hottest thing I'd seen all summer. He was taller than me by quite a bit—which didn't happen too often—with dark hair long enough to cling to his T-shirt collar, a long straight nose, and lips that quirked sideways in a smile. But I wasn't fooled. In the sober light of day, he probably ranked right up there with the eighty-year-old men who wore Speedos to the beach.

What drew me in despite my misgivings was the diamond stud in his ear. Who knew what he was trying to say with this fashion statement. Unfortunately for me, I was a sucker for a bad boy, and his earring flashed moonlight at me like a homing beacon under a banner that said THIS WAY TO PIRATE.

I told him, "I *might* be Tia." What I meant was, *For you, I am Tia. I'll be anybody you're looking for.* "Who wants to know?"

"Will Matthews. I just moved here." We were sitting too close for a proper handshake, but he bent his arm, elbow close to his side, and held out his hand.

"Really!" I exclaimed as our hands touched. Our small town was stuck in the forgotten northwest corner of Pinellas County, on the very edge of the Tampa Bay metropolitan area. The guidebooks called us a hidden gem because of the artsy downtown, the harbor, and our unspoiled beaches, but the thing about a hidden gem was that it tended to stay hidden. Some tourists came through here. A few newcomers did move here. But most of them were, again, elderly men in banana hammocks. The families who serviced the snowbirds and tourists had lived here forever. My friend Sawyer had shown up only a couple of years before, but even his dad had grown up here. New kids at school were rare. Girls were going to be *all over* this guy: fresh meat.

Will pointed toward the house. "I introduced myself to your friends inside. They told me I would find you by the beer."

"My friends are a riot." My best friends, Harper and Kaye, didn't drink. That was cool with me. I did drink, which was not cool with them. Over the years, though, Harper's reasoned arguments and Kaye's hysterical pleas had mellowed into concerned monitoring and snarky jokes.

This time their witty line wasn't even correct. I was *not* by the beer. Along with six or seven other people from school, I was sitting on a bench built into the porch railing, and the cooler was underneath me. Technically I was *above* the beer. Drinking on Brody Larson's back porch was standard operating procedure. Most of the houses near downtown were lined up along a grid, backyards touching. When parents unexpectedly came home, interrupting a party, somebody would grab the cooler as we escaped through the palm trees to another daredevil's house to start over. If this was the first thing Will learned about our town, he was my kind of guy. I reached into the cooler, my braids brushing the porch floor. I fished out a can for myself and handed him the beer he'd come for.

"Oh." He took the can and looked at it for a moment. He was expecting, maybe, a better brand of free beer? Then, without opening it, he swiped it across his forehead. "Are you even sweating? Perspiring, I mean."

"Why do you want to know whether I'm perspiring, Mr. Matthews?" I made my voice sound sexy just to get a guffaw out of him.

"Because you look . . ." He glanced down my body, and I enjoyed that very much. ". . . cool," he finished. "It's hot as an ahffen out here."

I popped open my beer. "A what?"

"What," he repeated.

"You said 'ahffen.' What's an ahffen?"

"An ahh . . ." He waited for me to nod at this syllable. "Fen." Suddenly he lost patience with me. Before I could slide away—actually I would have had nowhere to slide, because Brody and his girlfriend Grace were making out right next to me—Will grabbed my wrist and brought my hand to his lips. "Let me sound it out for you. Ahhhffen." I felt his breath moving across my fingertips.

"Oh, an *oven*!" I giggled. "You're kidding, right? It's ten o'clock at night."

He let my hand go, which was not what I'd wanted at *all*. "I've been here one whole day, and I've already gotten my fill of people making fun of the way I talk, thanks." He sounded halfway serious.

"Poor baby! I wasn't making fun of you. I was just trying to figure out what an ahffen was." I elbowed him gently in the ribs.

He still didn't smile. That was okay. I liked brooding pirates. I asked him, "Who made fun of you?"

"Some jerk waiting tables at the grill where my family ate tonight. We can't cook at home yet. Most of the furniture showed up, but apparently the refrigerator got off-loaded in Ohio."

"Uh-oh. Was that all you lost, or did the moving company also misplace your microwave in Wisconsin and your coffeemaker in the Mississippi River?"

"Funny." Now he was grinning at me.

Warm fuzzies crept across my skin. I loved making people laugh. Making a hot guy laugh was my nirvana.

He went on, "I'm sure we'll find out what else we're missing when we need it. Anyway, the waiter at the restaurant seemed cool at first. I think both my little sisters fell in love with him. He told me I should come to this party and meet some people. Then he started in on my Minnesota accent and wouldn't let go." Will pronounced it "Minne*sooo*da," which cried out for imitation. Plenty of people around here talked like that, but they were retirees from Canada. I decided I'd better let it drop.

"Was this grill the Crab Lab downtown?" I pointed in the direction of the town square, which boasted said restaurant where I'd worked until yesterday, the antiques store where I still worked (or tried not to), the salon where my sister Izzy cut hair, and Harper's mom's bed and breakfast. The business district was rounded out by enough retro cafés and kitschy gift shops that visitors were fooled into thinking our town was like something out of a 1950s postcard—until they strolled by the gay burlesque club.

"Yeah," Will said. "We had misgivings about a place called the Crab Lab, like there would be formaldehyde involved. If there was, we couldn't taste it."

"The Crab Lab may sound unappetizing, but it's an unwritten rule that names of stores in a tourist town have to alliterate or rhyme. What else are you going to call a seafood joint? Lobster Mobster? Hey, that's actually pretty good." I doubled over, cracking up at my own joke. "The slogan would be, 'We'll break your legs.' Get it? Because you crack open lobster legs? No, wait, that's crab."

He watched me with a bemused smile, as if waiting for

me to pull a prescription bottle out of my purse and announce that I'd missed my meds.

I tried again. "Calamari . . . Cash and Carry? I set myself up badly there. Okay, so Crab Lab is a stupid name. I'm pretty attached to the place, though."

"Do you eat there a lot?"

"You could say that. I just quit serving there. Did this jerk who was making fun of you happen to have white-blond hair?"

"That's him."

"That's Sawyer," I said. "Don't take it personally. He would pick on a newborn baby if he could think of a good enough joke. You'll be seeing lots more of Sawyer when school starts."

"The way my summer's been going, that doesn't surprise me at all." Will stared at the beer can in his hand. He took a breath to say something else.

Just then the marching band drum major, DeMarcus, arrived to a chorus of "Heeeey!" from everybody on the porch. He'd spent the past month with his grandparents in New York. A few of us gave Angelica, the majorette DeMarcus was leading by the hand, a less enthusiastic "Hey." The lukewarm greeting probably wasn't fair. It's just that we remembered what a tattletale she'd been in ninth grade. She'd probably changed, but nobody gave her the benefit of the doubt. As she walked through, some people turned their heads away as if they thought she might jot down their names and report back to their parents.

I stood as DeMarcus spread his arms to hug me. He said, "Harper told me you were back here sitting on the beer. I'm like, 'Are you sure? Tia is *in charge* of something? That's a first.' But I guess since it's beer, it's fitting."

"Those New Yorkers really honed your sense of humor." I sat down to pull out a can for him. Obviously it hadn't occurred to him that, unless a miracle saved me, I was drum captain. Starting tomorrow, the first day of band camp, I would be in charge of one of the largest sections and (in our own opinion) the most important section of the band. I'd spent the whole summer pretending that my doomsday of responsibility wasn't going to happen. I had one night left to live in that fantasy world.

As I handed the beer up to DeMarcus, Angelica asked close to his shoulder, "Do you have to?"

"One," he promised her. "I just spent ten hours in the airport with my mother."

Will chuckled at that. I thought maybe I should introduce him to DeMarcus. But I doubted my edgy pirate wanted to meet my band geek friend. Will made no move to introduce himself.

As DeMarcus opened his beer and took a sip, I noticed old Angelica giving Will the eye. Oh, *no*, girlfriend. I lasered her with an exaggerated glare so scary that she actually startled and stepped backward when she saw me. I bit my lip to keep from laughing.

With a glance at Will, DeMarcus asked me, "Where's Sawyer?"

Damn it! Sawyer and I hung out a lot, but we weren't dating. I didn't want to give Will the impression that I was taken. "Sawyer's working," I told DeMarcus dismissively. "He's coming later."

"I'm sure I'll hear him when he gets here," DeMarcus said. True. Sawyer often brought the boisterous college dropout waiters he'd already gotten drunk with on the back porch of the Crab Lab. Or firecrackers. Or both.

As DeMarcus moved along the bench to say hi to everybody else, with Angelica in tow, Will spoke in my ear. "Sounds like you know Sawyer pretty well. Is he your boyfriend?"

"Um." My relationship with Sawyer was more like the friendship you'd fall into when there was nobody more interesting in prison. Everybody at school knew he wasn't my boyfriend. We tended to stick together at parties because we were the first ones to get there and the last ones to leave.

I wasn't sure how to explain this to an outsider without sounding like a drunk floozy . . . because, to be honest, I was something of a drunk floozy. Not that this had bothered me until I pictured myself sharing that information with a handsome stranger.

I said carefully, "We've been out, but we're not together now." Changing the subject so fast that Will and I both risked neck injury, I asked, "What city are you from? Minneapolis?"

"No."

"St. Paul?"

"No, Duluth."

"Never heard of it."

"I know." He raised the unopened beer can to his forehead again. Perspiration was beading at his hairline and dripping toward his ear. I felt sorry for him. Wait until it got hot tomorrow.

"What's Duluth like?" I asked.

"Well, it's on Lake Superior."

"Uh-huh. Minnesota's the Land of a Thousand Lakes, isn't it?" I asked. Little had Mr. Tomlin known when he interrogated us on state trivia in third grade that I would later find it useful for picking up a Minnesotan.

"Ten Thousand Lakes," Will corrected me with a grin.

"Wow, that's a lot of lakes. You must have been completely surrounded. Did you swim to school?"

He shook his head no. "Too cold to swim."

I couldn't imagine this. Too cold to swim? Such a shame. "What did you do up there, then?" I ran my eyes over his muscular arms. Will didn't have the physique of a naturally strong and sinewy boy such as Sawyer, but of an athlete who actively worked out. I guessed, "Do you play football?"

His mouth cocked to one side. He was aware I'd paid him a compliment about his body. "Hockey," he said.

A hockey player! The bad boy of athletes who elbowed his opponent in the jaw just for spite and spent half the period in the penalty box. I loved it!

But my reverence for him in my mind didn't make it to my mouth. I had to turn it into a joke. "Ha!" I exclaimed. "Good luck with *that* around here. We're not exactly a hockey mecca."

"Tampa Bay has an NHL team," he reminded me.

"Yeah, but nobody *else* here plays. The NHL rinks are probably the only ones in the entire metropolitan area. A high school guy playing hockey in Tampa makes as much sense as the Jamaican bobsled team."

I'd meant it to be funny. But his mouth twitched to one side again, this time like I'd slapped him. Maybe he was considering for the first time that our central Florida high school might not have a varsity hockey team.

I sipped my beer, racking my brain for a way to salvage this conversation, which I'd really been digging. He held his beer in both hands like he was trying to get all the cold out of it without actually drinking it. His eyes roved the corners of the porch, and I wondered whether he was searching for Angelica as a way to escape from me if she and DeMarcus got tired of each other.

Before I could embarrass myself with another gem from my stand-up routine, the porch vibrated with deep whoops of "Sawyer!" The man himself sauntered up the wooden steps to the porch, waving with both hands like the president in his inauguration parade—but only if he'd bought the election. Nobody in their right mind would elect Sawyer to a position of responsibility. The only office he'd ever snagged was school mascot. He would be loping around the football field this year in a giant bird costume.

What didn't quite make sense about Sawyer De Luca was his platinum hair, darker at the roots and brighter at the sun-bleached tips like a swimmer who never had to come in from the ocean and go to school. The hair didn't go with his Italian name or his dark father and brother. He must have looked like his mom, but she lived in Georgia and nobody had ever met her. A couple of years ago, she sent him to live with his dad, who was getting out of prison, because she couldn't handle Sawyer anymore. At least, that's what Sawyer had told me, and it sounded about right.

After shaking a few hands and embracing DeMarcus, Sawyer sauntered over and stood in front of Will. Not in front of *me*. He didn't acknowledge me at all as he stepped into Will's personal space and said, looking down at him, "You're in my place."

"Oh Jesus, Sawyer!" I exclaimed. Why did he have to pick a fight while I was getting to know the new guy? He must have had a bad night. Working with his prick of an older brother, who ran the bar at the Crab Lab, tended to have that effect on him.

I opened my mouth to reassure Will that Sawyer meant no harm. Or, maybe he did, but I wouldn't let Sawyer get away with it.

Before I could say anything, Will rose. At his full height, he towered over Sawyer. He looked down on Sawyer exactly as Sawyer had looked down on *him* a moment before. He growled, "This is your place? I don't *think* so."

The other boys around us stopped their joking and said in warning voices, "Sawyer." Brody put a hand on Sawyer's chest. Brody really was a football player and could have held

Sawyer off Will single-handedly. Sawyer didn't care. He stared up at Will with murder in his eyes.

I stood too. "Come on, Sawyer. You were the one who told Will about this party in the first place."

"I didn't invite him *here*." Sawyer pointed at the bench where Will had been sitting.

I knew how Sawyer felt. When I'd looked forward to hooking up with him at a party, I was disappointed and even angry if he shared his night with another girl instead. But that was our long-standing agreement. We used each other when nobody more intriguing was available. Now wasn't the time to test our pact. I said, "You're some welcome committee."

The joke surprised Sawyer out of his dark mood. He relaxed his shoulders and took a half step backward. Brody and the other guys retreated the way they'd come. I wouldn't have put it past Sawyer to spring at Will now that everyone's guard was down, but he just poked Will—gently, I thought with relief—on the cursive *V* emblazoned on his T-shirt. "What's the *V* stand for? Virgin?"

"The Minnesota Vikings, moron," I said. Then I turned to Will. "You will quickly come to understand that Sawyer is full of sh—"

Will spoke over my head to Sawyer. "It stands for 'vilification.'"

"What? Vili . . . What does that mean?" Knitting his brow, Sawyer pulled out his phone and thumbed the keyboard. I had a large vocabulary, and his was even bigger, but we'd both found that playing dumb made life easier.

Will edged around me to peer over Sawyer's shoulder at the screen. At the same time, he slid his hand around my waist. I hadn't seen a move that smooth in a while. I liked the way Minnesota guys operated. He told Sawyer, "No, not two *L*'s. One *L*."

Sawyer gave Will another wild-eyed warning. His gaze dropped to Will's hand on my waist, then rose to my serious-as-a-heart-attack face. He told Will, "Okay, SAT. I'll take my vocabulary quiz over here." He retreated to the corner of the porch to talk with a cheerleader.

Relieved, I sat back down on the bench, holding Will's hand on my side so that he had to sit down with me or get his arm jerked out of its socket. He settled closer to me than before. With his free hand, he drummed his fingers on his knee to the beat of the music filtering onto the porch. The rhythm he tapped out was so complex that I wondered whether he'd been a drummer—not for marching band like me, but for some wild rock band that got into fistfights after the hockey game was over.

As we talked, he looked into my eyes as if I was the only

girl at the party, and he grinned at all my jokes. Now that my third beer was kicking in, I let go of some of my anxiety about saying exactly the right thing and just had fun. I asked him if he was part of our senior class. He was. It seemed obvious, but he *could* have been a freshman built like a running back. Then I explained who the other people at the party were according to the Senior Superlatives titles they were likely to get—Best Car, Most Athletic, that sort of thing.

My predictions were iffy. Each person could hold only one title, preventing a superstar like my friend Kaye from racking up all the honors and turning the high school yearbook into her biography. She might get Most Popular *or* Most Likely to Succeed. She was head cheerleader, a born leader, and good at everything. Harper, the yearbook photographer, might get Most Artistic *or* Most Original, since she wore funky clothes and retro glasses and always thought outside the box.

"What about you?" Will asked, tugging playfully at one of my braids.

"Ha! Most Likely to Wake Up on Your Lawn."

He laughed. "Is that a real award?"

"No, we don't give awards that would make girls cry. I'll probably get Tallest." That wasn't a real one either.

He cocked his head at me. "Funniest?"

I rolled my eyes. "That's like getting voted Miss Congeniality in a beauty pageant. It's a consolation prize."

A line appeared between his brows. He rubbed his thumb gently across my lips. "Sexiest."

"You obviously haven't surveyed the whole senior class."

"I don't have to."

Staring into his eyes, which crinkled at the corners as he smiled, I knew he was handing me a line. And I *loved* this pirate pickup of his. I let my gaze fall to his lips, willing him to kiss me.

"Hi there, new guy!" Aidan said as he burst out the door. He crossed the porch in two steps and held out his hand for Will to shake. "Aidan O'Neill, student council president."

I made a noise. It went something like "blugh" and was loud enough for Aidan to hear. I knew this because he looked at me with the same expression he gave me when I made fun of his penny loafers. He was Kaye's boyfriend, so I tried to put up with him. But we'd been assigned as partners on a chemistry paper last year, and any semblance of friendship we might have had was ruined when he tried to correct me incorrectly during my part of the presentation. I'd told him to be right or sit down. The only thing that made Aidan madder than someone challenging him was someone challenging him in public.

"Blugh" wasn't a sufficient warning for Will not to talk

to him, apparently. Aidan sat down on Will's other side and launched into an overview of our school's wonders that Minnesota probably had never heard of, such as pep rallies and doughnut sales.

"Time for everybody to get lost," Brody called. "My mom will be home from the Rays game in a few minutes."

"Thanks for hosting," I told him.

"Always a pleasure. Looks like this time you may have more pleasure than you can handle, though." He nodded toward the stairs, where Sawyer was waving at me.

Sawyer held up his thumb and pointer together, which meant, *I have weed. Want to toke up?*

I shook my head in a small enough motion that Will didn't notice, I hoped. Translation: *No, I'm taking Will home if I can swing it.*

Sawyer raised one eyebrow and lowered the other, making a mad scientist face. It meant, *You'd rather go home with this guy than get high with me? You have finally lost your marbles.*

I raised both eyebrows: *We have an agreement. We stick together unless something better comes along. This is something better.*

He flared his nostrils—*Well, I never!*—and turned away. He might give me a hard time about it when I saw him next, but Sawyer and I never really got mad at each other, because why would you get mad at yourself?

I turned to rescue Will from Aidan and saw to my horror that Aidan was disappearing back into the house. Will stared right at me with a grim expression, as if he'd witnessed the entire silent conversation between Sawyer and me, understood it, and didn't like it. "Don't let me keep you," he said flatly.

Damn Sawyer! We would laugh about this later if I wasn't so hot for the boy sitting next to me. This was not funny.

Heart thumping, I tried to save my night with Will. There wasn't any time to waste. If word that Brody was closing down the party got inside to Kaye and Harper before I left, they would try to stop me from hooking up with the new guy. They might have sent him back to meet me, but they wouldn't want me leaving with him. They didn't approve of Sawyer, either, but at least they knew him. Will was a wild card. They would find this frightening. I found him perfect.

I slid my hand onto his knee and said, "I'd rather go with you. Could you walk me home?"

And then some.

2

"FLORIDA ISN'T AGREEING WITH YOU SO FAR?" I asked Will, swinging his hand as we strolled down the sidewalk toward my neighborhood, old houses lining the street, palm trees and live oaks overhead.

"It's too soon to judge," he said. "So far it seems hot and weird."

"Are you sure that's Florida and not me?"

The warm notes of his chuckle sent tingles racing up my arm. "You're not weird. *That's* weird." He nodded toward the crazy monster face carved into the stump by Mrs. Spitzer's house.

"That's not weird either," I said. "That's artistic. Just ask the Chamber of Commerce. We have a large number of creative people in town, but that doesn't make us any stranger than a town in Minneso—"

We both stopped short. An enormous white bird, about a yard tall from feet to beak, stood in the center of the sidewalk in front of us.

Will arched his brows, waiting for me to take back my protest that Florida wasn't weird.

"That is a snowy egret," I said self-righteously. "They are very common. In Minnesota you have moose wandering the streets."

"You're mixing us up with an old fictional TV show about Alaska. Get behind me. I'll protect you." He nobly placed himself between me and the egret as we edged into the street to go around it, then hopped up on the sidewalk again. Will kept looking back at the bird, though, like he thought it would stalk us. "Honestly, more than the weirdness, it's the heat that's getting to me. Right now in Duluth it's probably in the fifties."

I shook my head. "If I lived there, I would lose so many parkas at parties."

"Parkas!" He gave me a quizzical smile. "You don't really have an autumn here, do you?"

"Define 'autumn.'"

"The leaves turn colors."

"No, we don't have that."

"Hmm. It doesn't even get cool?"

"Define 'cool.'"

"Below freezing."

"Jesus Christ, that's *cool*?" I exclaimed. "We would call out the National Guard for that. But it *has* gotten below freezing here before."

"When?"

I waved away the question, because I didn't know the answer. "There's probably a plaque commemorating the event on the foundation of the Historical Society building. Turn here." We walked up my street. Even if the power to the streetlights had gone out and the moon and the stars had been blocked by clouds, I would have known when we approached my house from the sound of the crispy magnolia leaves strewn across the sidewalk. Several years' worth.

He nodded ahead of us. "Isn't that the high school behind the fence?"

"In all its glory." I swept my arm in an arc wide enough that I pitched myself off balance and stumbled over a root that had broken through the sidewalk. Will grabbed my arm before I fell.

The campus didn't look too impressive. I'd had a good time for my first three-fourths of high school, but that was because I had a lot of friends and didn't do a lot of homework, not because the school was some kind of fun factory.

It was just a low concrete block labyrinth built to withstand hurricanes, although the gym and auditorium were taller, and our football stadium was visible in the distance. There were lots of palm trees, too, and a parking lot bleached white by the sun.

"That's a convenient location for you," Will said. "Though I guess you have to go all the way around the fence to get to the front entrance."

"Yeah, I ride my bike when I have time. Then I can go straight to work after school. But some mornings I'm running late. Well, most mornings. Then I go over the fence."

"What if you have books and homework to carry?"

"I don't do my homework, so I don't bring my books home."

"Oh." He followed me onto the front porch and waited while I unlocked the door. When I turned back to him, his head was cocked to one side like he was trying to puzzle me out.

I didn't play games with people. Mostly I told the truth. What you saw was what you got. Maybe that confused him.

"Come in?" I asked.

He stared at me a second too long, as if he couldn't quite believe what he was hearing. "Sure."

He didn't *seem* sure, though. The swashbuckling pirate I'd

wanted was retreating over the waves, and I didn't know why. He wasn't drunk. In fact, now that I thought about it, had he even opened the beer I'd handed him? Maybe he was tired from his move. I knew if I'd moved to Minnesota after living in Florida for seventeen years, I would have been stumbling around the frozen tundra, crying, *Where am I?*

To reassure him that everything was okay, I took him by the hand and led him into the house. I didn't flick on the light, because that would only have scared him. My dad and I hadn't finished unpacking from the last time we moved. It seemed futile, when the house wasn't big enough to hold our stuff. The space that wasn't taken up with furniture was filled with half-empty boxes. I tugged Will on a path so familiar I didn't need lights, through the den and down a short hall into my room and onto my bed.

He sat down next to me, his weight drawing me toward him on the mattress. Street lamps cast the only light through the window blind. Stripes of shadow moved up his broad chest and arms, his strong neck, and his sharp chin darkened with stubble. I wondered again if he could possibly look as good in broad daylight as he did in the sexy night.

Will might have been wondering the same thing about me. He pulled my hand toward him and clasped it in both of his, massaging my fingers. He looked me over—my hair, my eyes, my shoulders, my breasts—like he wanted to remember every inch of me. It was oddly touching but also strange. I kept getting mixed messages from him. He seemed to want me as much as I wanted him, but something was holding him back. Maybe he thought I'd be an ugly duck if he saw me walking down the street during the day. Or his reluctance might have had nothing to do with me. I wondered if there was trouble back home in Minnesota.

I reached up to rub my thumb across the line between his brows. "So worried," I whispered. "Relax." I swept my fingers through his hair and gently pinched his earring that I found so fascinating.

I'd hit upon his trigger. He sucked in a little gasp. Then he plunged both hands into my hair and held me steady while he kissed me.

I was surprised at how hot his mouth was. His lips pressed the corner of my mouth at first, then the other corner, then kissed me full on. His tongue teased my lips apart and swept inside.

We made out for a long while. He was a great kisser, gently controlling me. I could have stayed just like that with him for hours. But by this time, most guys would have made another move. When he didn't, I was afraid I'd mistakenly given him the message that I didn't want more. I took him by both shoulders and pulled him down on top of me as I lay back on the bed.

He held himself off me. I thought for a split second he was going to back away. But he was only arranging himself so that our bodies fit together, his mouth on my neck, his hands on my breasts, his erection pressed against me. He settled more of his weight on top of me, and I sighed with satisfaction.

"Wow," he whispered against my lips. "I like Florida better now." He kissed me deeply before moving to my earlobe.

I turned my head so he could reach my ear better. I was rewarded with a gentle explosion of tingles that spread down my neck and made the hair stand up all over my body.

"Do you like that?" he asked, inducing delicious shivers.

"Not really," I said drily.

He chuckled in my ear. This was the hottest thing he'd done yet.

He trailed one hand from my ear down my neck, traced his fingers lightly across my breastbone, and deftly undid the top button of my shirt. "Do you like this?"

"It's okay," I managed between gasps as his fingers continued downward. They blazed a trail of fire across my skin, paused to release another button, and traveled down again. When he reached the bottom, I panted in anticipation.

He reversed direction and smoothed one side of my shirt back against my shoulder. After fumbling underneath me to unhook my bra, he moved the satin out of the way too. With a light scratch of his stubble across my tender skin, he put his mouth on my breast.

"What?" I murmured.

He laughed against me, each puff of his warm breath sending a fresh chill across my chest. "You don't like this?"

"No, that I'm sure I like."

In agreement, he took me inside his hot mouth. For long minutes I was afraid I might explode with pleasure, holding my breath for each new thoughtful stroke of his tongue. Boys had done this to me before, yet not so slowly or thoroughly. Not like this.

I didn't want him to stop, but I couldn't be greedy. I took his cheek in my palm and brought his lips up to meet mine. Then I moved my hand down between us, under his weight, and into his waistband. I knew he was enjoying it because he forgot to keep kissing me.

"Do you like this?" I asked innocently, as if I didn't know the answer.

Will was holding his breath like I had been before. On a couple of quick exhalations, he grunted, "I haven't decided. Keep doing that . . . until I collect enough data."

This was something I pictured a good-looking, wholesome nerd like DeMarcus saying if Angelica ever had the courage to reach down his pants. But Will said it with the irony of a smart, worldly pirate. I giggled.

Through my laughter, I was careful to continue touching him. I didn't want to make him choose between feeling good and cracking jokes. This perfect boy, sent to sit next to me at a party, was quickly becoming one of my best friends with bennies. If he kept sounding so pleasantly shocked at what I was doing to him, he might even replace Sawyer as my favorite bad boy.

Brightness grew in the room. Headlights shone in from a car turning around in my driveway. The lines of light across Will's face changed and moved. As they caressed his jawline, I was surer than ever that his good looks weren't my imagination.

He was watching me again, and the worry line between his brows was back. "Don't tell me. Your dad's home."

"Oh, no," I assured him. "That's probably my friend Kaye—we talked about her, and I think you met her inside at the party—and her boyfriend Aidan. You know, student council president," I reminded him in a smarmy Aidan imitation. In a normal tone I said, "They stopped by to check that I got home okay before Aidan has to get Kaye back for her curfew."

It must have been a lot later than I'd thought. I didn't have a clock in my room, which was the way I liked it. I didn't want to feel nagged. But I did wonder about the time. It seemed like my night with Will had passed in an instant.

The bright light hung around for an annoyingly long time. I rolled out from under Will, crawled across the bed, stuck my hand through the slats in the window blind, and waved. The headlights retreated.

When I turned back to Will, he was sitting up on the bed, smiling at me. "You have good friends."

"Yeah. So good I want to kill them sometimes."

He pulled his phone out of his back pocket. "God, it's late. I'd better go. My mom's called me three times."

"That's so sweet!"

"Yeah. She's worried about me in a strange town and all, and I have to be somewhere at eight in the morning."

Something wasn't right here. Will didn't seem like the type of guy who went home so he would be rested for an early morning, or whose mother would check up on him. And even if she did, most boys I knew wouldn't admit this to a girl. But people were different. Maybe even pirates went to bed at a decent hour in Minnesota.

Then he motioned to a spot in front of him on the bed. "Come here, Tia."

JENNIFER ECHOLS

I could have made another joke out of it, crawling across the bed to him in a parody of a sex kitten. But he sounded so serious and looked so solemn that I simply slid closer.

He held my gaze as he maneuvered my bra back into place, then reached behind me to rehook it. He had some experience doing this, I gathered. Then he felt for my top button and fastened it, then the next. I'd never had a boy dress me before. As long as he watched me like I was the most beautiful girl he'd ever seen, he could put as many layers of clothing on me as he wanted. He fastened the last button, and his hand slid down to my thigh.

I asked him, "Do you know how to get home from here? Maybe *I* should walk *you*."

He squinted as he grinned. Then his smile faded. Stroking the corner of my mouth with one finger, he whispered, "I'd like that, if you would come inside and we could do this over again." He moved his hand to cup my jaw, coming closer until the tip of his nose rubbed mine. He kissed me again, so slowly, just tasting at first and then more deeply, like we had all the time in the world and he was going to explore each angle, enjoying every second. Finally drawing away, he said, "And then *I* could walk *you* home, and we could do it again."

I wished I *could* spend this night with Will over and over.

It had been one of the best nights of my life. Repeating it with no thought to consequences and no concern for what happened next . . . that made it perfect.

After one final stroke of his hand through my hair, he picked up his phone. "What's your number?"

I gave it to him. Since the night did have to end, I wanted him to be able to get in touch with me the next time he got the urge to drink (or not) on someone's back porch and walk me home. It could happen, but only in the next few days. Most guys seemed to love hooking up with me, at least at first, but they paired off with a possessive girl pretty quickly. Afterward they wanted to cheat on their girlfriends with me, and that was something I refused to do. Kaye might not believe it, but even *I* had morals.

Will wouldn't be any different. Alcohol wasn't fooling with my perception anymore. By now I was almost sober, and he was still incredibly handsome as he squinted at his phone in the dark. His soft lips pursed in concentration. His long hair fell forward into his eyes. Looking like he did, and being the new guy at our school, he would have girls hanging off him by lunch on the first day. He wouldn't need me for a hookup anymore. But he'd been heaven while he lasted, and I was glad I'd seen him first.

My phone rang in my pocket, a snippet of a salsa tune, and

vibrated too. I pulled it out and glanced at his number with an unfamiliar area code. "That's titillating. Call me anytime."

He laughed, and I sighed with relief. I hadn't realized how nervous I'd gotten when he looked so pensive.

I tensed right back up again when he asked, "Are you busy tomorrow afternoon?"

I countered suspiciously, "What do you mean?"

"I thought I could take you to lunch, and then you could show me around town."

I didn't know what to say. Truthfully, I would be busy tomorrow. But he wasn't asking about just tomorrow. I could tell from his tone that if I wasn't able to go to lunch with him, he would ask for another date. Eventually we would hit on a time that I could fit into my schedule. But I didn't *want* to fit it into my schedule, and I couldn't let him go on thinking that I did. I might have been a lot of things, but a tease wasn't one of them.

A hookup after a party would have been fine with me. But the idea of a deliberate-sounding date made my stomach twist. All three of my sisters had gotten excited about a date. They'd been smitten quickly. The boys they'd dated became the most important people in their lives overnight. My sisters left high school before graduation to be with those boys. Two out of three boys had already abandoned them.

"Let me guess." Will took my hand and stroked my palm

with his thumb, sending a shiver down my arm. "It's such a small town that showing me around would take five minutes, and then what would we do?"

I laughed softly, because his guess was so far off. I pulled my hand away. "No. It just sounds kind of serious."

His brows went down. "Serious? What do you mean? It'll be fun."

"I mean, you're moving too fast."

"Too fast!" He looked around the ceiling. "Weren't you the one who invited me into your bedroom when your parents weren't home?"

So I was a little, shall we say, open with boys. I didn't see how that hurt anything. What bothered me was when boys participated equally, and seemed to enjoy it, then complained about it afterward like I was somehow at fault.

"You know what?" he backtracked. "I'm sorry. I got to Florida yesterday. It's a huge change, and I'm going through some other stuff. Maybe what I said didn't come out right. I didn't mean to creep you out and move in on you. We could just have lunch and that's all. Or just ride around and that's all. Or . . ." Searching my eyes, he ran out of words.

"No," I said, "I mean I don't want a boyfriend. Period."

Not a muscle moved in his face. I couldn't read his expression. He stared at me for a long time, as if he'd never heard of such a thing as a girl who didn't want a boyfriend. He wasn't taking this well.

Finally he nodded very slowly, then looked toward the ceiling again. "What I said *definitely* didn't come out right." He stood up and walked out of the room, headed for the front door. His eyes must have adjusted fully to the darkness, because not once did he scream out in pain as though he'd veered off the path and hit something sharp.

As I trailed after him, I reviewed the night, searching for the point when it had gone wrong. He wasn't the type of guy who just wanted a hookup. How had I missed this? I *was* that type of girl and made a point never to hide it. Why did it surprise him now?

Surely he hadn't been so attracted to me that he'd known I was wrong for him but pursued me anyway. I was okay looking, nothing special. A lot of guys seemed to like my auburn hair, but that usually got canceled out when they saw that I was almost their height. And while some boys enjoyed a flaky girl, others said I was stupid and couldn't stand me. At least I wasn't so flaky that I didn't know I was flaky.

But I felt like the biggest flake in Florida as Will opened the door, letting the warm, humid night mix with the air-conditioning. As he turned to face me, his earring glinted, and I felt myself flush all over again with the longing I'd felt when I first saw him. I *did not* want a boyfriend, but it felt wrong to let Will go.

He looked into my eyes, then gazed at my lips. I thought he would kiss me again. And then—just maybe—we could return this night to the place where we should have left it.

No such luck. Without touching me, he stepped off the stoop and onto what was probably the sidewalk under all those magnolia leaves. "Good night, Tia," he said over his shoulder.

"Are you sure you can get home?" I asked.

"I have GPS." He took out his phone and wagged it in the air. "If I can remember my own address." When he reached the street, he walked backward as he called, "Go inside and lock the door so I'll know you're okay."

"It's my house," I said defiantly.

"I'll worry." He stopped and watched me.

I frowned, but I backed inside and turned the deadbolt. Even Sawyer made me lock the door when he left.

I navigated to my room, lifted a slat in the blind, and watched Will. He turned the corner and disappeared up a dead-end street. I waited.

Sure enough, he came back to the corner, focusing on his phone. Then he gazed up at the sky like a seafarer lost on his Great Lake, looking to the stars for guidance.

He headed down the street toward town.

3

I WOKE TO THE SOUND OF MY DAD'S TRUCK in the driveway, which meant it was seven a.m. Bright morning light streamed through the window blind. I scowled, remembering what had happened the night before. I didn't understand Will, but I knew enough that I didn't want to. He was so hot, and kissed so well, and that earring! He was the type of guy I could get really attached to if I wasn't careful. And though I might not seem like the most conscientious person most of the time, I was always careful about boys.

Besides, I'd never been one to lament what happened the night before. I had a great day ahead of me.

All summer I'd been looking forward to band camp. I'd spent two and a half months closed up in Bob and Roger's antiques shop. They'd given me a raise last month. They were talking about promoting me to assistant manager, so I'd have to boss around Marvin of the too-small T-shirts printed with cat designs and Edwina of the constant smoke breaks.

I'd have to quit soon if Bob and Roger went through with their threat of giving me more responsibility. Just in case, I'd taken a second job at night, waiting tables at the Crab Lab. That hadn't been ideal either. Sawyer's brother kept coming on to me, which was going to work if he gave me any more beer, and it was getting hard for Sawyer to keep him off me.

Just as something bad was about to happen, I was saved by band. Because there were only four days until school started and two and a half weeks until our first game, we would practice on the football field a *lot*: eight a.m. to noon, then six to ten p.m., splitting the day to avoid the ridiculous heat of a Florida August. There went half my shift at the shop, and going in to the grill wasn't even worth it.

I looked forward to seeing my friends, and beating the hell out of my drum. The only reason I dreaded band this year was that I was drum captain, by virtue of the fact that the three guys and one girl ahead of me last year had graduated. I should have been more careful to place lower during tryouts last spring, but thinking ahead was not my forte. Since then, the other snare drummers had refused to challenge me for drum captain, no matter how nicely I begged them.

So I was saddled with the responsibility of rehearsing all the drums and keeping them in line, which was going to require a constant vigilance of which I wasn't capable. If I didn't convince someone to take over my position, we would make a bad score at a band contest in the fall, I knew it. I didn't mind personal failure so much, but I did *not* want to cause anybody else to crash and burn.

I was holding out for a miracle.

I wandered into the kitchen, where my dad, in grease-stained jeans and a polo shirt with the logo of the boat factory where he worked, stared into the open refrigerator. Good luck finding anything in there. It was packed to the brim, and most of the contents were no longer edible. I was pretty sure the meat drawer contained ham that my sister Violet had bought before she moved out last March.

I kissed my dad on the cheek. "Morning."

"Hey there, *lucita*." He hugged me with one arm while drawing a questionable bag of bagels out of the fridge with his other hand. In Spanish he said, "I thought band camp started today."

"Not until eight," I answered in English. My Spanish was rusty now that my sisters were gone.

"I'm late getting home because we had a safety meeting." He glanced at his watch. "It's eight-oh-five."

"Shit!" I squealed. "I don't have time for a shower! Do I smell?"

He sniffed the top of my head. "On a scale of one to ten? Six point five."

"I'll take it." I didn't ask whether six point five was closer to the stinky or the odorless end of the scale. I dashed for the bathroom, scrubbed my face and brushed my teeth in thirty seconds flat, and grabbed sunscreen and a beach towel. I spent considerably more time in my bedroom looking for my drumsticks and my flip-flops and a big hat and a bag to stuff everything into. I didn't have time to stuff it then. It was just another part of the panicked bundle. I ran back to the kitchen for a sports drink, which was safe to drink because it was sealed, and a pack of Pop-Tarts from the box on the counter. I didn't feel too hungover, but something told me that might change in the heat of ten a.m. if I didn't put something in my stomach. "Love you," I called to my dad, who'd given up on the fridge and disappeared. He was probably in bed already.

Outside on the porch, I locked the door—my keys were still in my pocket from last night—and found my sunglasses in my other pocket. I dashed down the street to the school fence and pitched my drumsticks over, then the sunscreen and my drink and the towel and the bag and the Pop-Tarts.

I kicked off my flip-flops, knowing from experience that I couldn't climb the fence with them on, and hiked myself over. I was lucky I had long legs. Kaye refused even to try this stunt. Too-adventurous-for-her-own-good Harper had attempted it and gotten stuck with one leg hooked over. The trick was lifting myself high enough that the rough tops of the boards didn't scrape my thighs. Triumphant, I dropped to the other side and gathered up the stuff I'd thrown over.

The drums were already rehearsing. Their racket carried out of the football stadium, around the school, and across the parking lot. And then I realized that I'd left my flip-flops on the other side of the fence. There was no time to go back.

"Shit shit shit." I took off across the parking lot, loose shells from the pavement cutting into the soles of my feet. I couldn't even go straight to the stadium. I had to stop at the band room first to drag my drum out of storage. By the time I made it to the field, I was twenty minutes late instead of five.

The stadium entrance was at parking-lot level, but the bleachers rose above me and also sank into the ground. As I hurried through the gate, I was high enough in the stands to see that Ms. Nakamoto had put DeMarcus to work pushing flutes into place according to the diagram she'd drawn for the start of the halftime show. Ms. Nakamoto had backed the drums into a corner of the field and appeared to be lecturing them. Maybe I could sneak up behind her and pretend I'd been there the whole time. Maybe I would also be elected the senior class's Most Likely to Succeed. Fat chance.

As I left the stands, hit the grass, and hurried past the majorettes tossing their batons in a bored fashion, Angelica asked, "Isn't that the same thing you were wearing last night?"

Despite that I was *very late*, I stopped. Angelica wasn't normally one to confront people or throw insults—at least not at me. She was more crafty, getting people in trouble behind the scenes. For her to call me out like this, she *definitely* had shared a look with Will last night. Since I'd screwed up everything with Will, he was sure to move on to another girl. It was none of my business, but I didn't want that new girl to be old Angelica.

I told her, "Why, no. Last night I was wearing that new guy."

A couple of majorettes standing close enough to overhear us cackled loudly. My friend Chelsea said, "Girl, you are *crazy*."

"It's a little early to be dressed to impress," I told her, talking over Angelica's scowling head. Angelica would be sorry she insulted me before nine a.m. I was not a morning person. I turned my back on them and waded through the dewy grass to the drums.

One of whom was Will Matthews.

I didn't recognize him at first in his mirrored aviator shades. He hadn't shaved, so his dark stubble made him look even scruffier than he had last night. But he wore a Minnesota Vikings baseball cap. And he stood tall like a warrior, out of place in our dopey drum line. He'd already taken off his shirt in the oppressive morning heat. His snare drum harness covered most of his chest and hooked over his shoulders, but he held his muscular arms akimbo, with his hands and sticks folded on top of his drum. His earring winked at me from underneath his dark hair.

What was *he* doing *here*?

As I tried to sneak past Ms. Nakamoto into the end of the drum line, a rumble through the drummers told her I was coming. She glanced over her shoulder at me, then down at her watch. "Ms. Cruz!" she called sharply. "You've been challenged, and you were about thirty seconds from forfeiting."

"Yes, ma'am. Sorry," I said with a sigh, trying to sound sad that I would have to give up my drum captain position if someone beat me. Really I was ecstatic. I'd been saved!

And I'd arrived at just the right time. She wasn't making me forfeit. If she had, I would have been dead last in the snare drum line, which could have been a fate worse than being first. Then I would have had to stand between some scared freshman on snare and a timid sophomore on quads. I had a tendency to frighten underclassmen.

With everyone staring at me, including Will, and a couple of juniors, Jimmy and Travis, who were making a point of looking bored to death, I pitched everything I'd been carrying off the top of my drum. Sunscreen, bag, drink, towel, Pop-Tarts. Ms. Nakamoto watched the process like she'd come to count on this sort of thing from me. Then I started the part of the drum cadence that we used for tryouts.

As my too-loud notes echoed around the stadium, I felt that high I loved so much. Playing drum stressed me out a little, because there was no room for mistakes, and mistakes were pretty much my modus operandi. But when I was under pressure, I loved to put things in their proper places, like bubbling in the correct answers on a standardized test. Beating a snare drum was the ultimate pastime if you occasionally enjoyed precision in your otherwise scatterbrained life.

But this time there was a catch. I had to be very careful to make a mistake. Otherwise I'd end up right back where I'd started, as drum captain. And because everyone else had already taken a turn without me here to listen, I didn't know whether to make a bunch of mistakes or just one. In the end I settled for missing the syncopated part that tended to trip people up in the middle. I'd never heard Will play, but something told me my pirate hadn't missed a note.

Sure enough, a moment after I was done, Ms. Nakamoto made a mark on her clipboard, then read off the new order. Will was first on snare, and the new drum captain. I was second.

My hero! I could have relaxed all summer if I'd known that my knight in shining armor would ride out of nowhere—Minnesota, actually, which amounted to the same thing—to save me from my own success, and my certain failure.

There was a lot of confusion as drummers reordered themselves according to Ms. Nakamoto's ruling, purposely knocking each other with their drums as they reshuffled. Then they took off their harnesses and set down the heavy drums. Now that the challenge was over, we were just waiting for Ms. Nakamoto or DeMarcus to pull us into the proper position for the first set. We didn't need to wear our drums for that. Eight snares, four bass drums, three quads, and four pairs of cymbals lay on the grass like the excavated skeleton of a dinosaur. The drummers themselves borrowed space on towels to sit down with the trumpets and trombones near the back of the band, or moved up front and tried to tickle the majorettes.

Normally I would have made the rounds and talked to

all my friends whom I hadn't seen during the summer. But I wasn't passing up the perfect opportunity to question the mysterious Mr. Matthews on the percussion skills he'd suddenly acquired. I retrieved my towel from my pile of stuff and spread it out on the grass. "Join me?" I asked him.

"Ssssssure." He eased his big frame down onto half of the towel and leaned back on his elbows, showing off his abs. The guy had a six-pack. Every girl in band—and some of the guys—turned to stare, then faced forward again like they'd just been looking around casually. It wasn't that six-packs were unusual at our school. Athletics were important. But the chiseled chest was less common in band.

Allowing the uncomfortable silence to stretch on, I smoothed sunscreen across my arms, legs, and face. I held the bottle toward him. "Need some?"

"We're in the shade," he said.

True. The high bleachers on the home and away sides provided a lot of shade in the morning and evening, and the ends of the stadium were surrounded by palm trees and live oaks that shaded the grass even more. But because the field sat lower than the surrounding ground, it got no breeze. None. The heat turned the stadium into a hundred-yard pressure cooker and ensured that somebody, sooner or later, was going to die of heat exhaustion. Though the sun wouldn't make us crispy by the end of practice, skin as white as Will's would turn an unhealthy pink. The sun was sneaky and would find its way to him.

"Trust me," I said.

He took the bottle grudgingly and squirted lotion into his palm to spread along one muscular shoulder. "You're saying I look like I'm from Minnesota."

"You look like a hockey player from Minnesota," I clarified. The flutes stared unabashedly at him as his hands moved over his own body, as if he was putting on a peep show. I asked, "Want me to get your back?"

He watched me sidelong for a moment. At least, I thought he did. His mirrored shades were in the way. All I could see was the shadow of his long lashes.

"Sure," he said again, leaning forward.

I spread sunscreen across his broad back, kneading his shoulders and neck as I went. All the way across the field, the majorettes were looking. Chelsea actually pointed at me. I waved cheekily at her. I wished I could see old Angelica's face from this distance.

I said softly in Will's ear, "You don't seem as surprised to see me here as I am to see you."

Through my own sunglasses, I couldn't tell whether a blush crept across his cheeks. His long silence spoke volumes, though. Finally he said, "I told you last night that your friends had sent me to find you and introduce myself to you."

"Yes, you did," I acknowledged, "but—"

"When I walked into the party, I said I was new and I played percussion in the marching band. They said, 'Oooh, you have to meet Tia Cruz, the drum captain.'"

I liked the way he imitated Harper and Kaye—not in the high faux-girly voice boys used when they didn't think very much of girls. The pitch of his voice stayed the same, but he smoothed over the *oooh* like they'd made me sound delicious, and he'd agreed.

But I was sure he hadn't mentioned anything to me about drums last night. I would remember. I hadn't been *that* drunk. In fact, I'd watched him tapping his fingers to the rhythm of the music and wondered if he was a drummer, but I hadn't put two and two together. "I thought they sent you to me because you wanted to get drunk and hook up."

He shifted to face me on the towel. "They would meet a complete stranger at a party and send him to hook up with their drunk friend?"

He had a point. Kaye and Harper were way more protective of me than that. "I guess not," I admitted. "I was drunk as I was thinking this." I went back over what had happened last night when I looked up from my bench and saw a pirate. His explanation didn't make sense. "No," I insisted. "I thought you wanted a beer. I gave you a beer. You took it."

"I didn't drink it."

I glanced around, suspicious that I had been transported to a parallel universe where high school boys didn't drink the beer they were given. But there was still only one sun, mostly blocked by a tall palm, and I didn't detect extra moons or a visible ring around the planet.

As I thought about it, though, I decided I'd seen his true nature from the beginning—if not when he found me on Brody's back porch, at least by the time he walked me home and acted like a gentleman instead of the scoundrel I was expecting. I'd seen it, but I hadn't wanted to see it.

Yet if he *was* that innocent, what business did he have coming to a party and deliberately sitting next to the girl over the cooler? I pointed out, "We spent a lot of time together last night. You had plenty of chances to tell me that you're on the drum line, or that we would be seeing each other again soon, as in *this morning*."

He nodded. "You've got me. I didn't intend to hide it from you. Once we started talking, I was having fun with you, and I didn't want anything to ruin it."

That I understood. I'd felt the same way the countless times I'd thought, *This boy is not a real pirate.*

"And I hoped we were heading for something really good. If we'd started dating, which honestly was what I *assumed* was going to happen after last night, the fact that we'd have to spend so much time standing right next to each other would have been *good* news."

"It's still good news," I assured him. "I just don't want a boyfriend."

"I get it," Will said.

Ms. Nakamoto issued instructions through her microphone then, commanding all the drums to move our equipment so DeMarcus could place clarinet players in a curlicue where we'd been sitting. As we lugged our stuff five yards downfield and plopped on the forty-five, I pondered whether Will really did "get it," as he'd said. My reasons for not wanting a boyfriend ran deep. Not even my closest friends completely got what I only half understood about myself.

"Jesus. It's. Hot!" Will took off his cap, poured bottled water over his head, slicked his fingers through his hair, and put his cap back on.

"You'll get used to it," I assured him, munching a Pop-Tart.

"By the time I get used to it, I'll be gone."

This was true for a lot of the old people who thought they wanted to retire here. They came into the antiques shop to buy knickknacks for the cute cottage where they planned to live out their days. They told me it was a lot hotter in Florida than they'd imagined, and they asked if we were in the midst of an unusually hot spell. I told them no. When they reappeared a few weeks later to sell their knickknacks back to me, they admitted they were packing up and heading back to Cleveland. They weren't as sick of five feet of snow each winter as they'd initially thought.

But a high school senior couldn't do what he chose, obviously, so Will's words sounded bitter. I wondered again whether he was taking my no-boyfriend rule the wrong way: that is, personally.

I teased him, which was my solution to every problem. "If you want to stay cool, getting rid of the Paul Bunyan beard might help."

He rasped one hand across his stubbly cheek. "I can't find my razor."

"Your refrigerator and now your razor?" I poked out my bottom lip in sympathy. "We have razors in Florida, you know. And stores to buy them in. We're not *that* weird."

"I didn't want to be late this morning." He glanced sideways at me. "To beat you in the challenge."

"Ohhhhh!" I sang. "That hurt." It didn't really, but he'd seemed so straight-laced in the bright light of morning that the jab did surprise me. "By the way, how did you memorize the drum cadence so quickly?" I'd arrived too late to hear him, but he must have played the challenge perfectly to pull ahead of me.

"As soon as I knew I was moving here, I wrote ahead and asked Ms. Nakamoto to send me the music," he explained. "I'd already planned to challenge you on the first day. I mean"—he corrected himself when I raised an eyebrow— "I'd planned to challenge the drum captain. I didn't know it was you. Until last night."

Then he leaned over until his breath tickled my ear. By now just about all the boys in the band had pulled off their shirts, and some girls had too if they'd remembered to wear a bikini top or sports bra underneath. But I was very aware of Will's bare chest in particular, and the way he'd set my skin on fire last night, as he whispered, "You let me beat you, didn't you?"

I gazed at him, neither confirming nor denying, and hoped that, behind my sunglasses, my eyes were as unreadable as his. I didn't like to lie, but I wasn't willing to admit this either.

He whispered again, "Don't worry. I won't tell anyone."

Ms. Nakamoto was calling to us again: Everybody up. Back to our places. The drum captain had to provide a beat while the whole band marched through the first formation of halftime. Drummers scrambled toward us from all corners of the field. But Will and I sat watching each other. We understood each other better than either of us was comfortable with.

The moment passed. He stood and pulled me up after him. We marched elbow to elbow through the first thirty-two measures of the song, then stopped to let DeMarcus shift people a few steps up or back according to what Ms. Nakamoto hollered.

"So, this school's mascot is the pelican?" Will asked.

I was relieved that he'd dropped the serious conversation. Or maybe he just didn't care to have one while the third- and fourth-chair snares, Jimmy and Travis, and all the cymbal players could hear us. As long as he wanted to be jocular, I didn't care why.

"You've come to this realization only gradually?" I asked. "How did you interpret the large sign at the entrance to campus that says HOME OF THE PELICANS?"

"I thought it was a *home* for *pelicans*." He gestured to five of them flying in formation overhead, on their way from one inlet to another.

"You did not."

"School mascots are supposed to be fierce," he explained.

"Cardinals and ducks and pelicans are poor choices. If you're going to pick a bird, pick one that hunts prey or eats carrion, at least."

"Right. Let me guess. You transferred here from Uptight Northern High School, Home of the Vultures."

"We aren't vultures." With mock self-righteousness, he said, "Our mascot is the Wrath of God."

I snorted with laughter I didn't quite feel. Granted, he'd been in town only two days. But I wished he'd referred to his other team as "they" rather than "we," and in the past tense. He still identified himself as a member of his old school, not this new one. If he had his way, he probably *would* make it back to Minnesota before he got used to the heat. I watched a bead of sweat crawl down the side of his neck.

And I felt a fresh pang of guilt that I was part of the reason he didn't like it here. I certainly hadn't helped matters by taking him home and then brushing him off. But I wasn't about to change my no-boyfriend policy just to make a cute stranger feel more welcome.

I said calmly, "I see. And your marching band was called the Marching Wrath of God?"

"Please tell me this band isn't the Marching Pelicans." He sounded horrified.

"Yes," I said with gusto. We weren't really. We were called

the Pride of Pinellas County. "It's weird, but no weirder than lutefisk." Another score, courtesy of lessons on state trivia in Mr. Tomlin's third-grade class.

"Oh!" Will gaped at me in outrage. "No lutefisk jokes. That is *low*."

"Just preparing you for when school starts." Sawyer would be at the top of the list for making lutefisk jokes.

"The Tampa Bay Rays have a good name," Will said contemplatively. "Stingrays kill somebody every once in a while, right?"

"Well, they used to have a manta ray on the logo, but now the Rays are supposed to be sun rays," I informed him. "Like *that's* dangerous."

He took off his hat, wiped his brow with his forearm, and put his hat back on. "Depends on whether you're from Minnesota."

I laughed heartily at this. "I could be wrong. Maybe they're just a bunch of guys named Ray. Plumbers."

"And their logo is an exposed butt crack."

I pointed at him with one drumstick. "Perfect! We should clue Sawyer in. That would make a great look for the team mascot."

Will squinted at me over the top of his sunglasses. "Sawyer?"

"Yeah. He's the school mascot, our dangerous pelican."

"Sawyer, your boyfriend?" He gave me what I imagined was a steely glare through his shades.

I'd made clear last night that I didn't have a boyfriend. And I *thought* I'd made clear—as clear as I could make a relationship when it was admittedly a bit cloudy to begin with—that if I did *acquire* a boyfriend, Sawyer wouldn't be it.

But in Will's voice I'd heard that same bitterness from a few minutes earlier. He pressed his lips tightly together. I was doomed to stand next to this guy for the rest of the year, and he was making sure that I knew at every turn how jealous he felt.

I didn't want a guy *acting* like a boyfriend any more than I wanted the real thing. But as we watched each other, tingles spread across my chest as if he was kissing my neck.

An electronic beep interrupted us. "Hold on," he said, raising one finger. Obviously he thought it was important that we come right back to this stare-down when he finished his other business. He pulled his phone from his pocket and glanced casually at the screen. As soon as he saw it, though, his jaw dropped. He tapped the phone with his thumb again.

"Fuck!" he shouted in a sharp crack that bounced against the bleachers. He turned toward the goalpost, reared back, and hurled his phone—quite an athletic feat, considering he was still wearing his snare drum.

"Oh, God," I exclaimed, "what's the matter?"

Travis said, "Nice arm," and Jimmy agreed, "Forty, fifty yarder."

Will pointed at them with both drumsticks. Afraid he was going to launch into a tirade and get in trouble with Ms. Nakamoto, I put a hand on his chest to stop him.

Too late. Everyone in the band had turned around to gape at him. The ones who hadn't heard his curse whispered questions to the people standing next to them about what he'd said. And Ms. Nakamoto had definitely heard him.

"Hey!" she hollered, hurrying over from a row of trombones. She must have forgotten Will's name, because if she'd known it, instead of "Hey!" she would have shouted an outraged *Mr. Matthews!* She hustled right up to the front of his snare drum and frowned at him, hands on her hips, whistle swinging on a cord. She was at least a foot shorter than him. "Is that how you talked during band practice where you came from?"

"No." He should have said "No, ma'am," but I didn't think *that* was how people talked in Minnesota either, and he hadn't been here long enough to know better. I hoped she wouldn't hold it against him.

"Do you think that's appropriate language for the drum captain?" she demanded. "Do you think you're a good role model for freshmen when you lose your cool like that? Because I can give the responsibility right back to Ms. Cruz if you can't handle it."

"Let's not be hasty," I spoke up.

"I'm really sorry," Will told her. On top of his drum, he gripped his sticks so tightly that his knuckles turned white. "I got this . . . this . . ."

"Upsetting message on your phone, when phones aren't allowed in band practice?" she prompted him.

Officially we had a rule against phones, but Ms. Nakamoto didn't normally enforce it because a lot of band camp was spent hurrying up and waiting for something to happen. She wouldn't have come down on him like this if he hadn't hollered the *F*-word an hour after becoming drum captain.

But I could save him. Placing one hand on his back, I leaned forward and said quietly to Ms. Nakamoto, "We'll just go for a short walk, okay? Will moved here yesterday all the way from Minnesota. It's a big adjustment, and things aren't going smoothly." I assumed from his reaction to the message that this was the understatement of the century.

Ms. Nakamoto turned her frown on me, then pursed her lips. I couldn't see her eyes behind her sunglasses, but I hoped I'd caught her off guard with my offer of help, which was probably a first for me in three years of high school band.

She muttered something and turned away. Not wasting any time lest she change her mind, I gave Will a little push in the direction of his phone.

"While you're over there, see if you can find some change I dropped at practice last year," Jimmy said.

Will turned to him angrily, his drum knocking against mine. He was beyond caring, obviously, and anything was liable to set him off now. The bad-boy hockey player I'd seen in him hadn't been entirely my imagination.

I whispered to Jimmy, "Shut up. You don't want *me* back in charge, do you?" I put my arm around Will's waist—the way he'd touched me at the party the night before—and steered him downfield.

4

WHILE MS. NAKAMOTO WENT BACK TO ISSUING
orders through her microphone, and the giggles of the clarinets faded behind us, Will and I walked toward the goalpost
and ditched our drums. I spotted his phone in the grass and
pointed it out to him. He didn't move any closer but instead
stared at it in distaste, his nostrils flared like he didn't want
to touch it. I plucked it out of the grass for him. It wasn't his
phone, though. It was one half of its plastic cover, emblazoned with a logo of a sunset behind evergreen trees and the
words MINNESOTA WILD.

A couple of yards farther on, I picked up the other half
of his phone cover. It was printed with the slogan MINNESOTA
IS THE STATE OF HOCKEY. Sad.

The phone itself glinted in the sunlight—smack on the

white goal line. I dusted off some of the lime before holding it out to him.

"You can look," he grumbled.

I didn't want to invade his privacy. But I was dying to know what had happened. And clearly he wanted to tell someone.

I peered at the screen. It was a text from someone named Lance. All it said was "Dude." Attached was a photo of a dark-haired beauty with porcelain skin. She smiled sweetly into the camera, eyes bright. A cute guy with curly blond hair kissed her neck.

"Who's the girl?" I asked, my heart sinking into my stomach.

He verified what I'd been thinking. "My girlfriend. Beverly."

I nodded. "Who's the guy?"

"My best friend."

I looked up at him sadly. "Only two days after you left?"

"The same day I left," he said. "I mean, that picture was from last night, but I already heard they got together the night before that."

"So she didn't waste any time after you broke up?" I asked gently.

"We didn't break up," he snapped. "I'm going to be down

here for only a year, and then I'm going back to Minnesota for college."

"Oh," I said. Right. He wouldn't be here long enough to get used to the heat.

"We weren't going to have to do the long-distance thing forever. Less than a year. We were going to see each other at Christmas when I visit my grandparents, and maybe spring break. So we said good-bye two days ago, and I left in my car, right? My parents wanted me to sell it, if anyone would even buy it, because they didn't trust me to drive it down here by myself. But I convinced them." He was talking with his hands now. The car was important. He had this in common, at least, with boys from Florida.

"I was at a gas station in Madison when I checked my texts. I had ten different messages from *everybody* that she was cheating on me *right then* with my best friend at a party." He pointed to the phone in my hands, as though this was all the phone's fault. "I tried to call her, but she didn't answer. I tried to call him. I thought maybe I should drive back and confront . . . somebody. But what good would that have done?" He paused like he wanted me to answer.

"Right," I said. Going back to fix it would have been like trying to repair a house of cards with a window open to the breeze.

He looked toward Ms. Nakamoto as rim taps raced across the field to us. While Will and I were missing, Jimmy was beating the rhythm for the band to march into the next formation.

"I ended up driving around Madison for an hour," Will said. "I knew going back to Minnesota wouldn't do any good. And I needed to get here in time to try out for drum captain today. But the farther I drove from home, the less relevant I was going to be to any of my friends' lives. Then my dad chewed me out for being an hour late to the checkpoint in Indianapolis. He kept asking me where I was all that time. I was watching my entire life go down the drain, thank you."

I set my sunglasses down on my nose so I could look at him in the real light of day. "Therefore, when you came to the party last night, you *were* looking for a good time. A rebound girl. I didn't read you wrong after all."

He folded his arms on his bare chest like he was cold all of a sudden. "I'm sorry, Tia. For the first seventeen years of my life, I did everything right. For the past forty-eight hours, I've done everything wrong."

He hadn't kissed wrong last night. I wanted to tell him that to cheer him up. Then I decided against it because he seemed to be counting *me* as one of the things he'd done wrong.

A lot of boys considered me the wrong kind of girl. I

wasn't offended. At least, I thought I wasn't, until this came out of my mouth: "You didn't do the deed with her just before you left, did you?"

"I . . . what?"

"She cheated on you the same night you left. Last night she was at it again. That's why someone sent you this picture, right? Lance can't believe her gall."

"Right," Will said tentatively, afraid of where I was going with this. Good instinct.

"Any guy in his right mind would be outraged at her and think, 'Good riddance.' But you're devastated. You know what would do that to you? Finally having sex with her on your last night together. That's where people go wrong—*not* doing it for a long time, and putting so much emphasis on the act that when it finally occurs, it leaves you an emotional wreck. She probably wanted to do it for months, but you refused because she was a nice girl. She told you she wanted one special night with you, and then she would wait for you until you came back for college. Really it was her way of tricking you into sex and taking advantage of you."

"That's enough," he bit out. He held out his hand for his phone.

Feeling sheepish now, I gave it to him.

He pocketed it and picked up his drum.

I snagged mine by the harness and hurried back toward the drum line. Jimmy thought it was funny to speed up the beat until the band was practically running to their places rather than marching. That was going to annoy Ms. Nakamoto, who was probably nearing the end of her rope already. She would blame Will and threaten to give the drum captain responsibility back to me again. I started running myself, determined to prevent one tragedy today.

Will returned right after I did, taking over the marching rhythm from Jimmy. But the camaraderie between us was gone. He stayed utterly silent for the rest of the hour.

And I felt sorry for him. With only a little glimpse into his life back home, I could tell he was a nice guy. A hockey player and the drum captain, who had friends and a girlfriend. The friends he'd had and the titles he'd held were a big part of who he was. Rip him away from that and he wasn't even a nice guy anymore. Down here he was just an unknown hottie with no tan and a temper.

By the beginning of the third hour, I'd had enough. Will wandered away from me and sat on the grass. I spread my towel out right next to him and sat down. He stubbornly slid away. I picked up my towel again and moved it closer. He looked toward the press box, chin high in the air, but he bit his lip like he was trying not to laugh.

"What I said was way too personal," I whispered in his ear. If he'd been obsessing over our fight as I had been, he would know exactly what I was talking about. "I'm sorry. You said some personal things about me, and I pretended not to care when I really did, and then I jumped down your throat when you came to me for help."

He smiled with one corner of his mouth. "I'm sorry too. We've insulted each other a lot for two people who hardly know each other."

"We've also made out a lot for two people who hardly know each other. It all evens out. But we've got to find a way to make peace. Otherwise it's going to be a long year of standing next to each other. Almost as long as the last thirty minutes."

He gave me a bigger smile. "Agreed. Don't mention lutefisk again, okay?"

"I promise. I will also bathe from now on, or stand downwind of you." I tossed my hat onto the grass and pulled the hair bands off the ends of both braids, which probably looked like old rope on a shipwreck by now. I bent over to shake my hair out, then turned right side up again and started one French braid down my back by feel.

He watched me without speaking. When I finished, he said, "As long as you're tidying up, your shirt's buttoned wrong."

I looked down. Sure enough, one side hung longer than the other. "*You* did that," I accused him.

"What are you saying? That you want me to fix it?"

"If you dare."

He glanced over at Ms. Nakamoto, then at DeMarcus. He unbuttoned my top button and put it through the proper hole, then fixed the next button, periodically looking up to make sure he wasn't about to get expelled for molesting me one button at a time. He never rubbed me "accidentally" or undid more buttons than necessary at once, but the very act of letting him do this in public was enough to make chills race down my arms.

"I think we're sending each other mixed messages," he said.

"I think I've sent you a very clear message," I corrected him, "and you're choosing not to receive it."

His hands paused on the bottom button. "You mean you *do* like what I'm doing right now, but you *don't* want to date me."

"Date *anybody*," I fine-tuned that statement. "See? You *do* get it."

Ms. Nakamoto called through her microphone, "Mr. Matthews, take your hands off Ms. Cruz."

The whole band said with one voice, "Ooooh."

Will put up his hands like a criminal. This time, despite my shades, I could tell he was blushing.

Jimmy called from the next towel over, "At least Ms. Nakamoto knows your name now." Travis gave him a high five.

Will and I sat in companionable silence while the band lost interest in us. Ms. Nakamoto was making the trumpets into a square, which seemed fitting, knowing our trumpets. DeMarcus got into a shouting match with a trombone. A very stupid heron, even bigger than the egret from last night, landed near the tubas, and they followed it around. Out on the road past the stadium, a car cruised by with its windows open, blasting an old salsa tune by Tito Puente. Will absentmindedly picked up his drumsticks and tapped out the complex rhythm, which he'd probably never heard before, striking the ground and his shoe in turn to create different tones, occasionally flipping a stick into the air and catching it without looking.

I hadn't thrown that challenge after all. He really was a better drummer than me.

"Can I ask you something?" His voice startled me out of the lull of the hot morning.

We were trying to be nice to each other, so I refrained from saying, *You just did.* And I braced for him to probe me about my aversion to dating. He didn't seem to want to let that go.

"There was a girl at the party last night named Angelica."

He pointed across the field at her with a drumstick. "I saw her this morning. She's a majorette."

"You're kidding," I said.

"Shut up. I know you're making fun of me. She was with the drum major last night, but some of the cymbals told me they broke up afterward."

Wow. DeMarcus and Angelica had dated since the beginning of the summer. They'd texted each other constantly for the month DeMarcus had been in New York. I knew this because he would occasionally mention it online. And she'd broken up with him the first night he got back? I bet it was because he'd drunk a beer at Brody's party.

I could have told Will, *Better than her breaking up with him on the day he moves across the country, eh?* Instead I said diplomatically, "I hadn't heard that."

"My question is, were they really serious? Because if it was casual, I might ask her out. If they were serious, I wouldn't move in. I don't want people to hate me. Not my first week, anyway."

I had no skin in this game. But I wondered if he was playing me, to get back at me for turning him down last night, and saying what I'd said about his ex-girlfriend this morning. It didn't make sense that he would *really* be interested in both Angelica and me. The gap between the two of us could not be accounted for by the normal boundaries of taste.

So maybe he didn't *really* like *me*.

I told him the truth. I owed him that much, after the trials I'd put him through in the past twelve hours. "As far as I know, it was casual."

"Good," he said, and then, "Thanks."

We uttered hardly a word to each other for the rest of the time we sat together. The silence was as awkward as it had been before we made up, but this time it was because Will had designs on Angelica. I wasn't sure why that would turn him cold to me. For my part, I wasn't jealous, only disappointed that he had such poor taste in women besides me.

In the last hour of practice, gloriously, we got up, and the whole band played the opening number that we'd been marching through with only a drum tap all morning. I worked out my stress by playing a perfect rhythm, my beat fitting with the quad and bass and cymbal parts like pieces of a puzzle. During the pauses between run-throughs, I showed Will some of the tricks the snares had done at contests in the past, reaching over to play on each other's drums during some passages, and tossing our sticks in the air, which was only effective visually if the freshmen didn't drop them. Will taught me some even better tricks he knew from back home. We devised a plan to try some of these ideas in future practices and determine how well the worst players could handle them.

We'd joked around before, but now we were building solid mutual respect. Now we were friends.

Or so I thought. Then Ms. Nakamoto let us go for the morning, and Will didn't even give me a proper good-bye. "See you at practice tonight," he called over his shoulder as he made a beeline across the field to catch Angelica. Not wanting to witness their young love, I followed at a slower pace, saying hi to some girls in color guard and playfully threatening to bulldoze right over a mellophone player, snare drum first.

By the time I made it back to the band room to deposit my drum, word among the cymbals was that Will had asked Angelica to lunch. Lunch! I never heard of such a thing. He'd already whisked her off in his famous car. The way the other majorettes out in the parking lot were gossiping about them, Will and Angelica were an item already.

As I headed home, passing the majorettes on my way back to the fence, Chelsea said, "Wait a minute, Tia. I thought *you* were dating the new guy."

Still walking, eyes on the ground so I didn't step on glass in my bare feet, I told her, "That was yesterday." Not that I cared or that Will's date with Angelica was any of my business, because I didn't want a boyfriend. But some days this was hard to remember.

I snagged my flip-flops from where I'd left them on the wrong side of the fence. At home I grabbed a quick shower, which everybody would appreciate, and another pack of Pop-Tarts for lunch, then hopped on my bike to pedal to the antiques shop.

On the last day of school my sophomore year, I'd biked through the historic downtown, thinking that I needed a summer job. There'd been a HELP WANTED sign in the shop window. I'd walked in and applied. A job was a job, or so I'd thought. I never would have set foot in there if I'd known what I was getting into: Bob had cancer. When his treatments didn't agree with him, he needed time off from the shop, and Roger took care of him. I sat through a very stressful half hour while they explained this to me and asked me to work for them. I didn't want to take on that kind of responsibility. My aversion warred inside me against my desire to help them out and my blooming interest in the bizarre junk that cluttered their hideous store.

So I'd accepted the job. And I'd done whatever Bob and Roger asked me to do—a long list of responsibilities that had expanded over the past year and two summers to include inventory, bookkeeping, and payroll. When Bob took a turn for the worse, sometimes I got so stressed out that I cleaned and organized the shop. That just made them love me more, raise my pay, and load more responsibility on my shoulders. It was terrible. I didn't know how to get out of this vicious circle.

Today wasn't so bad. Bob was recovering from his last round of chemo, and he and Roger were both in the back office, so I wasn't technically in charge. I patted the shop dog for a few minutes, then took over manning the front counter from Smokin' Edwina. Almost as soon as I slid onto my stool behind the cash register, Kaye and Harper bopped in with a clanging of the antique Swiss cowbell on the door. I always welcomed a visit from friends, because it might make me look less responsible and more like a frivolous teen to Bob and Roger.

This time, though, I could have done without, because I knew what my friends were there for. They wanted the scoop on Will. I would rather have done payroll.

They both stopped to pat the shop dog too. Everybody did. But when they straightened in front of the cash register with their arms folded, without so much as a "How you doing?" I amended their mission. They didn't want a scoop. They were there to scold me.

"You left with the new guy last night before we could stop you," Harper said. Admittedly, it didn't seem much like a scolding coming from a soft-spoken artist in retro glasses and a shift minidress straight out of the 1960s.

"You sent the new guy out to meet me," I protested. "If you hadn't done that, I might not have met him at the party at all."

"Was he still at your house when Aidan and I came by?" Kaye demanded. She wore her tank top and gym shorts from cheerleading practice, and her hair stuck out all over in cute twists. No matter how adorable she looked, though, she made a lecture sound like she meant it. "At the time I thought Will couldn't have been at your house. It was so late. But after the rumors I've heard this morning, I'm not so sure."

"What's wrong with him being there late?" I asked. "You and Aidan were still out then."

"We were on a *date*," Kaye said. "Girls are supposed to say yes to a date, then no to manhandling. You're not supposed to say yes to manhandling, then no to a date."

Ah, so that's what this was about. It had already gotten around that I'd dumped Will at the end of the night. I needed to talk to him about revealing personal information to cymbals.

"First of all," I told Kaye, "*you* are not saying no to manhandling."

She uncrossed her arms and put her fists on her hips, cheerleader style. "That's different. Aidan and I have been dating for *three years*. You were manhandled by someone you knew for an hour."

More like two, by my estimate. "And second, I *want* the manhandling. I don't *want* the dating. That stuff is fake anyway. The guy is taking you on dates just so he can manhandle you later. You're not being honest with each other."

Kaye gaped at me. "Aidan and I have a *relationship* that is built on—"

"You know what?" Harper asked, sliding a hand onto Kaye's shoulder. "This is more confrontational than we talked about, and it's not productive." She flashed me a look through her glasses. We'd tried our best to support Kaye's relationship with Aidan. On paper it looked perfect. They were involved in a lot of the same activities, and they were neck and neck with a few more people for valedictorian. And we loved Kaye. We simply didn't like him.

"Tell us more about Will," Harper said. "He's *so hot*. Everybody stared at him as he walked through the party last night."

"That's because he's new," I lied.

"He seems kind of stuck up," Kaye said.

"Takes one to know one," I said.

"Hey!" Kaye stomped her athletic shoe in protest. The dog looked up at her reprovingly, like she had a lot of nerve, then settled back down.

Harper talked right over Kaye. "I heard he stands next to you in band."

"He does."

"I heard he took drum captain from you," Kaye said. "Did you throw it?"

"How could you accuse me of that?" I asked, looking her straight in the eye. "You and I had that talk recently about me taking personal responsibility. You speak and I listen."

Harper, heeding the signs that Kaye and I were about to lay into each other, switched the subject back to Will. "I heard that he took his shirt off during band, and he was very white and very built."

"He was wearing a drum harness," I said, "so I didn't notice."

Harper and Kaye muttered their disbelief. Because they were talking over each other, I couldn't hear everything they said, but I picked out "sunscreen" and "bullshit."

"But you probably got an eyeful last night," Kaye told me.

"Well, *somebody* got an eyeful of *somebody*," I admitted.

Kaye raised her eyebrows. Harper emitted a cute, embarrassed snort, wringing her hands as if the whole prospect worried her. "Is he like Sawyer?"

Girls at my school were captivated by Sawyer. He was fun to watch. He was likely to fly off the handle at any moment. And when he chose to be, he was downright sultry. One time he'd talked dirty to me during an assembly in the high school auditorium, just for fun, in a way that made me want to rip my clothes off for him right there in front of Mr. Moxley and the championship tenth-grade robotics team.

But most girls wouldn't hook up with Sawyer, in the same way that they wouldn't hook up with a train wreck. That task was left to me. And Harper and Kaye didn't want *me* hooking up with him either. They'd gotten very upset the first time they'd caught me with him in a compromising position at a party. Kaye told me that if she ever found me with him again, she and Aidan would not be my designated drivers anymore, and I would have to ride home from parties with the trumpets, who listened to a lot of lite jazz.

Kaye and Harper had gotten used to the idea of Sawyer and me after a while, and now, frankly, they were fascinated by our relationship. Harper was more obvious in her enthusiasm. Kaye listened quietly to my Sawyer stories. That told me she was more interested than she wanted to let on, since she was used to asserting herself in student council meetings and was rarely quiet about anything.

"Will is like Sawyer," I said, "but better."

"Better!" Harper exclaimed. "Better how?"

Better in that I felt myself flush every time Will looked at me. Sawyer and I had agreed a long time ago that we were too much alike to have any real chemistry. That didn't stop us from making out when nobody else was available, of course, but it had kept us from trying for anything more than friends with bennies.

The thing was, I didn't *want* more than that out of a relationship with Sawyer. Or even with Will.

"Better . . . taller," I said. Sawyer had only half an inch on me. It wasn't often that I encountered a guy who made me feel downright dainty. I thought of Will looking down at me during band practice, and wondered again what he'd been thinking when I couldn't see his eyes behind his aviators.

"It doesn't matter, though," I said. "Will's out to lunch right now with old Angelica."

"Angelicaaaaaa!" Harper and Kaye moaned in despair. Once, in ninth-grade science class, they'd been passing a note back and forth about Kaye's crush on Aidan. Angelica, instead of passing it along the row like she was supposed to, had turned it in to the teacher, who had read it out loud. That had led to Aidan asking Kaye to homecoming. So the outcome could have been considered a good trade-off if you thought Aidan was a prize, which I didn't.

Or if you had not been completely mortified by the incident, which Kaye had. I could hear it in her voice still as she cried, "How could you let *Angelica* have Will?"

"It wouldn't have worked with Will and me," I told them honestly. "He would get as exasperated with me as you are right now."

They both opened their mouths to say awww, they weren't exasperated with me (Harper), or they *were* exasperated with me but only because I consistently sold myself short (Kaye). I was saved by the cowbell on the door. After petting the shop dog, a customer asked to see the women's jeweled watches I'd posted to the shop's website. That was going to take a while because we had fourteen, which was why I'd been trying to move them out of inventory. I waved good-bye to Kaye and Harper and led the customer back to the display case, with the dog following.

And I tried to shake the uneasy feeling my friends had left me with. Will and I had shared an unwise night together. Okay. We'd had another argument this morning, yes. But we'd made up, and when things had gotten awkward between us again, that was probably because he was preoccupied with asking Angelica out. Things would be better tonight, and for the next three days of band practice. By the beginning of school on Friday, we would have no problem getting along in the drum line.

I honestly believed this, because I was not the best at foreseeing trouble and planning ahead. I had no idea our friendship was about to go south.

5

BAND CAMP WENT OKAY AT FIRST. I HAD TEN times more fun with Will than I'd ever had standing between a past year's seniors. They'd taken their shirts off, all right, but they hadn't looked as good as Will did, or laughed like he did at my jokes. And they hadn't had an earring. I'd become a big advocate of the earring.

The thing about Will was, he took being drum captain *very* seriously, and he seemed determined to prove his worth to Ms. Nakamoto after his Monday-morning meltdown. A lot of drum lines I'd talked to, from high schools on the University of South Florida side of town, had student teachers as percussion instructors. Up here in our far corner, we were on our own. And that meant when the drums broke off from the rest of the band, Will ran rehearsal, with Ms. Nakamoto

BIGGEST FLIRTS

occasionally peeking her head into the palm-tree grove where we'd retreated for shade, making sure we hadn't all killed each other yet.

She would have been right to worry if I'd been in charge. I would have pulled out my braids the first hour I had to deal with these people. But Will was an amazing drum captain. Jimmy and Travis might give him a hard time when Ms. Nakamoto reprimanded him on the field, but they didn't cross him in drum sectionals. Maybe it was because he obviously knew what he was doing and cared that we got the music right. When the bass drums got tangled up in their complicated rhythms, he took the time to figure out exactly which sophomore was tripping them up and why, and he taught that guy a new, less confusing way to count off the measures. He was equally patient with the cymbals and their crashing-at-the-wrong-time issues.

More likely, nobody crossed him because he seemed so serious most of the time, with the worry line between his brows visible behind his shades. And that's what made it all the more delicious when I got a giggle out of him. Sometimes he looked like he wanted to shush me on the field when Ms. Nakamoto or DeMarcus frowned in our direction, but he couldn't shush me if he was too busy laughing.

Best of all, our friendship had stabilized. Will didn't hint

81

about asking me out or being jealous of Sawyer. He was dating Angelica now. And I didn't worry too much about what he was *doing* with Angelica. With night practice lasting until ten, she probably didn't let him so much as come over to watch TV and feel her up, because she needed to be fresh for insulting other girls' outfit choices the next morning. They had only the afternoon to spend together, and how much trouble could anybody get into in the afternoon?

The one thing that bothered me about my week with Will was that we kept touching each other and getting in trouble for it with Ms. Nakamoto. The whole band turned around to stare at us when this happened, including Angelica with her arms crossed. It wasn't like we *meant* to touch each other. We just started talking about TV or music or, God, I don't know. We could make a joke out of anything. And then I pretended to sock him for something he said, and he grabbed me, and we were in trouble again.

Boys with girlfriends had propositioned me before. This made me uncomfortable. I had turned them down. I didn't want to feel like the mistress of a married man. But I wasn't Will's mistress. He wasn't married. This was just being friendly without fooling around. And if he did have some exclusive understanding with Angelica that he was not to touch other girls, that was his problem, not mine.

The only reason I felt uneasy was that I liked him so much. Every time he put his hands on me, I liked him more. This was dangerous.

As problems went, however, it was a happy one to have. I wasn't late to band again, because the minute practice was over I was pretty much dying to see Will again. But toward the end of the week, a couple of things happened to ruin my paradise.

First, at band practice on Thursday, instead of breaking at noon and then meeting up on the football field again at six, we reconvened on the beach at four. Attendance had already seemed pretty good at practice, and you could bet all hundred and eighty of us would be at a party. DeMarcus's dad grilled hamburgers and hot dogs for us. A lot of other parents brought delicious grub. Ms. Nakamoto laid down her whistle, donned a little white one-piece, and frolicked in the surf with her husband and her children like a real person.

As far as sexytimes went, there wasn't much new to see, because most of us had already taken off our clothes during band. But something about Will lying on a towel in the sand with his front to Angelica's back, both of them apparently asleep, got my blood boiling. Sure, for the past three days he'd sat on my towel in band with his shirt off, and I'd taken my shirt off too to show my bikini top underneath. The only differences between that scene and this one were that he was now wearing a bathing suit instead of shorts, she was wearing bikini bottoms instead of shorts, and they were lying like lovers.

Oh—and the girl by his side was Angelica, not me.

I sat with Chelsea on a big rock under palms, taking pics of the great view: the Gulf, the boats sailing in and out of the town's small harbor, and all the boys we claimed not to like *that way*. I didn't take a pic of Will, though. I couldn't believe Will voluntarily lay in the sunshine rather than the shade. His tan wasn't dark enough yet to protect him. And he definitely hadn't gotten used to the heat. Sometimes in band he seemed almost sick with it. He and Angelica must have lain down when that part of the beach was in shade. Now the sun had moved.

As I was steaming about this, I got a text from Sawyer, just a question mark. He was asking if I wanted to hook up after he got off work.

I texted back, "At marching band party, geeking out. Come crash. Great food. I will find you some vegan." I really did want to see him. I wanted Will to see me *with* him even more.

No such luck. Sawyer texted, "KILL ME NOW."

And a second later, when he realized that was a little mean, even for him, "Thx but no thx."

I plopped my phone down on my lap in frustration. I ordered Chelsea, "Go down there and tell old Angelica she has to get Will out of the sun. He doesn't understand that the five o'clock rays will still fry him."

"I'm not getting in the middle of this," Chelsea said.

"In the middle of what?" I asked innocently. But I felt myself blush at the idea that Will and I were in a messy love triangle.

"Besides," Chelsea said, "if that player fries, he deserves it."

"What?" I asked. "Will? Why is he a player?" My heart sank at the thought that he might have dropped Angelica off to go night-night after practice, but he had another girl on the side. This hadn't occurred to me.

Chelsea gasped. "He went home with you after Brody Larson's party, then dumped you for Angelica the next day, and now he's here feeling her up at the beach after he basically felt you up at band practice all morning! Don't you even care?"

I wasn't sure what she meant when she said he'd felt *me* up. True, at every practice, Ms. Nakamoto called through her microphone, "Mr. Matthews, get off Ms. Cruz." In fact, Jimmy had taken to looking at his phone and announcing the elapsed time between her reprimands—"One hour, forty-five minutes"—like we were going for a record. But in one of those instances, Will had been helping me adjust my snare harness. It only *looked* like he was molesting me. On another occasion, he caught me in a headlock, which I really enjoyed, after I mentioned lutefisk to see what he would do. So that was my fault. And several of those times, he was spreading sunscreen on my back at my request. Ms. Nakamoto simply didn't catch me when I was lotioning *him* up.

"He's cute, though," Chelsea said. "I look forward to seeing that around school this year. I'm not helping you, but, yeah, you should go warn him before he gets burned. Hey!" When she called out to DeMarcus, who was passing by, he helped her backward off the rock. They walked toward the open-air pavilion where the food was, abandoning me to carry out my own mission.

I scrambled down to the beach. But as I moseyed toward Will and Angelica, who were oblivious that I was about to disturb their romantic moment, I felt less and less like a friend aiming to avert a medical tragedy and more and more like a scheming bitch. Will was seventeen years old, and he could put on his own sunscreen. He couldn't reach his back, though. And he didn't seem to have a lick of sense when it came to the Florida sun. I ought to let Angelica take care of him, but obviously she wasn't willing or able.

So I knelt in front of them—I knew I should not be doing this as I did it—and said in a low tone that spoke of my mature health concerns, "Angelica, you can't let Will get burned out here, no matter how much you're enjoying second base." I waited only until she sat up and scowled at me in outrage. Her movements jostled Will's sunglasses down on his nose. He opened one eye and frowned at me.

Mission accomplished. I walked down the beach and got drafted into a volleyball game, baritones versus tubas. They thought I would be good to have on the team because I was tall. By the time they figured out I *wasn't* good at volleyball, it was too late for them to kick me out. I ate until I was stuffed—I realized suddenly that I'd been living on Pop-Tarts for the entire week, now that I wasn't working at the Crab Lab and scarfing free food—and then lounged on the beach with my friends, swam, and got into a splash fight with Jimmy and Travis (which I won).

I had a lot of fun, like always. But the entire time, I was aware of where Will was, and what he was doing with Angelica. My scolding seemed to have shaken them out of sun-worshipper mode, and they secluded themselves on a shady bench. When the sun went down, they joined everyone in the pavilion. DeMarcus's parents had hauled in their huge TV and hooked up their dance-competition video game. Dorks who didn't mind embarrassing themselves in public (including me) participated in the dance throwdown (which

Chelsea won). Will and Angelica sat to one side, near a fan, close and still like a mature couple too lost in each other to have fun with anybody else—another reason never to have a boyfriend. I didn't envy Angelica if dating Will meant acting like they were already in the nursing home.

Yet despite everything else going on, I went over and over that scene in my mind, Will lying behind Angelica on the beach, her body folded into the sheltering curve of his body, his hand on her bare skin, and wondered what that had felt like.

Thank God they stayed until the end of the party. I suspected he took her straight home afterward.

Because Friday was a school day! And that was the second thing that shook me out of my comfort zone with Will. Homeroom was combined with first period, which for me was calculus, through no fault of my own. Years ago the principal and the teachers had conspired to keep me in the college-track classes no matter what I said or how little homework I turned in. At the back of the class sat Will, also not too much of a surprise now that I knew more about him. And just as on the first day of band camp, he looked completely different from the previous night. I walked through the door, headed for the desks, and actually exclaimed to the already half-full classroom, "Your eyes are blue!"

"And your eyes are a lovely shade of shit brown," DeMarcus told Aidan, not missing a beat in their conversation.

"Shut up," I told them as I passed them in the row.

Will watched me as I approached, waiting for me to explain what was so astonishing about the color of his eyes. I'd never noticed in the five days I'd known him. His Minnesota Vikings baseball hat and aviator shades seemed like a part of him. But when I saw that devastatingly handsome guy with intense blue eyes staring back at me—that's when I realized what I'd been missing.

I slid into the desk behind him, then shrugged helplessly. "I've only seen you from a distance, or wearing your sunglasses, or in the dark."

"In the dark, huh?" asked Brody, across the row from me. "Yeah, that's what I heard happened after my party."

"Do you mind?" I asked him.

But when I turned back to Will, he gave me a small smile like the interruption didn't faze him. He leaned over the desktop between us and squinted at me. I'd thought from the beginning how adorable he was when he squinted. Coupled with the blue eyes, the look made my heart flutter. He said, "Your eyes are so dark, I can't see your pupils. Do you even *have* pupils?"

"Yes, or I wouldn't be able to see," I said, because when I was under pressure, I was nothing but romantic. In my defense, his own comment about my invisible pupils was the kind of pickup line you'd hear at a sci-fi convention. Or possibly he wasn't *trying* to sound romantic, because *he had a girlfriend.*

As if sent to remind us of this fact, Chelsea walked in, calling, "Uh-uh, not during school. Break it up, you two. Keep it classy."

We both straightened the slightest bit—knowing she was right, but not wanting to give in to her teasing, either. And I wasn't done with Will. "Your hair," I said quietly, reaching out to finger the back of it, which was gone. All the bad-ass length of it had been cut short. Yet he retained that look of dangerous energy, possibly because there was no hiding his earring now. He watched me with such an intense expression that I hardly dared touch him. But of course I did, running my fingers up his shorn nape. "Oh my God, you weren't kidding on the field," I said. "You *were* hot!"

"Let me tell you something, Tia," he deadpanned. "I'm *still* hot."

I threw back my head and cackled at that, not really caring who heard me, because now it was close to time for the bell, and the room was crowded and loud.

When I collected myself and grinned at him again, he

was grinning at me, too, and doing that cute squint. "I didn't want to cut it. I just hated the thought of band practice today. Mornings and nights were bad enough, but from two to three in the afternoon? It's going to be so hot out there."

"Like an ahffen!" I exclaimed.

Before I could back away, he'd pushed me to the side of my seat and bent me over in the aisle with his arm around my neck—gently but very firmly. He growled in my ear, "Every time you make fun of the way I talk, you're going in a head-lock."

"Do you promise?" Admittedly, catching a girl in a head-lock was less something he would do to Angelica or his beautiful, treacherous girlfriend back home, and more some-thing he would do to one of his little sisters. But his arm was around my neck, his breath was in my ear, and I was very aware that this was the most fun I would have the whole school day, until band last period.

"Mr. Matthews, get off Ms. Cruz," DeMarcus called through a rolled-up sheet of paper in an excellent imitation of Ms. Nakamoto.

Will released me. I sat up and flipped my braids back over my shoulders like nothing had happened. "Who cut your hair so fast?" I asked. "Did you let your sisters go at it with Barbie scissors?"

He put both hands on the back of his head in horror. "Does it look that bad?"

"No," I promised him. "I have to stare at you for an hour a day. Two hours, if Ms. Reynolds lets me stay in this desk. When you start falling down on the job, I'll let you know."

He put his hands down. "I was driving to school this morning and stopped in at a shop downtown that opened at seven."

"That was my sister Izzy!" I said with more enthusiasm than I'd felt about her in three or four years.

He pointed at me. "I *thought* . . . well, I did and I didn't. You look a lot alike, but you're completely different."

I nodded. Izzy wasn't funny.

"Are you two close? You've never mentioned her."

"We used to be, a long time ago. I have three older sisters, and all of us were close when they lived at home. They've moved out, though. And I had an argument with Izzy at the beginning of the summer. I stopped in the shop and asked if she needed help taking care of her kids on my nights off from the Crab Lab—"

"*Kids?*" Will asked. "How old is she?"

"Twenty-two." I glossed over his real question, which was *How old was she the* first *time she got pregnant?* Because the answer was *Younger than me.* "Anyway," I said, "she laughed at me. Admittedly, I'm the last person in the world anybody would want to take care of their kids, but if I offer to help, I don't want to be laughed at."

He frowned. "And then what?"

"And then nothing. I haven't seen her since then."

"Even though you worked just down the street from her all summer?" When I nodded, he said, "Wow, that's some chip on your shoulder."

Yeah, I guessed it was.

The bell rang to start first period. As it clanged, instead of facing the front, he reached across my desk to cover my hand with his. "Have a good senior year, Tia."

"Awww!" I said, a bit mortified that I seemed so pitiful and needed this boost, but also touched that he would think of lifting me up this way, when he was the one who'd moved clear across the country and had to start over. "You too."

As he turned around, Ms. Reynolds was already passing out write-in ballots for the Senior Superlatives elections. Mostly I filled in the names of my friends according to the titles I figured they wanted, until I got to Most Academic. There I jotted my own name on the female side, because I knew I wouldn't get it, and I didn't want old Angelica to have it.

At the last second I felt bad about this. The little egghead deserved (and probably coveted) that title. If the tally was close, my throwaway vote could have denied her dream, all because I was bitter about her boyfriend, whom I myself had turned down. But by the time I made a move to snatch back my ballot, Will had put it on the bottom and passed the stack to the guy in front of him.

His was on top, completely blank. I'd tried to tutor him on who was who in the senior class, but not everybody remembered stuff the first time they heard it like I did. I doubted he knew anybody's full name except mine.

We didn't get another chance to talk during class. As I'd suspected, he was one of those people who actually did calculus during calculus. But I also had AP history and AP English and study hall/lunch with him. Angelica didn't. I hung out with him during those periods so that he had a friend.

In my classes without him, and while traveling the halls, I heard girls talking about how hot he was, and how stuck up. It didn't help that he had a Yankee accent people couldn't quite place, like an elderly snowbird. When I heard them talking behind his back, I tried to help him out by explaining that he was from Minnesota. This elicited moans of "Minne*soooooooo*da!" which did nothing for his popularity.

It also didn't help that he had his eyes on his phone all the time. And since Angelica didn't have her eyes on hers, I figured he wasn't anxiously awaiting her texts. He was probably obsessively checking his friends' photos for more evidence of his ex gallivanting with his so-called best friend. But he'd told me about that disaster in confidence. It wasn't my info to share. And if he hadn't shared it with Angelica, I didn't know what it would do to their relationship when she found out that she was the rebound girl. I didn't like him dating her, but I wasn't going to sabotage it—at least, in a way that he would know about—and make my own relationship with him worse.

I knew about his ex and how lost and lonely he was, because I'd stood next to him in band camp. But he dropped plenty of other hints that he wasn't the prick everyone made him out to be. There was the dancing, for one thing. He might have seemed serious, but he was often dancing. Not flailing like a freshman at a teen club, mind you, but understatedly boogying to his own beat. It was the drummer in him. Anytime music came on—rap spilling out of a car outside the school, or pop blasting over the loudspeakers in the gym for a girls' PE class—he was part of it somehow. It might be his head or his toe or just one pointer finger tapping on his thigh, but he was beating out the music as if it was his own.

There was his shyness, for another thing. When someone approached and spoke to him—someone besides me—his lips parted, but he stayed silent. A stricken look entered his blue eyes, and it took him five seconds longer than it would have taken most people without a speech impediment to come up with an answer. He wasn't stuck up. He just had a hard time meeting new people. Transferring to a new school must have been his nightmare. I was more sure than ever that, driven by fury at his ex, he'd been bluesing for a hookup when he bravely walked into Brody's party the first night.

Kaye and Harper tried to talk to him in the halls and commented to me later how hard he was to draw out. I felt like I needed to defend him more than ever. But I couldn't, not to them, because they'd think I still liked him despite not wanting a boyfriend, and then they would never leave me alone. The worst thing in the world would be for those two to decide to "help me through it." I couldn't stand to obsess about Will any more than I already did.

It pained me to know that my friends didn't like him. I'd tried and failed to help him fit in. But a sneaky part of me enjoyed knowing things about him that they didn't. I doubted his ex had noticed his fingers drumming on his desk to any little beat. Surely if she had, she would have waited for him to come home to Minnesota next May and never let him go. Angelica might have noticed, but I couldn't picture her appreciating his love for a beat the way I did. Only I understood him, and in some small way, in a tiny warped corner of my mind, that made him mine.

6

"YOU'VE BEEN LYING TO ME," WILL SAID IN MY
ear. A chill shot down my neck in the blazing afternoon.

I straightened and stared at him. We'd both been retriev-
ing our drums from the trunk of his car. His 1970s Mustang
gave away, yet again, that this uptight boy had a wild streak.
Years of Minnesota winters had rusted the wheel wells like
he'd been driving through acid, which was why he'd been
able to afford the car, and why his parents had wanted him
to leave it behind.

I had mixed feelings about the Mustang. I wished his
dad had forbidden him to bring it. Then Angelica wouldn't
have shown up in it to night band practice last Monday after
their lunch date, waving languidly out the window like a
homecoming queen on parade. But I was glad he had this

car, because he parked it just outside the stadium. The trunk gave me the perfect place to stash my drum so I didn't have to lug it back and forth to the band room.

Now I tried to read his expression behind his shades. When he accused me of lying, my mind automatically shot to the fact that I liked him way more than I wanted to let on. Rather than melting under his stare into a pool of hysterical shame, however, I reached for my drum again and commented, "Yes, I have. Which lie do you mean, specifically?"

With an impatient huff, he reached into the trunk, too—it was shady in here, our heads were close together, and if it hadn't been a hundred and sixty degrees, it would have been a great place to make out—and he dragged out my drum and held it up for me so I could get my shoulders under the harness. "You've given me the impression, on purpose, that you're some free-spirited surfer girl who doesn't care about school or your future or much of anything at all."

Uh-oh. I had an idea where this was going, and I tried to spin the conversation in a different direction. "We don't have a lot of surfers," I pointed out. "The Gulf is too calm. You'd have to go to the Atlantic side of Florida for that."

"You know what I mean," he said. "You pretend to be an airheaded beach bum. If that were true, your friends should be stoners."

"Well—" I started to point out that Sawyer, though not someone I'd call a stoner because those people had absolutely nothing else to do, had been known to partake. But I wouldn't get Sawyer in trouble, even for the sake of a joke. And how well did I really know Will, anyway? Maybe old Angelica's tattletale ways had rubbed off on him.

As Will dragged his own drum out of the trunk, he was saying, "But your best friends are the photographer for the yearbook and the head cheerleader. Something doesn't compute."

"Oh," I said, relieved that was all he'd meant. I'd never thought about it, but Harper and Kaye and I did make an odd trio. "I'm friends with them because we were in gifted class together starting in elementary school." When he stared blankly at me, I explained, "At your school, maybe they called it enrichment class? Sawyer calls it the loser class." I held my fingers to my forehead in the shape of an L, Sawyer style.

I jumped as Will slammed his trunk. "That's just more fuel on the fire. I heard you're going to be a National Merit Scholar."

"Ha! That's what the guidance counselor *says*, based on my test scores. But I have to get a teacher to vouch for my dedication to academics." I poked him in the ribs with my drumstick as we entered the stream of the band flowing from the school into the stadium. I said more quietly so we wouldn't be overheard, "I took the PSAT last year. Fifteen minutes before I went in, I'd just had this huge fight with Jason Price. I'm sure you haven't met him yet."

"I heard about him." Will pointed one drumstick at me. "Stoner."

"Why, yes," I said, proud of Will for identifying someone in our class by first and last name after all.

"You dated him," Will said.

"Well, not *dated*," I said. "Why are you all over me for having winner friends if you also know I had a loser hookup?"

Will was giving me the look that people gave me whenever I purposely misled them and they lost track of what I was telling them and why. I didn't fool him for long, though. We carefully descended the stadium steps, glancing to the side of our drums so we could see our toes, the air growing hotter as we went. Finally we reached the grass, and he could concentrate on what I was saying rather than on whether he was about to tumble to his death. His brain caught up with my mouth, and he exclaimed in exasperation, "Because if the guidance counselor says you're going to be a National Merit Scholar, you must have made an almost perfect score on the PSAT!"

"Shhh!" I hissed, looking around to see who'd heard. "You'll ruin my reputation. See, I was stressed out about Jason, and when I'm stressed, I like to put things in order."

"But *only* when you're stressed." He must have been thinking of his glimpse inside my dark house.

"Obvs. I find multiple-choice tests soothing."

"That only makes sense if you know all the answers," he grumbled.

"Of course I know all the answers. I mean, I know them if I'm actually trying to figure them out. So, to make a long story short, I made an almost perfect score because the test caught me on a bad day."

"Are you talking about her PSAT score?" Kaye asked, jogging over. The cheerleaders had practice on the football field last period, at the same time as the band. We used the middle of the field, they stayed on the sidelines, and we tried not to plow through their pyramids. Normally I would have hugged her hello, but she was about to say something to make this convo with Will worse, I could tell.

Sure enough, she volunteered, "Tia's an underachiever. She works very hard at it. One year she made a C in Spanish even though she's bilingual."

Will looked to me for verification.

I shrugged. "Just because I can speak it doesn't mean I can

spell it." In Spanish I told Kaye to take her little cheerleader shoes and tumble on over to the sidelines and stay there.

In response, Kaye uttered the only Spanish curse I'd ever taught her, which really was not appropriate for this situation. But she ran across the field toward the other cheerleaders, tossing in a couple of handsprings and a layout as a *so there*. Good riddance. I turned back to Will and grinned like our pleasant small talk had been interrupted but now the children had left us alone again.

"You are incredibly dumb for a smart person," he said.

I laughed. "I've never denied this."

"You're just confirming, over and over, that you've been lying to me."

"I haven't," I insisted. I knew he was only teasing, but something about being called a liar, by Will, when I really hadn't meant to mislead him that first night, ticked me off. "*You're* the one who's so closed minded that everything has to line up perfectly or it doesn't make sense. Why can't I be an underachiever? This is America. I can be anything I want. Besides, *you're* the one who lied to *me*. When we first met at Brody's party, I thought we were kindred spirits. You gave me the impression that you were a pirate, with your earring."

"Oh." Surprised, he put his hand to his earlobe like he'd forgotten all about his earring.

"I had no idea you turn in your homework," I said. "Traitor."

"You mistook me for something else, and that's the only reason . . ." As we reached our starting spot on the field and faced the home side, his voice trailed off, but his silence told me the rest of what he was thinking. All of it was true. Yes, I'd lured him home last Sunday night only because I thought he was a slacker like me. Yes, he'd ruined everything by being an upstanding Future Pharmacist of America. Yes.

He nodded as if accepting his fate. "So listen, I wanted to ask you something. It's *not* about a date."

I laughed to show him I wasn't uncomfortable that he'd read my mind. And then I kept laughing uncomfortably.

He talked over me. "I'm trying out for Spirit of Atlanta in late November. My parents promised me I could try out for drum corps this year, but that was when we lived in Minnesota and there were three corps right next door in Wisconsin. Now that Atlanta is the closest one, I wondered if you wanted to try out with me."

My heart was beating so hard it hurt. He'd said he wasn't asking me for a date, but he was issuing me an invitation for something sweet, something kind, something I almost *wanted*.

Drum corps were basically marching bands with super-powers. They took only the best players from high school and college. They toured the country, competing against each other. It sounded like the perfect place for Will to pass the summer between high school and college—especially if most of it was spent bopping around the northern states, where he wouldn't overheat at eight a.m. I could tell from the way he talked so wistfully about it that this was one more thing he'd had to give up when he moved.

"I don't see what my PSAT score has to do with trying out for corps," I said.

Gathering his thoughts, he tapped his stick on my drumhead a few times. "When I met you, I thought you were a random person who randomly was an excellent drummer. Now I know you're an excellent drummer on purpose, the type of person who goes out for corps."

"You're wrong about me," I insisted. "You were right the first time. I'm random. When I succeed, that's the mistake."

"You make a lot of mistakes." He sounded hurt. I hoped we weren't going to have another silent practice like after we argued last Monday.

But he was only waiting for Jimmy, Travis, and the rest of the drummers to arrange themselves in line. When they'd passed, he said quietly, "It would be better to have a friend in corps than to go knowing absolutely nobody, don't you think? Plus, you have to be there one weekend a month during the school year for practice, and my parents don't want me to make that seven-hour drive twice in one weekend by myself."

I turned to look at him. He wasn't the bad boy he'd seemed at first. Another admission that his mom wanted to keep him safe shouldn't have surprised me. But that just didn't jibe with the tall drummer in front of me, looking so serious with his hair cut short, his expression inscrutable behind his mirrored shades.

"What do you think?" he prompted me. "Would your dad let you spend the night in a car with me?"

He was kidding. This was exactly the kind of joke I ribbed him with constantly.

But I found myself speechless. I was imagining spending the night in Will's car with him. Driving through the night to Atlanta. Talking. Touching. Keeping each other awake behind the wheel.

Then I was thinking about my first night with him. How good he'd made me feel. How I'd decided that one night was enough. How wrong I'd been.

"Tia," he said.

I snapped, "My dad wouldn't notice."

Will's dark brows knitted behind his sunglasses, and that worry line appeared. "You should try out, then."

"I couldn't afford corps." This wasn't exactly true. My dad worked so much, and our house was in such a state of disrepair, that a lot of my friends assumed we must be at the brink of bankruptcy. We weren't. But my dad *was* very tight with our savings. He'd had to support Izzy and Sophia and their kids for a while. Violet hadn't gotten knocked up and abandoned yet, but we figured she would. By now we both expected the worst.

For that matter, I could have paid for corps myself. I'd saved a lot working two jobs. But saying no to Will was a foregone conclusion. I wanted to get involved with him, but I just couldn't do that to myself. I knew what would happen next.

Will had an answer for everything. "It's expensive, but you could apply for a scholarship, or you could get some business in town to sponsor you."

A business like the antiques shop, I thought grimly as I pulled my vibrating phone out of my pocket and glanced at the screen. I used to answer every time Bob and Roger called, because I was afraid Bob had taken a turn for the worse. But lately they'd started calling me about the *shop*, of all things— where the vintage handbags were on the network of shelves, and how to access the catalog of sterling flatware I'd set up in their computer so they *wouldn't have to call me.*

As I slipped my phone back into my pocket, unanswered, Will was saying, "I mean, corps isn't for everyone. Don't let me talk you into it if you're not a fan."

"No, I love corps," I said. "People complain about traveling the whole summer, eating peanut butter sandwiches three meals a day, and sleeping on school gym floors all over the country, but that sounds fun to me. And not too far removed from my current life. I always wanted to try out."

He moved his drumsticks apart, a drummer's version of spreading his hands to shrug. "Why didn't you?"

"I figured I wouldn't make it." A half truth this time. I had a lot of confidence in my ability as a drummer, because I'd listened carefully and compared myself to other players when our band went to games or contests. But I had no confidence in my ability to lead a section or arrive at practice on time. God only knew what I'd be getting myself into in an organization that was actually rigorous.

"You would make it." He looked sidelong at me beneath his shades. "But maybe you don't want to chance getting stuck next to me again."

The highlight of my day, even a fun first day of school like this, was standing next to Will. But I brushed him off.

"Maybe *you* don't want to chance getting stuck next to *me* again, and you regret bringing it up."

He shut me down. "Nope. So let's make it official. Will you drive to Atlanta with me for tryouts in November?"

The last thing I wanted was to have a real conversation with Will in which we confronted our issues. But he was watching me with his brows raised behind his shades, which I interpreted as hope in his eyes. Just like Sunday night all over again. I knew he would keep bringing up the idea and I would continue to string him along to avoid either committing to him or disappointing him, unless I went ahead and cut him off. I said, "You think you've got me all figured out, but you're way off the mark. I don't do stuff like that."

"Stuff like what?"

"Stuff requiring effort." As I said this, I turned away from Will. DeMarcus motioned to call the band to order and open practice. It was the drum captain's job to play a short riff that the rest of the drum line echoed, snapping the whole band to attention. I did the job this time, startling Will.

The entire band went completely still, except for Will, who really had gotten caught off guard. He eased his head forward and slowly folded his sticks on top of his drum in our attention position so he wouldn't get in trouble for failing to keep his eyes up front.

The whole standing-at-attention thing was just a little game we played for a few seconds at the beginning of band sometimes. It was a tool Ms. Nakamoto used to make us listen to her if she couldn't convince the trumpets to shut up otherwise. Usually it bored me to death. Today I heard the cars swishing by on the street outside the stadium, the cries of seagulls gliding overhead, a breeze through the palms that definitely didn't make it down to the bottom of the bowl we were standing in, the tiniest tap as Will finally set his sticks down on his drumhead, and his long sigh. Maybe he sighed with relief that he hadn't gotten caught. I was afraid he sighed with frustration that I was playing impossible to get.

Most boys who pursued me stopped trying eventually, frustrated. I would miss Will. I hoped he wouldn't stop trying for a while.

Of course . . . he had already, when he asked out Angelica. Funny, even though I could see her from where I was standing, way up near the home bleachers in the majorette version of standing at attention with her toe pointed and two batons crossed on her hip, I'd forgotten all about her when Will stood so close.

"At ease," DeMarcus hollered. "At ease" didn't mean "collapse," but that's what happened. The tubas and drums slid their instruments off their shoulders and dumped them on the ground. While Ms. Nakamoto told us through her microphone what we'd be rehearsing for the next hour, Will took off his harness, handed me his hat and shades, then pulled his shirt over his head, just like in every other practice this week.

Much as I wanted to see this, I told him quietly, "You can't take your shirt off."

"Yes, I can," he said through the material. "Watch, it's stretchy."

"No, I mean . . ." I said to his naked torso.

I stopped and just watched him. This was the hottest thing I'd ever seen at school. His paleness had mellowed into a gentle tan that would protect him from the sun, and his strong build gave him the look of a proud lifeguard. He took his hat and shades back from me. The lenses reflected the palm trees behind me.

"Not during school hours," I managed. "It's against the dress code."

"Suddenly you care about the rules." He cracked a lopsided grin at me, twirling his shirt cheekily in one hand.

"Mr. Matthews," Ms. Nakamoto called through her microphone. "Put your shirt on. We don't allow students to break the dress code when school is in session."

I started to taunt him but thought better of it. He really

might be upset that he'd gotten in trouble, and for something so silly.

Just as I was thinking this, he roared back at Ms. Nakamoto across the field, "It's. Three. Thousand. Degrees!"

"Mr. Ma-*tthews*?" Ms. Nakamoto's tone had changed to the one I'd heard her use only on me, last year, when I overslept and made all four buses half an hour late leaving for a contest in Miami.

"He's doing it," I called to placate her. I held out my hands and snapped my fingers for his hat and shades.

He gave heaven a sour look for a second, then obediently passed me his cap and sunglasses again while he pulled on his shirt. Then he took his hat and shades back. From the side, I could see he'd closed his eyes behind the lenses as he inhaled a long, calming breath through his nose.

With Ms. Nakamoto issuing clipped instructions through her microphone, I whispered to Will, "What are you thinking about? Revenge?"

"Snow."

Ms. Nakamoto drilled us for most of practice, so we didn't get to chat. We played and marched through the opening number probably eleven times. In the pauses between, while Ms. Nakamoto stood way up in the stands with DeMarcus and they pointed at the lopsided loops in the formation (not our problem; drums stood in rows), we watched Sawyer working the field in his pelican costume. It was impossible not to watch him.

Sawyer and I were good friends. I knew there was a lot more to him than being the screwed-up son of a felon. But I'd been just as astonished as everybody else when he tried out for school mascot last spring—and made it. He'd told me excitedly about the school paying for him to go to mascot camp a few weeks ago. He'd learned a ton, and he was over the moon the day the school handed him the mascot costume they'd ordered. The new pelican wasn't especially for him, of course. It was just time for a new one. The old pelican had been shedding faux feathers and looked like it had spent time in an inland pond and caught a disease that caused its beak to disintegrate. When the drum line had been bored in the stands at a lackluster football game last fall and feeling snarky, we'd taken to calling it the Pelican't.

This was our first time seeing Sawyer the New Pelican in action, and his hold on everyone's attention had very little to do with the bird's blinding whiteness. He performed an exaggerated version of the cheerleaders' chants and dances while standing right behind Kaye, and he wasn't dissuaded when Kaye frequently spun around and slapped him. His outfit was padded. Eventually he wandered over to bother the majorettes until Ms. Nakamoto called, "Mr. De Luca, remove yourself from the band, and keep your wings to yourself."

The band and the cheerleaders burst into laughter. Sawyer folded his wings and stomped his huge bird-feet back toward the cheerleaders in a huff. Chuckling, I said, "He's going to be good."

"Or dead," Will grumbled. "How does he wear that getup in this heat?" I could see why Will was concerned. Even in his shorts and tee, with his hair as short as Izzy could have cut it without shaving it, sweat dripped down his temple, and his cheeks gleamed with it.

"I told him not to put on the costume in practice during the heat of the day," I said. "He says he wants to get used to it so he doesn't pass out during a game."

"So you're seeing him again?" Will asked. "You didn't tell me that."

His question shocked me. He hadn't mentioned Sawyer, or sounded particularly jealous, since Monday.

No, I wasn't seeing Sawyer. That is, I'd never been *seeing* him in the way Will meant. And something about bantering with Will during practice had made me feel almost like I was seeing *him*, and going out with Sawyer would be cheating.

Of course, if that was true, Will was cheating on me every night with Angelica. And Will had no business thinking I should keep him updated on whether I was *seeing* Sawyer or not.

Logically I knew this. But Will and I were operating on a different plane from everybody around us, it seemed to me. He was in a relationship. He thought I was in a relationship. We shouldn't have feelings for each other, but we did, and they were more important than anything else—at least when we were together.

"Um," I said as he tapped one stick lightly on the rim of his drum, nervous for my answer. Part of me wanted to tell him I *was* seeing Sawyer, just to give him a taste of what I'd felt like when he'd lain on the beach with his hand on Angelica.

The school bell rang through a speaker on the outside of the school, loud enough for us to hear across the parking lot and down in this hole. It was the signal for the end of the period and the beginning of announcements. The rest of the school sat in classrooms and listened to the principal go over test schedules, game schedules, and threats of *no more artificial sweetener for anyone* if students kept sprinkling Equal on the floor of the lunchroom and yelling "blizzard!" Though the announcements had never struck me as earth shattering, the principal thought they were so important that she typed them up and e-mailed them every afternoon to DeMarcus so he could read them to the band and cheerleaders (and insane school mascot) using Ms. Nakamoto's microphone. I explained this to Will, and we dumped our drums and harnesses onto the grass.

DeMarcus's reserved monotone was great for being the guy in charge of the band, but not so good for reading announcements. Bo-ring. In fact, though we were supposed to be paying attention, I thought we were veering toward dangerous territory where Will would ask me again whether I was seeing Sawyer. I preferred to let the question hang there, unanswered. That way, I wasn't telling a lie, but Will had to wonder about Sawyer and me.

So, to spice up the announcements a bit, I started translating them into Spanish in an even worse monotone than DeMarcus's. After an initial burst of laughter that made the cymbals turn around, Will pressed his lips together while I entertained him with the Telemundo version of soporific crap.

"That's all wrong," he said. "The Spanish I've learned has been super animated. I thought that was part of the language." He took a stab at the next announcement, enunciating it like an overenthusiastic thespian.

"You just mixed up 'swimming pool' with 'fish,' and

'swimmer' with 'matador,'" I informed him. "I'm glad you're not really announcing this, or people would be dressing very strangely for the swim meet tomorrow."

"That's it." He grabbed me and wrapped his arm around my shoulders, threatening the headlock.

"No fair!" I squealed. "The terms of the headlock are *very clear*. I did not mention lutefisk."

"Mr. Matthews, get off Ms. Cruz," Ms. Nakamoto called through the microphone. When Will stood me up straight, she was handing the microphone back to DeMarcus so he could finish the announcements.

Turning around on the towel he was sharing with a trombone, Jimmy tapped his watch and told Will and me, "Fifty-six minutes. Not a personal record, but a damned good time."

In answer, Will held one drumstick out beside him, flipped it into the air so that it tumbled three or four times, and caught it without looking at it. This was his answer to pretty much everything drummers said to him that he didn't like, and it was effective at awing them into silence.

"How do you do that?" I asked. If he managed to escape back to Minnesota early and left me high and dry as drum captain, I could sure use a trick like that. I'd never awed anyone into silence in my life.

"Like this," he said, showing me his drumstick in his palm. I imitated him. "Now . . ." He raked his thumb under the stick and flipped it into the air. He caught it neatly. I tried it and accidentally launched the stick at his head. He caught that, too.

"Not quite," he laughed. "Look." He took my hand in his, pressed my stick into my palm, and showed me how to scoop the stick out and upward with my thumb. I wanted to learn this trick, really. All the warmth spreading across my cheeks had everything to do with excitement at learning a stunt, and the oppressive heat of the afternoon, and nothing to do with Will standing inches from me, his hands on mine.

"Oooooh," the band moaned loudly enough that I glanced up to see what the commotion was. The entire band, all hundred and eighty of them extending in lines and curlicues across the grass, turned around in one motion to stare at us.

At least, that was my first impression—that they were staring at both Will and me. Maybe DeMarcus had paused in his drone to hand the microphone to Ms. Nakamoto, who'd scolded Will and me for touching again, and we hadn't heard her over our own laughter. But DeMarcus was still reciting the announcements.

I hit on the answer. The band was staring at Will, not

me. I still didn't know why, but I wasn't surprised anymore. People stared at Will a *lot*, even when he *was* wearing a shirt. I spent a good portion of my day trying not to do it myself.

No, that didn't seem right either. Girls might gaze longingly at Will as they passed him on the grass, but the whole band wouldn't turn around to say "Oooooh!" unless he'd gotten in trouble.

"What is it? I wasn't listening," I said to Will as a joke, because the fact that I hadn't been listening was pretty obvious.

"I don't know," he said, giving the band a suspicious once-over, "but they're still pointing at us."

At *me*, I thought. I glanced around the drum line to pinpoint someone I could ask, but everybody else had abandoned their drums to sit down with trumpets or clarinets who had towels to spread out. Will and I were the only ones left standing. Nobody was offering an explanation.

"Whatever it is," Will said, "it must be very good, or very bad." He mouthed a question to Angelica way across the field. It was probably my imagination, but I thought she turned away on purpose.

Maybe I would have better luck. I peered in the direction of Kaye and the group of cheerleaders huddled up front. Sure enough, she was waving her arms, trying to catch my attention, mouthing something. I read her lips. "Biggest fart," I said. "I let out the biggest fart? I am sure I did *not*. Only freshman trumpets have contests like that."

"I've got it," Will said. "Biggest Flirt."

"Oh!" I understood now. DeMarcus must be announcing the winners of the Senior Superlatives titles we'd voted on first thing that morning. In fact, he was calling out Most Athletic right now. And while I wasn't listening, I'd been elected Biggest Flirt. "I'm not sure I like this. It has a slut-shaming flavor, like they really wanted to give me Biggest Ho."

"No, Tia." The worry line formed between Will's brows as he explained, "We're *both* Biggest Flirts."

"*You?*" I laughed. "Why would anybody elect *you* Biggest Flirt?"

"Because of you!" Those bright blue eyes glared at me over his sunglasses.

I'd withstood the Florida heat for an hour with no problem, but suddenly I felt sweat break out on my forehead. Will had been chosen Biggest Flirt because of me? The school thought we were flirting with *each other*?

Well, if I was honest with myself—a twisting pain settled in the pit of my stomach, which was what I got for being honest with myself—I *had* been flirting with Will all week. I just hadn't known anybody had noticed. Except for

Chelsea and Brody and DeMarcus. . . . The list got longer as I remembered all the people who'd asked me about Will in the past few days. For some reason I'd had the impression we were invisible here at the back of the field with the whole band turned the other way. Now I knew we'd been in a fishbowl for anyone to see.

Worst of all, Will had been elected Biggest Flirt too. I'd felt like I was only teasing him, but the school thought he'd been flirting back. That gave me a head rush. Will secretly liked me.

Or, he *had*. I could tell by the way he was looking up at the sky that he was angry. Angelica had turned her back on him because she didn't like her boyfriend being named Biggest Flirt with another girl. And that meant my delicious friendship with Will was about to come to a screeching halt.

7

STRANGELY, WILL SEEMED LESS CONCERNED about what Angelica would think, and more concerned about what his parents would think. With DeMarcus announcing Senior Superlatives titles in the background, Will told me, "You don't understand what a big deal this is. My parents are going to look through my yearbook next May and see I won Biggest Flirt. If they make friends and start talking to other parents, the rumor may get back to them even sooner."

"So?"

"So, I'm trying to convince them I'm responsible enough to drive up to Atlanta for drum corps in a couple of months, and to go to college in Minnesota like I always planned. They say the extra expense for out-of-state tuition has to be worth their while. In other words, I can't screw up or seem like I'm not serious about school. If I'd stayed in Minnesota, I would have been Most Academic."

"There's no way you would have gotten that here," I said. "A lot of people are in the running for valedictorian, but Xavier Pilkington sewed up the title of Royal Nerdbait in third grade when he made a working dishwasher out of Legos."

"Right. I understand that. I don't belong here, and everything's already taken. So why couldn't I get no title, rather than Biggest Flirt? If the school puts that stuff on the Internet, my friends at home are going to see it."

"Your friends who cheated on you within two minutes of you leaving?"

He drew back from me and stood up straighter, looking down at me over his shades with astonishment and hurt in his blue eyes.

"Cheap shot," I admitted, "but you have taken on an accusatory tone. You're standing here blaming *me* when we *both* got elected Biggest Flirt. We achieved that honor together. It's like a guy blaming a girl for getting pregnant."

Instantly I was sorry. I'd blurted out my resentment from a fight Izzy had had with her ex a couple of years ago. Will already had a low enough opinion of me. I hadn't meant to make it worse.

His mouth flattened into a grim line. I thought he was going to yell at me.

Instead, he opened his arms and slid them around me, stepping forward until he was giving me a full-body hug. My ear pressed against his damp T-shirt. He was getting me sweaty. I didn't mind. I could hear his heartbeat thumping as the low notes of his voice vibrated in his chest. "I'm not blaming you," he said. "I'm sorry. I didn't mean to make you feel that way."

I allowed myself to stay in his arms, enjoying the way his body made mine feel, for three deep breaths before I started to back away.

"Mr.," Ms. Nakamoto said through the microphone, which she'd taken away from DeMarcus again, "Matthews."

Will put his hands up, a drumstick in each, in the pose he assumed at least once per practice.

Jimmy called from his towel, "Double header!"

Ms. Nakamoto gave the microphone back to DeMarcus, who resumed his slow recitation of the senior titles.

"Are you okay?" I asked Will. His eyes were closed behind his shades.

"It's so hot," he said. "I might vomit."

I glanced toward the sidelines. The lunchroom work-ers had already taken away the cooler of water they'd set out for us at the beginning of practice. "You don't have any water left?"

He tapped the plastic bottle in his back pocket, which made a hollow sound, and shook his head. A drop of sweat slid from his cheek, over his chin, and down his neck.

"Here," I said, trying not to sound alarmed. I handed him my own half-full bottle from my pocket.

"Thanks." I watched his throat working as he drank all of it in one long draw and tossed the bottle toward his drum on the grass. Then he pulled up the hem of his shirt to wipe his face. Glancing over at me, he said, "I'm okay."

"You worry me."

"I just get kind of dizzy sometimes," he said. "I feel like a dork."

"You *are* a dork," I said, "but not because of that."

He started toward me. I recognized his headlock stance by now.

"Mr. Matthews," I warned him in Ms. Nakamoto's voice.

"Kaye Gordon and Aidan O'Neill." DeMarcus's monotone had continued through the microphone all this time, but he caught my attention only when he mentioned my friend. "Most Likely to Succeed."

That was perfect! Or it would have been, if I'd liked

Aidan. At any rate, I could tell *Kaye* was happy about it. She curtseyed, grinned, and gave everyone a two-handed wave like she'd just landed a perfect vault and won the Olympics for the US gymnastics team. I cheered and clapped for her along with everyone else.

One of my hands was jerked down from clapping by something large and fuzzy. I was being attacked by a killer stuffed animal. Glancing behind me, I saw it was Sawyer the Pelican. I stopped fighting him and relaxed my arm before he pulled it out of its socket.

Wrong move. He'd caught Will's arm too. I realized right before it happened that Sawyer was trying to make us hold hands.

I jerked my hand away and cried, "Stop!" because yelling in the middle of announcements was a great idea when I didn't want people staring at me anymore. At the same time, Will jerked *his* hand away, uttering an outraged "Hey!" His face was as red as a sunburn.

"Come on," I said to Sawyer's enormous bird head, which I assumed had an ear hole in it somewhere so he could hear me. "Will's already in trouble with the boss lady."

"Sawyer De Luca," DeMarcus droned.

Distracted from Will and me, thankfully, Sawyer put his weird, furry pelican hands up to his huge beak like he could hardly stand the suspense of what title he'd been given. Most School Spirit, of course. But if that had been his title, a girl would have been named along with him. He must have won an award we didn't give to girls because it would make them cry.

"Most Likely to Go to Jail," DeMarcus called.

"Oh!" I exclaimed. That was low. The title had seemed funny to me when it was a joke. It wasn't amusing anymore when the winner's dad had *actually* gone to jail.

I stopped feeling sorry for Sawyer when he grabbed both my drumsticks. I sighed in frustration and put my hands on my hips. I didn't want to be part of his act. Maybe another day, but not right now, when I felt so mortified that I was partially responsible for mortifying Will. "Give them to me," I told Sawyer.

He shook his huge head. His googly eyes gazed at me, but staring angrily at him did no good because I wasn't sure which part of the head he was actually looking out of.

Will stepped forward to intervene. "Back off, bird."

Good. If Will was defending me, he couldn't be *too* resentful.

Sawyer put one hand over his beak, like he was horrified, and used the other wing—with my drumsticks in that hand—to cover his bird crotch.

"I said *back* off," Will said, laughing, "not *jack* off."

Will was laughing! Now I felt even more relieved—until Sawyer put my drumsticks into his enormous bird beak.

"Oh, Sawyer," I sighed. Almost as if he'd anticipated being named Most Likely to Go to Jail, he'd been stealing things all period and slipping them into his beak—sunscreen, hats, cheerleader pompons so voluminous they didn't quite fit and hung over the edges of his mouth like he'd tried to swallow an octopus. When his victims finally convinced him to give their stuff back, he shoved his wing into his mouth, fished around in there, pulled out the possessions in question, and wiped them on his ample tail like they were covered in bird saliva before handing them back, pretend-wet. I didn't want this to happen to my new Vic Firth sticks. After purchasing them last spring and promptly losing them, I'd found them Tuesday night under my bed and brought them to practice. Will had been impressed. But everyone seemed powerless in the face of Sawyer's act, and I was no exception.

Apparently, Will *was* an exception. He leaped forward and put both hands around Sawyer's padded neck to choke him. This was a pretty funny sight because normally Will was taller than Sawyer, but Sawyer in the costume was taller than everyone. Will growled, "Cough them up, pelican." Sawyer shook his head stubbornly.

Will let him go. "Have you drunk any water since you've been out here? You've got to be dying in that getup."

Sawyer picked up the empty bottle Will had thrown down and tipped it up over his beak.

"That's awesome," I said. "Pantomiming hydration. Seriously, Sawyer, you've got to take your head off for water breaks."

"Harper Davis and Brody Larson," DeMarcus intoned.

DeMarcus had been reading on and on as Will and I argued with the world's largest bird, but at this announcement, Will looked at me in confusion. Sawyer scratched his bird head.

I'd given Will a few possible titles for Harper. And I'd told him Brody might be voted Most Athletic because of his football skills, or Most Likely to Die on a Dare because of the time he jumped from the top of the inflatable water slide on Fifth-Grade Play Day and had to go to the hospital. But Brody and Harper were so different from each other that I couldn't think of a single thing they *both* might have won. I could tell from Will's expression and Sawyer's pantomime that they were thinking this too.

"Perfect Couple That Never Was," DeMarcus said.

"What?" I exclaimed. "How bizarre." It was so strange for Harper to get paired romantically with a guy she probably had nothing in common with and hardly knew—especially when that guy already had a girlfriend, and Harper had a boyfriend.

"Almost as bizarre as the two of us getting voted Biggest Flirts." Will looked over at me, and the big grin he'd been wearing slowly faded.

I don't know what he saw in my face that made him regret his joke. I didn't have a crush on him, exactly. To me, a crush implied that I wished we would get together someday. I didn't wish this for Will and me. The only way we would ever hook up again was if we both got plastered at a party—which happened to me often enough, and likely never happened to Will.

But I did admire him. Long for him. Enjoy teasing him more than I'd ever enjoyed telling another uptight guy dirty jokes. He must have detected this with his Super X-Ray Tall Girl Vision, because his eyes shifted away. He opened his mouth to say something to get us out of this awkward conversation, but he must not have been able to think of anything and closed his mouth again.

Sawyer turned his bird head pointedly to Will, then just as pointedly to me.

"What?" I yelled at Sawyer. It was bad enough that Will was embarrassed to be associated with me. Having a huge bird exaggerate the situation made it worse.

Sawyer had told me before that he never talked in costume, which might have been the weirdest thing about his act, because when he wasn't wearing the bird getup, he never shut up. This time he didn't even pantomime a reaction to me shouting at him. He simply reached into his beak, pulled out my drumsticks, wiped the imaginary spit on his big bird ass, and handed them to me between two fingers like they were so gross that he was reluctant to touch them.

The field was full of noise and movement. DeMarcus must have finished the announcements. Most of the cheerleaders and the band moved toward the stadium exit, with a few trumpets playing runs, like anybody was going to be impressed. Those of us who'd ditched our heavier instruments during the announcements bent to pick them up now, Will and me included.

Normally this would be the time at the end of practice when Will and I would get in one last laugh for the road, some meta-analysis of the sorry excuse for a newscaster that was DeMarcus. But Will was very obviously keeping himself turned away from me as he hooked his snare onto his harness to carry it off the field. It was like we were having a sullen lovers' quarrel without the benefit of making out first.

Across the field, Kaye turned toward me. Anticipating

her move, Sawyer had crept up behind her, if that was possible while wearing three-foot-long bird shoes, and stepped into her path. She ran right into his padded belly. "Ooof!" she cried. "Get out of my way, pelican!" Sawyer pumped her hand up and down, congratulating her on being named Most Likely to Succeed. When she didn't protest, he tried to put his wing around her. This time she shoved him away.

She walked toward me with her arms out for a hug. I put my arms out too. We couldn't really embrace because my drum stuck out in front of me like I was fifteen months pregnant, but we leaned around the obstruction and patted each other on the shoulder, then walked toward the stadium exit together.

"Congratulations, princess!" I sang. "I want to go down on record as the first person to ask you for money. I'll give you ten years to become a millionaire before I cash in, but I'm asking you in advance."

"So noted," she said, like we were in one of the club meetings she ran so well. "And congratulations to you!"

Despite myself, my gaze floated ahead of us to Will. Every band practice after the first, Angelica had waited for him, smiling brightly, at the gate separating the field from the stands. Today she frowned at him, hands on her hips.

I had mixed emotions about this. I could actually feel the

emotions churning like a couple of different kinds of acid in my gut. If Angelica broke up with Will for being named Biggest Flirt, that would make him available for me again. But I'd already decided I didn't want him. It would be my fault if he lost his girlfriend, and I was afraid he wouldn't forgive me.

Dejected, I asked Kaye, "Congratulations for *what*?" I doubted she'd be happy for me, even in jest, for being elected Biggest Flirt. Not after her lecture at the antiques shop last Monday.

"For *not* getting elected Biggest Party Animal," she explained. "What if a college admissions board saw that when they looked you up online?"

"I beg your pardon," I said. "That's your neurosis, not mine." I planned to go to college, eventually, when I got around to it, but not one with an admissions board that ran background checks through Homeland Security.

She stomped her petite cheerleader shoe in protest that I wasn't taking this seriously. "What about your dad? Your dad might have grounded you."

This was Kaye's vivid imagination. She was superimposing her own family life on mine. My dad would never find out what I'd been elected. I could have been voted Biggest Ho, or Greenest Teeth, and he wouldn't have noticed. And he couldn't very well ground me even if he wanted to, since he was either asleep or gone whenever I went out. Parents who made their kids stay home had to be home themselves.

"Dodged a bullet there," I said.

"Of course, getting elected Biggest Flirt with Will Matthews when he already has a girlfriend is pretty awkward too."

"Can it, would you?" I knew she was only teasing, but I wasn't in the mood. "You haven't given me helpful advice about boys since the sixth grade."

"Yeah. That was the last time you turned one down."

I glared at her and considered giving her a good whack with my drum, but we were on the stairs.

"I'm kidding!" she exclaimed. "Come on. You've cultivated this reputation yourself. You act like you're upset that you got the title."

"I just didn't think Will and I were attracting that much attention," I confessed. "We're friends, and we horse around, but I wouldn't have thought we would stick out to the whole school after four days of band camp."

"You're hard to miss," she said. "You're both six feet tall."

"We are not." I looked up at Will, who was cresting the stairs with tiny Angelica beside him. I was only five nine, which admittedly was tall for a girl, but not so tall for people in general. Will, on the other hand, had a good four inches on me, maybe more. I corrected myself: "*I* am not."

"The two of you are probably six feet tall on average," Kaye said as we reached the top of the stairs ourselves. Out in the parking lot, Will stood in front of the open trunk of his car, talking to Angelica. He leaned way down. She gave him a peck on the cheek. She flounced smiling across the melted asphalt, toward the band room. Obviously being elected Biggest Flirt hadn't hurt his relationship with Angelica after all.

He pulled off his T-shirt, rubbed it across his muscular chest and arms, and ducked into his trunk again for a dry one. He had a whole pile of them in there.

"Wow," Kaye said reverently.

"Yeah," I agreed.

"And we're heading over there," Kaye noticed, "when he's half-naked, his girlfriend just kissed him, and you and he were chosen Biggest Flirts together? This is messed up."

"He invited me to keep my drum in his trunk," I explained as we reached him. Considering our new title, I thought it might help to remind him that this storage option had been his idea, not mine.

"Oh," Will said, turning around with the fresh T-shirt in his hands. Glancing at Kaye and then back at me, he said, "You can't anymore, because of the flirting thing."

"Wait a minute." I didn't mean to raise my voice, especially not with Kaye standing there. But I felt baited and switched, so I lashed out. "I can understand why we shouldn't flirt anymore because of the title, but not why I can't leave my drum in your car. This is how it ends, after all our time together? What about the mortgage? What about the *kids*?"

His grim mouth slid to one side, like he was frustrated with me and also trying very hard not to laugh. I could hear shouts and slamming doors in the parking lot now that school was dismissed and people were getting in their cars and driving away. His blue eyes swept the area over my head, alert for anyone who might have overheard me and would *tell Angelica oh noes.*

My phone vibrated in my pocket. "Hold on," I told Will, exasperated with absolutely everybody. The shop was on the line, and I figured I'd better answer since I'd ignored their call a few minutes before. "Bob and Roger's Antiques," I said sarcastically. "How may I help you? *From band practice?*"

While Roger complained to me in one ear that Bob couldn't remember where he'd stored any of the Depression glass, I put my hand over the other ear and tried to shut out Will commenting to Kaye, "The shop calls her a *lot*."

"She's their golden child," Kaye explained.

"I don't know," I told Roger, because if I kept helping him and Bob when they called me, they would keep calling me and appreciating my help, which would surely lead to a promotion and more responsibility.

Kaye was telling Will, "They have so much shit in that shop, they have no idea where it is or what's even in there. Lucky for them, Tia has a photographic memory."

Though Roger was still talking, I held the receiver away from my mouth while I told Kaye, "I do not." She'd said this before. I wasn't sure whether she was right. I never really put myself in that category or thought about my memory that way. More than being amazed with myself for remembering stuff, I got annoyed with other people for *not* remembering stuff.

She continued to recount the wonders of my brain to Will. Roger kept lamenting to me that Bob's memory was going—what was left of it, that is. Will flexed his thick triceps as he pulled his clean shirt over his head.

And Sawyer wandered over from the boys' locker room, his blond hair soaked from a shower, wearing a crisp yellow polo shirt and madras shorts, a lot like Aidan's preppie style except that Sawyer also wore flip-flops that looked like he'd walked around the world in them. He stuck his hand out to shake Will's. This could not be good. Alarm bells went off in my head. I was trying to get off the phone so I could intercede before something terrible happened, but I was too late.

He told Will, "Congratulations on being elected Biggest Flirt with my girl instead of yours."

8

"SAWYER!" I SNAPPED. I DIDN'T CATCH WHAT Will growled at him, but it must have been ugly, because Kaye's eyes widened. I told Roger, "I have got to go. I'll be there in half an hour anyway!" Hanging up on him, I told Sawyer, "Would you stop? All of this is getting blown completely out of proportion. It's just a dumb title. The *definition* of flirting is that it *isn't serious.*"

"I'll tell you how it's defined." Sawyer pulled out his phone and typed on it with his thumbs. Kaye gamely looked over his shoulder, as though making things worse between Will and me was the most fun she'd had since her last pedicure. Irked, Will sat on his bumper and felt around in his trunk for his sunglasses without looking at me.

Reading his screen, Sawyer gasped dramatically and slapped his hand over his mouth.

I sighed with relief. The more horrified he acted, the less there was to be horrified about. That's how Sawyer worked. "What does it say?" I asked drily, to get this over with.

"'Flirt,'" Sawyer read in the clipped tone of a fourth-grade know-it-all. "'To flick or jerk.' *Jerk?*" He opened his eyes wide at Will in mock outrage.

"That's not it," Kaye said. "There's another definition."

Sawyer went back to his screen. "'To make love' . . ." He gaped at Will and then me. "Dirty!"

"What?" It was Will's turn to sound outraged.

". . . 'playfully,'" Sawyer finished. "To make love playfully? According to this, you've been getting it on out on the football field, but it's all been in fun! Thank goodness. Not to worry. I can't imagine why Angelica is so pissed."

With a nervous glance at me, Will grumbled, "Give me that," and grabbed the phone from Sawyer. Peering at the screen, he said, "When they say 'make love,' they don't mean sex. They mean, you know, flirting. Playing around. They're using 'make love' that way because this definition was probably written in 1962, when people still wore hats." He handed the phone back to Sawyer.

"I guess that's what I get for downloading the free app instead of the one for a dollar ninety-nine," Sawyer said.

"You still haven't found the right definition," I said. "You're defining 'flirt' as a verb, 'to flirt,' but in the title Biggest Flirts, it's a noun."

"Always thinking, aren't you, Cruz?" Sawyer tapped his temple with one finger, then looked at his phone again. "'Flirt. Noun. A person who dallies with romantic partners, having no intention to commit.'" He pointed at Will. "That's you!"

Will pointed at me. "That's *you*."

I pointed at Sawyer with one drumstick. "That's *you*."

Sawyer pointed at Kaye, who wagged her finger and said, "I don't *think* so."

"Anyway," Sawyer said, pocketing his phone, "you're right, Tia. Angelica shouldn't be upset at *all* that her boyfriend is labeled as someone who's playing her."

"Could you guys let me talk to Tia alone?" Will's words were polite but clipped.

"Yes," Sawyer said, "but don't dally. Ha!"

Kaye rolled her eyes. Bumping fists with me, she put her arm around Sawyer and pointed him across the parking lot.

"Congrats on being Most Likely to Succeed," we heard him say. "Can I borrow some money?"

"Tia asked first," Kaye said. They walked toward Aidan,

who sat on his front bumper, glowering at them, like he was annoyed with Kaye or Sawyer or both.

Join the club. I turned back to Will. "Sorry about that. You were saying? Angelica doesn't want my junk in your trunk?"

He gave me the lopsided smile I loved. "Look, from the time I left the field to the time I made it back to my car, four people called me a dog. Everybody thinks I've been flirting with you but dating Angelica."

"You *have* been flirting with me but dating Angelica."

"No." He shook his head emphatically. "I asked her to lunch on Monday. I wanted her to show me around town—you know, like I asked *you* to lunch first—"

I nodded with my eyebrows raised, acting like I was only politely interested, not hanging on every word about what he'd done (or not done) with Angelica.

"—but she didn't seem to know anything about this town, even though she said she's lived here all her life. I brought her back to band practice that evening, and except at other practices, I didn't see her again until the party last night."

"Where you placed your hand on her bare tummy," I reminded him.

He pointed at me. He looked strange doing this without a drumstick in his hand. "I sat down by myself, under a tree, because I had started to feel sick from the heat."

So my instincts *hadn't* been wrong. I wanted to find Chelsea right then and vindicate myself for being concerned about his health last night. "Were you in shade when you first sat down? And then the sun moved?"

"Yes! I'm not stupid."

"Why didn't you go in the water to cool off?" Really, he was going to die here before he made it back to Minnesota.

"It was sunny in the water. So, Angelica sat down with me. We talked for a while, and then I lay down and closed my eyes, just hoping I'd feel better if I rested for a little bit. The next thing I knew, you were waking me up."

"With your hand on her bare tummy," I repeated.

"She must have pulled my arm around her," he said.

I gave him a slow, assessing look, letting him know I was not born yesterday.

"I don't care whether you believe me or not," he said lightly. "*You* won't go out with *me*, remember?"

Tingles spread across my face and chest, and I stepped a little closer to him. He hadn't given up on me in favor of Angelica after all. But something didn't make sense. "No, you hung out with her for the rest of the night."

"Because I've been following *you* around like a puppy all week. It's embarrassing."

"Oh." In my defense, I really had assumed he was dating

Angelica. But now I saw what I'd been putting him through. I was his best friend in town, yet I'd made it clear I didn't want to hang out with him any more than necessary. That had to be a blow to the new guy's ego.

"I shouldn't have hung out with her, either," he said, "because she assumed what everybody else assumed, that she and I would go out a second time. She confronted me down on the field just now and told me she wasn't going to date me again if I kept flirting with you. On Monday, when she asked me about you, I said we stand right next to each other throughout band practice, and we're friends. Just friends. I guess that made sense to her then."

I guessed not, judging from the way she'd glared across the field at me. "Right," I said.

"But this label changes everything," he said. "The whole senior class is basically telling her that I'm a liar. Now they'll be watching you and me. It's like being accused of a crime. Even if you're proven innocent, people always suspect you when a wallet goes missing."

I was one hundred percent sure that this analogy had nothing to do with Will's real life. Of *course* this nice boy (in his own mind, at least) would never be accused of stealing a wallet. And of *course* he hadn't meant to flirt with me. He had no feelings for me. It was all a big misunderstanding.

"I finally asked her out on a date," he said. "Tonight. And that means you can't keep your drum in my car anymore."

Suddenly the sun was bothering *me*. I wished he would move over and make room for me in the shade of his trunk. "It kind of sounds like you wouldn't have asked her out again if we hadn't been elected to this stupid title."

"This stupid title is all anybody here knows about me," he said. "I'm the asshole who took Angelica out and flirted with you. Well, now I'm not going to flirt with you, and I'm going to make it up to her."

"What for?" I burst out. "Is this another one of those things you need to prove to your parents so they'll let you out of the nest? You're supposed to be elected Most Academic and have a steady girlfriend?"

"That's enough," he said sharply, just as he had when I'd jabbed at him about his Minnesota ex on Monday.

I felt my face turn beet red. The sun was burning a hole through the back of my neck.

He stood, turned around, and dragged my backpack out of his trunk. "Look," he said more gently, "this is a record for me. I've lost three girls in one week. It's too much." He tried to slip the backpack onto my back for me. I kept my arms stubbornly by my sides. He pried one arm up and then the other, which would have looked *suspiciously like flirting* if anybody in the parking lot had been watching. Then he attempted to hand me my purse. I wouldn't take it. He plopped it onto my drum. The snares rattled. The noise echoed against the wall of the stadium.

"All this is really heavy," I whined. Seriously, the drum weighed twenty pounds. My purse on top of it weighed a lot too. I rarely cleaned it out, and God only knew what was in there. My backpack actually had books in it today. On a whim I'd thought it might be fun to do something unusual this weekend: homework. I poked out my bottom lip, fluttered my eyelashes, and asked Will, "Could you give me a ride over to the band room?"

He just stared at me without laughing this time, without twisting his mouth to keep from laughing. The joke was over. "See you Monday."

Fine. I whirled around—he dodged at the last second so I didn't whack him in the gut with the drum—and I walked through the parking lot, picking spaces to pass through that cars had already pulled out of, because the drum and I were too wide to edge through the path between two parked cars. We would have taken off some paint.

Harper waited for me behind the school, already astride her bike. She could use her granddad's car whenever she wanted, and she drove me to school on the rare occasions when it rained. The rest of the time, she biked. *Voluntarily.* She said it helped her feel more a part of the community. Harper was kind of a kook.

"Hey!" she called. "You told me you were keeping your stuff in Will's car. Why do you still have your drum?"

"He kicked me out of his trunk. I've got to dump this in the band room, but I'll just be a sec." I dropped my purse and backpack beside my bike in the rack, then walked through the entrance of the school, into a courtyard full of palm trees where people hung out during midmorning break and lunch. This was a bad design on the school's part, because the courtyard was walled in by classrooms with windows that definitely were not soundproof. Teachers let us escape out here, then shushed us constantly. It was like standing next to Will in band.

All the frustration of the last thirty minutes—or the last week, more like it—hit me suddenly. I felt an uncontrollable urge to make some noise. Marching through the courtyard, I tapped out a complicated salsa beat while singing a Marc Anthony tune at the top of my lungs. He was born in New York City and was about as Puerto Rican as I was, but the dude could really write a salsa. And though drumming was second nature to me after years of practice, when I really listened to myself, I was surprised at how good I was and how fast my sticks could strike the drumhead.

I saw movement behind one of the windows. Though school was out, the teachers were still here, planning our demise for Monday. They wanted *quiet*. In the next second someone would slam open a window and tell me to be *quiet*. Until that happened, I beat my drum as loudly as I could, even threw in some rim taps that would take the skin off an unprotected ear canal. As I backed through the band room door, I saw Harper had stopped her bike a few yards away. She frowned at me with both hands over her ears.

"Sorry," I said. Feeling a little better, I dumped my drum into the storage room and came back outside. "So, what's this I hear about you being the perfect couple with Brody Larson? You're both dating other people, and you hardly know him. You move fast, don't you? Slut."

"Shut it." She removed one of her hands from the side of her head and placed it over my mouth. Then, as I walked through the courtyard to retrieve my own bike, she pedaled beside me. "The artistic side of me says, 'How cool and random for a boy I hardly know, some jock who isn't on the yearbook staff or the newspaper staff or even in the drama club, to be chosen as my perfect boyfriend!' The artistic side of me wants to write a poem about it. Meanwhile, the rational side of me is saying, 'What the fuck?' Also, 'His girlfriend is going to kick my ass.'"

"I'm not rational at all," I pointed out as though this were not obvious, "and I'm saying 'What the fuck?' also. But the difference between you and me is, the second he and Grace broke up—and this is probably going to happen, because Brody never dates anyone for long—I would try to hook up with him just out of curiosity."

"You're forgetting Kennedy," Harper said.

I was *not* forgetting her boyfriend, Kennedy. I simply thought if her choice was between responsible Kennedy and wild Brody, there was no contest. Bring on the hot mess! But that was me, and Harper was Harper. I figured I'd better let the subject drop before I got myself in trouble.

As we emerged from the courtyard again, I gazed across the parking lot, which was almost empty of students' cars now. Of course Will had *not* waited to watch me emerge from the school so he could rush over and apologize. His car was gone. He'd probably picked up old Angelica on his way off campus. I bet she'd slipped her little hand in his before they even passed the HOME OF THE PELICANS sign.

"Worry about your own mismatched boy," Harper said. "Tell me what happened between you and Will. You were elected Biggest Flirts, and that's why he kicked you out of his trunk?"

"Yes! He broke up with me!" As I unlocked my bike from

the rack and launched myself down the palm-lined street, I told her all about my argument with Will.

"Let me get this straight," she said. "You want him to like you enough that he doesn't ask anyone else out, even though you've turned him down because you don't want a boyfriend."

"Correct."

"That's just selfish of you."

"I agree."

"You're not a selfish person."

"Apparently Will's my downfall."

"But . . ." Harper pondered this for a couple of blocks before finally asking, "Don't you think it might be worth considering bending your no-boyfriend rule for Will? People at school are talking about you two a *lot*. It's hard to believe this is just a passing hookup."

"A past hookup," I clarified. "I'm sure he wouldn't even take me back now. He wants exactly what he has. Angelica is a tiny blond girl. I'm a gangly *puertorriqueña*." We'd reached a row of shops where we had to get off the sidewalk and stick to a narrow bike lane. I shot ahead of Harper, trying to escape this discussion.

"Tia," Harper called, "that's just weird. If Will has a problem with you being part Puerto Rican, you don't want him anyway."

"I *don't* want him anyway," I threw over my shoulder.

"And you're not gangly. You're tall, which would be an asset on the modeling runway."

"I am not on the modeling runway, however. I am riding a bike through suburban Tampa/St. Petersburg, and my knees are touching my ears." As I pedaled, I bent my head to try to make this happen. I swerved dangerously toward the comic book store we were riding past and straightened just in time to avoid crashing through the window and shocking the nerds.

Harper was laughing her ass off behind me. "I promise you're not gangly. To be considered gangly, you would have to walk funny. In that case, Kaye would have shown up at your house before now to conduct an intervention."

We talked about Kaye then. Harper hadn't seen her after school. I told Harper how happy Kaye had seemed at being elected Most Likely to Succeed along with Aidan—as if either of them needed to be reassured.

Harper asked me how closely I'd listened to the announcements. She said she was taking the Senior Superlatives photographs for the yearbook starting Monday morning, and Will and I should meet her in the courtyard right at the beginning of second period.

News to me. I wondered whether I should call Will to

pass along the information. This would violate our new pact to cool it. Angelica would interpret *phone call* as *hot sex* and Will would hate me. No, I would not call him. I could go into the yearbook under the heading Biggest Flirt by myself.

As we approached the antiques store, Harper waved and said brightly, "Ta! See you Monday," as though the coming photo session sounded like good times.

"Ta." I didn't want her to look back and see me watching her mournfully. I locked my bike in the rack and went into the shop.

When we'd first started riding our bikes together, and I'd been headed home instead of to work, I'd always begged Harper to come inside with me—if she would be very, very quiet and not wake my dad—or I would suggest we hang out at her mom's bed and breakfast. She'd explained that I was an extrovert, and extroverts got their energy from being around other people. She was an introvert, and introverts got their energy from being by themselves. She needed to go home, be by herself, and work on her photography project of the moment so that the next time we saw each other, she would have more energy to give me. This scenario made me sound like an alien sucking her brains out through a straw, but it also kind of made sense. It explained why, now that my sisters had moved out and my dad was always at work or asleep,

I felt so down at home. But that knowledge wouldn't do anything to fix a long, lonely weekend.

Luckily I was super busy at work, dealing with customers while simultaneously finding things in inventory for Bob and trying to explain to Roger how computers worked. Three hours flew by. Then we closed, and I was out on the sidewalk again, unlocking my bike. I gazed down the street at the salon where Izzy worked. I could forgive her, I supposed, for what she'd said to me months ago about watching her kids. But Izzy could be harsh, and the idea of her saying something else snide was enough to keep me away. Besides, if she'd been at work to cut Will's hair at seven this morning, she was long gone now.

I rode to my house, lifting my bike over the front lawn so I wouldn't crash through the magnolia leaves and wake my dad. The house was deathly quiet, and I hated it. Much as my sisters had annoyed the crap out of me while they lived at home, I would have given anything to ignore Izzy's orders as I walked in the door, and tease Sophia about the fantasy novel she was reading on the sofa, and yell at Violet because I caught her stealing a shirt out of my closet in the room we shared.

It wasn't going to happen. With a deep sigh that nobody heard but me, I nuked a frozen dinner, cleared off a space at the kitchen table, and drew my calculus book out of my backpack. This actually happened. I thought about Will, and what a good student he was, and what a good student old Angelica was, diligently ciphering in anticipation of that bright, shining day in spring when she could take the AP test. Maybe Will would like me better if I wasn't so lame in school.

But I knew I shouldn't do stuff just because Will would like me better for it. That was exactly why I didn't want a boyfriend. There were other reasons to do my calculus homework, such as not flunking. I pulled out my notebook and turned to the page where I'd written down the assignment. This was more difficult than it sounded. Usually I wrote things down on whatever page I opened to rather than starting from the beginning and working through to the end like *some* academically obsessed drum captains. I took a bite of dinner, started the problem . . . and then lost myself in it. I had a hard time starting my homework because I dreaded it, but once I got into it, I forgot what I was doing and didn't mind so much. Until—

HOOOOOOOOOOONK.

I scraped back my chair and ran outside without even looking to see who'd pulled into the driveway. The only important thing was to get the horn stopped before it woke my dad. I rushed blinking into the dusk. When I was halfway across the lawn, I saw Sawyer grinning at me from the cab of his truck.

I sliced my finger across my throat. "My dad's asleep."

Sawyer took his hand off the horn. "Sorry." He wagged his eyebrows at me. "Does that mean I can come in?"

"No." I didn't have to think about that one. Except for Harper, my friends always assured me they could come inside my house and be quiet. They were wrong. They always forgot, somebody laughed really loudly, and my dad woke up.

"You're afraid we'll make some noise?" Sawyer asked.

"I know we will." Bantering with him was easier than explaining that no, I was serious, my dad actually had to work tonight, and this was the last sleep he would get. Sawyer understood a lot about life—way more than he probably should have at seventeen—but he didn't understand factories that ran all night, or trying to support a family on third shift.

"Why'd you give me such a hard time about Biggest Flirt today?" I griped. "And you called me your girl in front of Will. What was that about?"

"You need to stay away from that guy," Sawyer said. "He's a player."

"He's not," I said. "*You* are."

"But you *like* him," Sawyer pointed out. "That makes him dangerous. I don't matter. So come out with me."

"Can't," I said. "Homework."

"*You?*" he asked, astonished. "Are doing your *homework?*"

Normally I wouldn't have been offended by a comment like that, but what Will had said about me making so many mistakes—that must have gotten to me. "It's been known to happen," I said haughtily.

"I'm more fun than homework," Sawyer said.

I was about to point out that cleaning the toilet was also more fun than homework, and I had no intention of doing that, either.

Then an airliner roared over us, bringing the last of the season's tourists. Labor Day was coming up in two weeks, signaling the end of summer—for Yankees, anyway. I cringed at the noise, crossing my fingers that it wouldn't wake my dad.

Yeah. Sawyer was better than homework. He was way better than another night of staying very quiet until my dad finally dragged himself up grumpily, refused to eat what I'd heated for him because he wasn't hungry when he first woke, and left. It was like living by myself except for an outdoor cat we'd once had that passed through the house only to use the litter box.

"Come on," Sawyer said. "My brother's bartending tonight. Come sit on the back porch of the Crab Lab and get wasted with me."

I said, "Just let me lock up."

9

ONCE I'D GIVEN IN TO SAWYER FRIDAY NIGHT, it didn't make sense to turn him down Saturday night or Sunday night. That's why, when Will and I sat on a bench in the school courtyard Monday morning, waiting for Harper to finish photographing Mr. and Ms. Least Likely to Leave the Tampa/St. Petersburg Metropolitan Area, it was like he and I had traded personalities. I was a little hungover, so I wasn't my usual laugh riot. And Will must have had a banner weekend with old Angelica. He was in a great mood, regaling me with all his ideas for the picture being taken in front of us.

"Chain them to the palm trees," he said. "Build a box and pour concrete around their feet."

"Have them get married at seventeen," I suggested. "Find

the guy a factory job with lots of overtime and give them so many kids that he keeps the factory job and takes all the overtime he's offered so he can feed everybody."

Will frowned at me. "Who are you talking about?"

"My dad." I pressed my fingertips to my throbbing temple.

"Did something happen? What's wrong?" His brow furrowed, and he took a closer look at me, his gaze lingering on my mouth. Which made me look at *his* mouth. Which made me mad.

"Yes, something happened," I snapped. "You broke up with me Friday. You can't decide to be friends with me again today. Go over there." I pointed to a bench on the opposite end of the courtyard. I'd spoken loudly enough that Harper looked up from her camera and raised her eyebrows. I shook my head at her.

I thought Will would be offended all over again. Maybe I *wanted* him to be offended. It was kind of a letdown that he gamely crossed the courtyard and sat where I pointed. Then he called through his cupped hands, "Do we have to stay in the courtyard? We could take them to the beach and bury them up to their necks in sand."

He grinned at me, but his smile faded as I glared at him. Harper was dismissing Mr. and Ms. Loser. They disappeared back inside the school as Will and I continued to watch each other. I didn't know what he was thinking. *I* was thinking that he was the hottest guy I'd ever known, slouched on the bench with one ankle crossed on the other knee, his arms folded defensively, and his pirate earring winking in the sun. I wished he would go back to the frozen tundra and leave me alone.

He called, "You ruined the curve, didn't you?"

He was talking about the test in our AP calculus class. I shifted uncomfortably. The concrete was awfully hard all of a sudden. "That is an ugly thing to accuse me of."

Harper looked up from flipping through the images on her camera. "What curve?"

"Tia was the only one who didn't have her calculus homework this morning," Will explained. "Ms. Reynolds chewed her out and said she'd heard about Tia from other teachers and she was *not* going to have a repeat performance of that in *her* class."

"Oh my God!" Harper gaped sympathetically at me.

"Then we had a test on what the homework had covered," Will said. "Ms. Reynolds graded the papers while we were getting a head start on tonight's homework. In the middle of it she announced, 'You can all thank a very surprising person for making one hundred on this test and ruining the curve for you.' She sounded pissed. And at the end of class, when she passed the tests back, Tia shoved hers in her purse before anybody could see it."

Protectively I tucked my purse closer to my hip on the bench.

"Tia, damn it," Harper cried. "Was the curve just for your class or for all of them?" She told Will, "We're used to her ruining the curve in math, but doing it on the second day of school is pretty obnoxious, even for her."

"Aren't you in Angelica's class?" I asked Harper. "Even if I didn't ruin your curve, Angelica will." I was making this up. Math wasn't Angelica's thing. She was more of a prim-and-proper-English kind of girl whom incorrectly corrected people's grammar.

Harper gave me a quizzical look over her glasses, knowing I was only trying to get Will's goat. "Well, hooray. It's your turn for a yearbook photo." She held out a hand toward Will and a hand toward me, her fancy camera hanging around her neck. I wanted to tell her that Sawyer had already tried to get Will and me to hold hands, with lackluster results. Instead, I stopped a few feet away from her outstretched hand and eyed Will.

"Look," Harper said, "I know this title has caused you two some pain, but I have a job to do here. The yearbook is counting on me. I have to take a flirtatious picture of you both. You didn't win Most Awkward." She turned to Will. "Since you're so great at coming up with photo ideas, what's your brainchild for this one?"

He glanced uncomfortably around the courtyard, into the tops of the palm trees, up at the sky, the same deep color as his eyes. "I hadn't thought about it."

"That's what I suspected," Harper said in a tone that made it sound like she had suspected the opposite. Her retro glasses were adorable, but when her art was at stake and she got in this no-nonsense mood, the glasses made her look like a stern 1960s librarian. "I'll give you a hint," she said. "For this photo, you need to flirt."

"What does that mean?" I asked uneasily.

She shrugged. "You're the flirts. You should do what you were doing to get voted Biggest Flirts in the first place. I never actually witnessed it."

"We were just standing next to each other on the foot-ball field," Will said. "That's all."

"Oh, come on, Will. That's not *all* we were doing," I said just to bother him.

It worked. He cut his eyes at me, and his cheeks turned pink. He wasn't smiling.

"Sorry," Harper said, "but you can't just stand next to each other. Not in *my* yearbook photo. We need some action."

It was strange, but my headache was going away now that Will seemed hot and bothered. His discomfort was some sort of elixir for me. I bounced a little and clapped. "What kind of action?"

"He could drag you into the bushes," Harper said. "That's been done in a lot of yearbooks."

"Yes!" I exclaimed. "Drag me into the bushes!"

"I'm not dragging you into the bushes," Will said. "The bushes are prickly."

"So are you." I snapped my fingers. "There's an idea. I'll drag *you* into the bushes."

He folded his arms on his chest and looked down his nose at me. "You will not."

That sounded like a challenge. "Get your camera ready," I told Harper. I slipped both hands around his upper arm, just where it disappeared under the sleeve of his T-shirt.

Then I paused. I'd known all too well that he was built, but I was surprised at how solid his arm was. I wouldn't be able to move him. But I'd threatened to, and it obviously bugged the shit out of him, so I had to go through with it. I pulled on him and said, "Drag." I gave his arm a couple more cursory jerks. "Drag, drag."

Harper had her camera to her glasses, still clicking away,

but she said, "Not enough action. It's less flirtatious and more mournful and hopeless."

I laughed, because it was true. That's exactly how I'd felt about Will all weekend, and it was gratifying that Harper was able to see that through the camera lens. Even Will laughed a little.

In fact, he looked so carefree in that moment, like the Will I'd had fun with in band practice last week, the one I'd lost when we got elected to this stupid title, that I couldn't resist. With one hand still bracing myself against his rock-hard arm, I stood on my tiptoes and moved in to give him a quick kiss on the corner of his mouth, just where his smile turned up. Harper would get the shot, and Will could sigh with relief and go back to his beloved schoolwork. At least until he had to stand beside me again in band.

Just as my lips were about to reach him, he seemed to realize what I was doing and turned his head slightly. Instead of my lips touching the corner of his mouth, his lips met mine.

I was so confused about whether he'd made the move on purpose or not, and so surprised at the zap of electricity racing through me, that I stood paralyzed for a second. Which I shouldn't have done. We weren't even kissing, really. Our lips only pressed together. If I'd stepped away from him and acted embarrassed, we could have laughed off the whole thing like it had been a mistake.

Instead, his lips parted, and so did mine. We were kissing for real. Neither of us had tripped into this one. I wore a sleeveless minidress, so I shouldn't have gotten overheated, but my skin felt like it was on fire.

As quickly as it had begun, it was over. Will unceremoniously took a step back from me.

He turned to Harper and commanded her, "Delete those pictures. You can't let Angelica see them."

A hoot of laughter drifted to us. It didn't sound loud, but it must have made quite a noise inside the building for us to hear it through the closed windows. I glanced around at the windows and saw boys' faces pressed against the glass. They'd been watching us the whole time.

"Great," Will exclaimed. "Now Angelica will find out for sure. Those assholes will run right back and tell her. Angelica may even be *in* that class." He glared at me, then turned and stalked toward the door. Actually, I don't think he stalked. Stalking was uncool and self-righteous, and Will didn't move that way. He sauntered toward the door and threw it open like a rock star.

And I stared after him with my mouth open, desperately grasping for something funny to say to lighten his mood. He would stop, turn on the step, and give me a grudging grin. I would know that, even if I'd messed up things between him and old Angelica, at least he didn't hate me, and we'd be back to normal soon. But without a joke, I was lost.

I turned to Harper. "Think of a joke."

Harper gaped at Will too. Without taking her eyes off him, she said, "I've got nothing. And I don't think a joke would fix this."

The door slammed shut. Will was gone.

"Of course a joke would have fixed it!" I squeaked. "Normally you're hilarious. What kind of friend are you if you can't think up jokes on cue?"

She looked at me somberly through her glasses. "I'm the kind of friend who will support you during what comes next. If you two Biggest Flirts keep claiming you're not going to flirt anymore, you're going to blow each other's lives wide open."

Angelica did indeed find out about her brand-spanking-new boyfriend kissing the girl he'd sworn off. And then everybody else found out from Angelica. During the break after history, I heard her before I saw her in the crowded hall outside my English class, looking small and dead serious as she pointed her finger in Will's face and raised her voice at him. I gave them a wide berth and ducked into class without either of them seeing me, I thought—which didn't change the fact that everybody in the room stared at me as I walked toward the back and plopped down, four rows away from where I'd sat behind Will on Friday.

Will walked in on the bell, mouth set in a grim line, a pink flush crawling up his neck. I wondered if he'd gotten so angry with Angelica that he'd given her the "That's enough!" line I kept getting from him when I pushed him past his breaking point. He didn't look angry, though. He looked mortified. Apparently he got angry at a girl giving him heat only when he didn't deserve it.

Band that afternoon was exactly as awful as I'd suspected. Unlike in the other classes I shared with Will, I couldn't avoid him. I was stuck right next to him for the whole hour. And he didn't say a word to me unless he was barking orders to the section. He'd brought two bottles of water for himself so he wouldn't run out, and he must have spread sunscreen on the back of his neck already. He sat on the grass by himself instead of sharing my towel. It was the first practice we'd had in which Ms. Nakamoto didn't have to tell him to get off me.

As we rehearsed the halftime show over and over, the hour flew by. But the heat was terrible, even to me, and Sawyer's antics in the pelican costume weren't funny. I tried to lose myself in the music and just enjoy it, forgetting Will was there. This was difficult when I was often sliding one stick sideways to play on his drum while Jimmy played on mine. Then we reversed direction, with me playing on Jimmy's drum and Will's stick in my personal space.

I fantasized about switching places with Jimmy, so that I stood between him and Travis. Just moving one person down in the drum line would make all the difference. I wouldn't feel Will beside me constantly, his arm brushing against mine and suddenly pumping my body full of adrenaline. I wouldn't smell the spicy scent of him that dragged me back, against my wishes, to our hopeless night together. With him finally out of my life, I could spend my spare time floating in the waves at the beach rather than trying to party thoughts of him away.

All it would take was one person in the snare drum line to challenge somebody else. Then we'd all have to try out, and I could carefully throw the competition so that I came in third. Problem was, except for Will, our snare drum line wasn't very ambitious. I hadn't convinced them to challenge me after begging them all summer. I wouldn't convince them to challenge Will now.

I could, however, challenge Will myself.

That fantasy turned into an idea. The idea turned into a plan, because I had plenty of peace to think it through without the pesky drum captain teasing and distracting me. By the time DeMarcus started reading the end-of-day announcements, I'd made up my mind. Without a word to Will or Jimmy, I hefted my drum onto my shoulders, marched across the field, and climbed the stadium steps, making a beeline for Ms. Nakamoto. I whispered in her ear.

When DeMarcus finished his monotone of the day, Ms. Nakamoto held out her hand for the microphone. "One last announcement," she said. "Snare drums, report to the band room before school tomorrow. Ms. Cruz is challenging Mr. Matthews for drum captain."

"Oh, man!" was the first cry to come out of the snare drums, followed by some lower-key cursing—likely because they didn't want to come to school early, not because they were worried about keeping their positions in the section. Then came a swell of "oooooh" as the rest of the band realized I must be trying to make Will's life as miserable as possible.

While I had their attention, I used my drumstick to point at him far away across the field, like a tough boxer talking smack at the press conference before a big match: *You, my friend, are dead meat.*

I wasn't sure I'd ever cried at school before. My decision never to have a boyfriend had come early, so nothing much had bothered me even during middle school when everything bothered everybody and girls broke down because a stranger insulted their sandals.

And now, as a senior, I'd been alternating between swallowing tears and outright sobbing for hours, since I'd beat Will and all the other drums in the challenge to become drum captain.

"This is so frustrating," Kaye said. "Why do you get upset when you do well? It makes no sense!"

She and Harper and I stood in the hall outside Mr. Frank's classroom before study hall. Kaye kept Sawyer and other curious boys at bay with the glare of a student council vice president. I ached to talk to Sawyer about what I'd done too. He understood my problem with responsibility a lot better than Harper and Kaye. But he and they did not get each other at *all*. I couldn't talk to the three of them at the same time.

"I'm not upset for doing well," I grumbled. "I always do well on drums. I'm a good drummer. I just don't want to come in first, because first chair is drum captain and has to be in charge."

"If you didn't want to be drum captain," Harper puzzled, "and Will was drum captain before, why'd you challenge him?"

"Because he's furious with me for breaking him and Angelica up, and I didn't want to stand next to him every day for the rest of marching season. I challenged him and intended to get third."

"Get *third*," Kaye repeated. "Like, you can decide ahead of time what your rank will be."

"Absolutely," I said. "Will should have played perfectly and snagged drum captain again, like he did last week when *he* challenged *me*. Travis is good, but he has trouble with the roll at the beginning of the bridge, so he should have placed second. Jimmy doesn't quite understand the syncopation in the chorus, so he should have placed behind Travis. Actually, he did. The drum line goes downhill from there. All I had to do was throw a couple of minor things and I could have slid in perfectly between Travis and Jimmy at third chair. That way I wouldn't have to slum with the freshmen at the bottom of the section, but I wouldn't have to stand next to Will anymore."

Kaye and Harper shared a look. Harper said, "We know you've thrown challenges before, but I had no idea you were approaching this with the precision of a brain surgeon. Is this how you always try out?"

"Yes."

"So what happened?" Kaye asked flatly. I could tell she was exasperated with me, but she was humoring me. For now.

"I was upset about the whole thing with Will"—I paused to sniffle—"and I forgot to mess up. Now he's even madder at me for taking drum captain away from him. But I didn't want it!"

"That's ridiculous," Kaye said firmly. "You've told us some doozies before. You've been irresponsible and a goofball. But trying to throw a challenge when you love band borders on insane. I can't believe you! You're so smart, Tia. You're so smart that you can pull off looking like an imbecile, just because you don't want to be in charge? You're going to let a guy be in charge so you don't have to take responsibility?"

I had stood there through Kaye's lecture, taking it. I was used to her talking to me like my mom. I didn't mind most of the time, since my mom was gone. It wasn't as if I was getting it twice.

But by the end of Kaye's speech, I was ticked off. She wasn't even through, but I was done listening.

I straightened to my full height, feeling like Godzilla rising out of the Gulf of Mexico to tower over Greater Tampa Bay, and pointed down at her. "You're *vice* president of the student council," I said. "Your boyfriend is *president* of the student council. Is that because you ran for president and he beat you? No, it's because you ran for vice president in the first place. And how did that happen? Either he decided he was going to take the front seat while you took the back, and he informed you of his decision, or *you* decided to take the back seat, so he wouldn't be mad at you."

Kaye's mouth crumpled in a little frown, and her dark eyes blazed. "And how is that worse than what *you're* doing, trying to make sure Will is in charge instead of you?"

"It's worse because *I'm* not giving *you* a damn lecture!"

She stomped off. All I could see was her hair twists bopping down the hall. I had tunnel vision, which happened to me when I got really angry, about once a year.

"Breathe," Harper said.

I'd forgotten she was standing there. Looking around the hall, I saw that I'd attracted everyone's attention, which I was getting really good at lately. Sawyer leaned against the lockers, watching me, waiting to listen to me when I was ready.

Will stood talking with Brody and some other guys from the football team. I was glad Brody had reached out to Will, because otherwise Will probably didn't have a friend in the school. He watched me too, his face stony. When he saw me looking in his direction, he turned away.

I didn't blame him. I'd taken him down in the most public way possible—on purpose, he thought. For the millionth time that morning, I remembered pointing at him with my drumstick yesterday, in front of the whole band. A lot of my problems would be solved if I stopped trying so hard to be funny. I took a long breath. "Do you hate me too?" I asked Harper.

"No. Kaye doesn't hate you either."

"We've never had a fight like that before."

Harper shifted the strap of her camera bag to her other shoulder. "You never told her she was wrong quite so firmly before."

"Do you think I was right, to tell her that?"

Harper raised her eyebrows. "You didn't have to yell in front of everyone. I've never seen you act like this. Will has really thrown you for a loop."

I looked around the hall again. A few people who'd still been staring at me turned away. I didn't want to sit under their gaze all through study hall. I definitely didn't want to spend study hall in the same classroom as Will. "I'm going to clean the band storage room."

"Uh-oh," Harper said. "Like last March?"

"Maybe." I'd gone on a cleaning spree when Violet moved out.

"What are you going to do about Will?" Harper asked.

"I can't *do* anything."

She shook her head. "If you don't try to fix it, it won't get fixed."

"I tried to fix it by challenging him on drum. You see how that turned out."

"I don't mean cook up some cockamamy scheme," she

scolded me. "Actually talk to him, face to face, and explain how you feel."

I didn't think that was possible. I wasn't sure how I felt myself. And even if I had known, the last person I would have wanted to explain it to was Will.

"Later." I held up my hand until she gave me a fist bump. Then I told Mr. Frank I was spending study hall in the band room. Over in Ms. Nakamoto's office, I grinned and sounded perky as I respectfully requested that she loan me a spray bottle of cleaner and a rag.

"Uh-oh," she said, looking up from her desk. "Like last March?"

"Everybody seems to remember that episode as if it was so horrible," I said, dropping the upbeat act after a total of ten seconds. "You got your sousaphones scrubbed, remember?"

"What's happened?" she asked. "Are you upset about the challenge?"

"Yes," I said, actually relieved that she'd guessed.

"Do you want to talk about it?"

"Yes," I repeated with gusto. "I want to undo the challenge and go back to the way we were before, with Will drum captain and me second."

"No." So much for talking about it. She found the cleaner and rag on top of a filing cabinet and handed them to me.

The storage room was tall and narrow, snaking back thirty feet underneath the stage and the auditorium, and lit by a single bulb in the ceiling. The ceiling itself was so high that the janitor had to use a special ladder when the bulb went out, which meant it was sometimes dark in here for days, with everybody falling all over each other trying to locate their instruments and drag them out of their cases. It wasn't much lighter in here even when the bulb worked.

I decided to start with the shady shelf at the back of the room and work my way forward. This involved tugging tubas down and cleaning the dusty wood underneath. Right away I found the trumpet mute that Shelley Stearns had lost and accused the trombone section of stealing last February.

I heard Will's voice out in the hall, creeping into the storage room and echoing weirdly against the concrete block walls. "Wait a minute," he said. "Why do you want to retake a yearbook picture in the storage room? It's dark in there even with the light on."

Suddenly Will came reeling into the room, shoved from behind. Off balance, he couldn't catch himself until he'd already tripped over some trumpet cases and hit the wall.

"Enjoy!" came Harper's voice. The big door slammed.

Will leaped back over the cases and jogged for the door, but the sound of the key turning in the lock outside already echoed through the storage room. He rattled the knob, then pounded the door. "Harper!" he roared. When there was no answer, he called, "Ms. Nakamoto?"

"She's gone to lunch," came Harper's bold little voice through the steel. "I'll come back to let you out at the end of the period. I hope you don't have to pee."

"Damn it, Harper!" Will backed up a pace and rammed the door mightily with one shoulder. It made a terrific noise but didn't budge.

To stop him before he hurt himself, I spoke up. "It's my fault. I left the key in the lock. I should have known she'd try something like this."

He whirled around, squinting in the dim light.

I stepped out from the dark shelves, where he could see me. "She locked us in here together so we'd have to talk about what happened."

His shoulders sagged. "I hate Florida."

10

WELL, I HADN'T WANTED TO TALK TO HIM, either, but the idea of five minutes of conversation wih him wasn't loathsome enough to make me despise the entire state.

"Tia," he said softly. "Don't look like that."

How did he want me to look? Like a girl who didn't mind being insulted? I tried that, crossing my arms in front of me, which was awkward because I was still holding the filthy rag in one hand and the spray bottle in the other.

He frowned. "What are you doing in here?"

"Cleaning."

"You?"

"You know, just shut up. If I never bathed, you would have smelled me by now. The sun makes that worse. Another reason for you to hate Florida."

He put his hands in his hair, looked perplexed, and then took his hands away again, as if he'd forgotten momentarily that his long hair was gone. "*You've* ruined *my* life, but you're going to make me feel like *I've* done something wrong."

I squinted to keep the tears from slipping out of my eyes. I didn't feel like I was totally to blame for our kiss yesterday, or for us getting elected Biggest Flirts. But I *was* to blame for boasting about knocking him out of drum captain, and then actually doing it. I'd been angry with Will, but I cared about him—way too much—and the last thing I'd wanted was to ruin his life.

I'd never been a girl who cried or otherwise showed my emotions just to get my way. I did occasionally let an emotion slip, but never to manipulate anyone. I'd noticed, though, that my mood swings really worked on Will. He was a sucker for a sad girl. He actually watched my face in band, and if I looked genuinely hurt at a pretend insult he'd thrown at me, he apologized. Now his voice softened. "Hey."

I was too far gone already. Cleaning for a few minutes had helped me put my brain on the right track, but now I was back where I'd spent the whole morning, in tears. "I didn't mean to beat you," I sobbed. "I know you won't believe that now, but you thought last Monday that I'd thrown the challenge. I meant to throw it again. I wanted to get third. I didn't want to stand next to you when you hate me." Stating the case that plainly, I sounded like a kindergartener, but the truth was simple.

He put out one hand, pulled me toward him, and sat me down on a tuba case. With a big sigh, he sat down next to me. The flagpoles behind us, probably twenty of them wrapped in their flags, slid sideways along the wall and draped the silks over us. I had always thought "silks" was a strange thing to call band flags, because clearly they were made of polyester.

"Okay," he said, batting the weird orange cloth off us. "You're not totally to blame for what happened yesterday. You started to kiss me, and I kissed you back. And I agree we were both at fault for getting elected Biggest Flirts. But you *are* ruining my life. You won't go out with me, but you've made sure nobody else will want to go out with me either."

I looked into his eyes. He seemed to be admitting again that he was still attracted to me—which meant asking Angelica or anybody else out was just an exercise.

"Why is it so important to you to date right now?" I asked. "You've been here a week, and you keep saying you're booking it to Minnesota the first chance you get. So the drive to find a girlfriend, any girlfriend, in Florida doesn't make a whole lot of sense." I felt like the lowest of the low as I said this. I really wanted to know, but Harper's words from Friday echoed in my head, pointing out that I was selfish when it came to Will.

His nostrils flared a little, like when I'd tried to hand him his phone on the football field, as though he found the thought of Minnesota distasteful. "I *did* want to go to Minnesota. That was my original plan, and it took me a few days to get used to the idea that it was gone. I don't want to go back. My girlfriend is screwing my best friend now."

I nodded sympathetically, thinking of that beautiful girl getting kissed by that blond boy. "You wish you'd never moved."

"No, not even that," he said. "I wouldn't want to go back to the way things were before I moved, now that I know she's the kind of person who would cheat on me the second I left town. Even if I'd never given her that opportunity, she was *still* that kind of person."

"What?" I asked, puzzling this out. "She was a latent cheater? A cheater waiting to happen?"

"Exactly," he said. "So now, my life here sucks, and I have the knowledge that my life there sucked too. I just didn't know it at the time. My life would suck anywhere. It's completely fucking tragic."

"That's not true," I said, a little alarmed. "You're in a bad spot, Will. Moving is stressful, and you're only one week out.

Your girlfriend cheating on you was awful. You feel bad about that. There would be something wrong with you if you didn't."

He gave his head a dismissive shake, telling me I had no idea what he meant. "That's not all." He reached down for a flag and rolled the neat hem between his fingers. "I was supposed to be drum major back home."

"You were?" I could see him as drum major.

"Yes. And student council president."

I could not see him as student council president. He'd never glad-handed a stranger like Aidan did. "You?"

"Yes," Will said bitterly. "Thanks."

"Sorry. I'm so sorry." I put one hand on his knee so he wouldn't pull away from me completely. "It's just that in my experience, that job requires skills you don't seem to possess, such as talking."

He nodded. "Right."

"What do you mean, you were *supposed* to be?" I asked. "You were going to run for these positions in Minnesota this year?"

"No, I'd already been elected."

"Oh my God!" My voice echoed against the concrete walls. "Why did your parents make you move, then? Couldn't they wait another year until you graduated?"

Will sighed. "My dad's office closed down. If he didn't

transfer to manage the branch office here, he would have been laid off. So, no."

"Oh."

"And my mom said since I'd done that stuff at my old school, I could do it at my new school. I believed her. Nothing I'd ever been through told me otherwise. It was only when I got here . . ."

"We already had a drum major and a student council president," I finished for him.

"Even if DeMarcus hadn't snagged one office and Aidan the other, I wouldn't have gotten them. I'm not the man my parents thought I was, or *I* thought I was. I'm . . . I think I'm . . ."

I held my breath, my mind spinning at what he might say.

"Shy," he sighed.

I burst into laughter. "Well, you've got that one right."

"It's not funny," he said.

I considered him beside me, looming over me, really, when he was sitting so close, his muscular body making the room seem smaller. He had a big personality, too, one that didn't seem aptly described by the word "shy." "You're introverted," I corrected him.

He shrugged.

"You get your energy from being by yourself," I guessed.

This was Harper's description of the strange phenomenon I did not understand. "Having to talk to a bunch of people at once, especially people you don't know, makes you feel drained."

"Exactly!" he exclaimed, surprised that I had any insight. "I guess I never noticed at home. Here, where I have to start over, it's debilitating. I fell asleep as myself one night and woke up the next morning as a loser. This is coming at a really bad time for me. My parents are telling me that I can't follow in my dad's footsteps. If I'm a terrific manager, all that will get me is threatened with a layoff and transferred across the country. I have to be better than my dad. I have to be perfect at everything. So my parents are like, if you can't be drum major, be the next best thing. Be drum captain. I thought I'd done that. And then—"

Before he could say, *A disorganized mess of a girl took that away from me too. IS THERE NO JUSTICE?* I broke in with, "I'm sorry." Again.

"It's not your fault," he said. "You won fair and square. I was afraid you would. I practiced for hours beforehand, but I still missed a beat when we played the cadence during the challenge, and you didn't. End of story."

I thought about him in his room late last night, lying on his bed with his eyes closed, beating out the cadence on a practice pad propped up on his knees—that's how *I* practiced, anyway, when I practiced—over and over until he thought his head would explode. I hadn't practiced at all, since I hadn't wanted to win. But I had a three-year head start on him, having played this cadence countless times throughout high school. He'd been no match for an experienced drummer so scatterbrained that she forgot herself and won.

"My mom keeps saying if I act the way I acted in Minnesota, I'll have what I had in Minnesota. If I stay the same person, I'll have the same great friends. Well, now it turns out my friends there weren't so great. And no one here cares who I used to be back home. Nobody would believe me anyway."

"I believe you," I piped up.

"You actually know me," he said. "You've been forced to stand next to me. I can't go around the school making people stand next to me for forty hours just so they'll see what I'm made of. People believe the rumors, believe what the Senior Superlatives title says about me, believe what Sawyer tells them."

I snorted. "I doubt anybody in their right mind believes anything Sawyer tells them, ever."

"Well, I'm even less credible than he is, because I'm just the Fucking New Guy. Right?"

I *had* heard Sawyer refer to Will as the Fucking New Guy. I would have to talk to him about that, because, although the consensus in the school was that Sawyer was full of shit, his nicknames for people did catch on. "Sawyer has a chip on his shoulder," I explained. "He hasn't been here very long himself. He used to live with his mom up in Georgia. He only moved here a couple of years ago when his dad got out of jail."

"That sounds about right," Will grumbled.

"Now, wait a minute," I said. "You're judging him the same way that you don't want to be judged."

"Good," Will said. Normally he backtracked when I pointed out that he was being a hypocrite, but I'd noticed he had a tendency to shut down when Sawyer was mentioned. "Anyway, he's not the only one talking smack about me. Back home I was just me, Will. Everybody had known me forever. They knew that I try to stay in shape all year so I don't get killed in hockey, not to show off. I would never take off my shirt unless I thought I was going to pass out from heatstroke, and I would never, ever cheat on my girlfriend. Here I'm a completely different person, and my whole life is changing to match it—all because of this label that I got saddled with."

"Will, it's not that bad," I lied. It was pretty bad.

"Everybody hates me," he said.

"They do not!" Hate was too personal.

He gave me a stern look. "I've overheard you trying to convince your friends that I'm not the stuck-up shit they thought I was."

He certainly had. "I don't see why you care so much," I said. "You have to sit out one year of high school, not doing some of the stuff you thought you were going to do. It'll be over in another nine months. You'll go to college and get on with your life and forget all about us."

"No, that's exactly it. The person I thought I was—that was the fake. I was successful because everybody had known me since we all started kindergarten. But pluck me out of there and set me down in a new school, and I'm completely unrecognizable. I don't have Aidan's charisma or Sawyer's . . . whatever Sawyer has."

"Penchant for catastrophe."

"Yes, that. If the senior class had voted for the Superlatives titles and I'd gotten nothing at all, I would feel better. Nobody had time to notice me. But what do I get voted? Biggest Flirt. With you. Why? Because I want to be around you all the time. You're the only person here who makes me feel like I'm at home."

I waved away his compliment, if indeed that's what it

was. "People always tell me I could have a conversation with a rock."

"Exactly. What am I going to do when I start college? Or I start a new job, where my dad thinks I have to be the star performer on day one or else? There's not always going to be someone like you there, following me around, giving me someone to joke with, and talking other people out of hating me."

I resented this. I hadn't thought of myself as *following him around*. And *giving him someone to joke with* sounded like I was his e-reader.

But I wasn't going to get in a fight with him when he was already upset about not getting along with everyone else. I said, "I don't think this is a permanent condition, Will. Yeah, you may have a harder time making friends than you thought. But in the week you've lived in Florida, you've also been angry. You're mad at your parents for moving. You're mad at your dad's company, and now you don't want to work for The Man. You resent everyone here who holds the positions that were yours in Minnesota. All that anger changes what you are, reserved"—I opened my hands—"and turns it into dour." I cupped my hands together in a ball to show Will how he'd closed down. Then I put one hand on his knee again.

"You don't get it," he said. "You're saying everybody is

looking at me differently in Florida from how they saw me in Minnesota. I'm saying *I'm* looking at me differently too. I really am not the person I thought I was. When you kissed me for the photo yesterday—"

"Hello, *you* kissed *me*!"

He put his hands up in the air like he did when Ms. Nakamoto scolded him through the microphone. "Whatever happened, that wasn't supposed to happen. I'm not like that. That wasn't me. I really didn't *want* it to be me, because if I cheated on Angelica, I was doing to her exactly what Beverly did to me when I left Minnesota. That was never my intention. I mean, if I'm going to do that to Angelica, I can't really be angry with Beverly, can I? And I would like to be angry at her for a while longer."

"Okay," I said, laughing. I knew he was serious, but I enjoyed hearing him admit to being base and petty every once in a while. It helped to know he wasn't as superhuman as he looked.

"So I'm sorry for the way I acted after the picture yesterday. You didn't know what's going on with me. I came down a lot harder on you than you deserved. And I understand why you challenged me. I drove you to it. I wouldn't want to stand next to me either." He looked down at my hand on his knee. Then he glanced over at the door like he hoped Harper would relent and open it. I wished he would put his hand on mine, some sign that we were cool again, but he seemed only to want to be alone.

"I consider you a friend," I said quietly. "I think we're having such a hard time getting along because, the first night we met, we read each other completely wrong. We went a lot farther than you were expecting, and I was surprised at how you reacted."

He held my gaze and said grimly, "That's not why."

As I watched his eyes, looking dark now rather than blue in his shadowed face, I felt warmth spread across my chest and up my neck. I was more confused and more turned on than I'd been yesterday morning when we kissed, because his words were weightier than his lips on mine. We both understood we had a connection. I'd told him, over and over, that I didn't want a boyfriend. He'd made progress toward getting a different girlfriend. And whatever we said we wanted, we kept ending up close to each other, touching.

That scared the hell out of me. I took my hand off his knee.

He glanced toward the door again, nodding like he accepted what I was telling him: that we would never be together. Not the way he wanted. And he was ready for Harper to come along and let him go.

He'd confessed his feelings to me, and his motivations. I was glad Harper had made us talk. But when he walked out that door, he would still be lost in Florida. The school would still view him as the dog who couldn't stick with one girl-friend—even worse than Sawyer, who at least was up front about his inability to commit. And Will would still be second chair on snare.

"Will you challenge me?" I asked him. "Tell Ms. Nakamoto during band this afternoon, and we'll have another tryout tomorrow."

"No," he said firmly. "You won. I lost. If we went through it again tomorrow and *you* lost, I'd know you threw it. So would everybody else. You've already undercut any authority I might have had with the drums."

"That's not true. You get your authority from being a great drum captain. I don't *want* to be in charge. You'll see in practice this afternoon. If we're so unfortunate that Ms. Nakamoto tells us to have a sectional, Jimmy and Travis will laugh me out of the parking lot."

His brows knitted, deepening the worry line between them. "Can I ask you something personal?"

"More personal than 'Do you like it when I put my mouth on your nipple?'"

A blush shot through his face. He pursed his lips, trying

hard not to laugh. I noticed that goose bumps broke out on his skin too—possibly the only time in the last week that he'd felt a chill, unless he'd been taking cold showers. I wondered if he realized he was rubbing his arms with his hands to warm himself as he said, "I'll take that as a yes. The question is, what were you in charge of that you screwed up?"

I shrugged. "Nothing. I've never been in charge of anything."

"Then why are you so scared?"

"I *will* screw it up," I said.

"How do you know?"

"Everybody tells me I will. Everybody says, 'Oh, you'd better not put Tia in charge of anything—watch out.'"

"Who says that?"

"My sisters. Everybody at school. You heard the drum line, and DeMarcus. They were so freaking relieved that *anybody* was drum captain besides me."

Will squinted at me. "Don't you think that's because *you* go around saying, 'You'd better not put me in charge of anything'? It's a self-fulfilling prophecy."

What he was telling me seemed to glimmer in front of me. "No," I said. "You wouldn't think that if you'd known me for more than a week. The people around here have known me forever."

"I just got here," Will said, "and that's exactly why I can see you so clearly."

Suddenly I was the one who was cold. I crossed my arms but tried to disguise the move by putting my chin in one hand.

"Girls look up to you."

"Ha!" I crowed. "That is the saddest thing I've ever heard." I felt my smile dropping away as he watched me silently without laughing along. I asked, "Are you serious?"

"Yes. The girls in the drum line, especially. They watch your every move. They practice the twirls you do with your sticks when you're thinking about something else."

I suspected he was making this up. "I never noticed."

"They wait until you're walking away."

"Well, God help them," I said. "If I can do one positive thing for them between now and when I graduate, it will be to give up drum captain and never be put in charge of anything again."

"That's not a goal," he said. "It's an anti-goal. It's an aggressive stance against any sort of goal, like *that's* going to help you."

I let out a frustrated sigh. He was starting to sound like Kaye. Besides, *I* wasn't the one who needed help. *He* was the one who feared the school would show up at his house with pitchforks and torches. And I could use that to my advantage.

"Listen, would you challenge me for drum captain if I did you a favor?"

He grinned at me. "What kind of favor?"

He looked so adorable when he smiled. I *wished* I was suggesting that kind of favor. "I'll explain the situation to Angelica," I said. "I'll tell her the picture yesterday was my fault."

"It wasn't your fault," he murmured. "Not totally. We agreed on that."

"Still, I'll try with her. I'll convince her to give you another chance. You can go out with her again. You and I will keep our hands off each other. Then all your problems will be solved."

His fingers tapped a beat on one knee. "Knock yourself out."

"And you'll challenge me?"

"Yep." He was looking at the bare bulb in the ceiling. He didn't seem very invested in this conversation. I would show him, though. Getting out of drum captain was at stake here.

Then he asked, "If Harper really doesn't come back until the end of the period, we have a few minutes. How should we spend them?" There was absolutely no innuendo in his voice. I knew Will, though. He was flirting with me again, whether he meant to or not.

I handed him the spray bottle.

11

THANKS TO OUR EFFORTS—ACTUALLY MORE
Will's efforts, because I lost interest in cleaning once I felt
better—the storage room was organized. Or, not *organized*
per se, but no longer ready to avalanche its contents on top
of anybody. At the beginning of band practice, I was able to
extract my drum pretty quickly rather than struggling to free
it as usual from a tangle of harnesses and cases and music
stands and "silks" and sketchy-looking lost-and-found hood-
ies. I hurried across the parking lot (yes, while banging out a
salsa beat—why not?), where I blew a kiss to Will, who was
standing behind the trunk of his car. This was not flirting at
all. I carefully descended the stadium steps and found Angelica
exactly where I thought I would: on the sidelines, practicing
baton twirls that she could perform perfectly already, working

hard despite the heat because she was so dedicated to her craft, ten minutes before the start of band.

I marched right over. "Hey there, old Angelica. How's it hangin'?"

She lifted her chin and looked down her nose at me. Possibly I deserved this. I wasn't making things any easier by greeting her in the style of drug dealers at a downtown Tampa gas station.

I started again. "Can we talk for just a second?" I even removed my harness and propped my drum nicely against the fence so that my distracting protrusion wouldn't hover between us.

She swallowed before saying, "Sure," almost like she was dreading this convo as much as I was.

"Can you lay down your weapons?"

She bent at the knees to place her batons daintily on the ground, then followed me along the fence to stop a few yards beyond where Chelsea and the other majorettes would gather. When they arrived, they could still inch toward us to overhear, but only if they wanted to be super rude. Which I did not put past them, honestly.

I took a deep breath and belted it out. "I just wanted to say I'm sorry for kissing Will when we were taking year-book pictures yesterday. It wasn't planned. We were together at Brody's party, when you were still with DeMarcus." I thought it might help my case to remind her that she wasn't the only lady getting around, even if hers was a G-rated version of playing the field.

She grimaced, still sensitive about her breakup with DeMarcus. Good.

"Will and I are friends," I said. "Definitely. But we're nothing—"

I stopped as a large foam beak blocked my view of Angelica. Sawyer stood beside us in his pelican costume, nodding at me as if he was participating in the conversation.

"Sawyer," I snapped, "I swear to God."

Sawyer put his wings up, just like Will put his hands up when he got in trouble. I watched Sawyer sashay along the sideline toward the cheerleaders, exaggerating the wag of his big bird booty, until I was sure he couldn't hear us.

I turned back to Angelica. "Will and I are nothing more than friends," I said. "Except for that one night, we haven't seen each other outside of band and school. And the picture . . . we were discussing what to do in the picture, and then the kiss just sort of happened." I was telling the truth, and yet not. It was an accurate depiction of the events, if not of how I'd felt when they happened. Funny how everything that had gone down between Will and me since that first night had been pretty innocent on the face of it, and underneath, so very guilty.

"Will was upset about the picture," I said, "because he was worried about what you'd think. With good reason, judging from the way you chewed him out yesterday."

She raised her artfully plucked eyebrows at me. Her meaning was clear: *And your point would be* what?

"I promised him I would try to explain it to you," I said. "He's sorry about what happened and how it looked. He knows he embarrassed you. He was embarrassed too. He's been cheated on himself, and, um." I still doubted he'd told Angelica about Beverly, and I didn't think his treacherous and extremely recent ex back home was a selling point. "He would like to go out with you again."

She faced Will across the field, lowering her chin to look at him through long, thick lashes. I didn't turn around to follow her gaze. I was trying to get these two back together so I could hand off the drum captain position to Will and keep him as a friend. But if I actually saw him gawking at this girl like I imagined he was right now, I wasn't sure my heart could take it.

"You know," she said, still gazing in his direction, "Will is sooooo good looking."

Yeah, I knew.

"And he's pretty nice."

Pretty nice? Try *nicest guy ever*! What was wrong with this chicklet?

She opened her hands and let out a high-pitched sigh. "I don't have to settle for a good looking, pretty nice guy who acts half the time like he prefers another girl."

I nodded, but I was frowning. "Or a guy who will have a beer at a party."

"Or a guy who will have a beer at a party," she confirmed, enunciating her words and opening her eyes wide at me, like she'd already had this argument with DeMarcus and her perspective should have been obvious by now.

I stepped back and looked at Angelica, really examined her, maybe for the first time ever. She gave the impression of being a gorgeous girl, but she wasn't really, or wouldn't have been without carefully applied makeup and a flattering top hanging at exactly the right length over her shorts. She had taken a lot of shit throughout high school for stuff she'd done in ninth grade, but I'd never heard of her breaking down about it. She just took care of herself, came to school, and plowed through. I'd always viewed her as a stubborn stick-in-the-mud with no personality, but now I was realizing that being a stubborn stick-in-the-mud *was* her personality, and she deserved kudos for being true to herself.

Surprising myself, I told her, "I like you, old Angelica."

She didn't seem moved by this admission. "You like everybody." Then she nodded at something over my shoulder. "We've got to go."

Turning around, I saw that DeMarcus was on his podium. "Oh, shit," I said. He officially started band practice every day by calling us to attention, but we were supposed to keep track of time and find our places on the field before he did that, so people weren't scrambling. As I ran for my drum, I tossed over my shoulder, "Thanks for the talk, Angelica. See you around!" I thought she rolled her eyes at me, but I didn't hang around to see.

I grabbed my harness and tried to fit it over my shoulders while hightailing it across the field to the drum line. Panicked about getting caught on the forty-yard line when DeMarcus called us to attention, but elated about the way Angelica and I had resolved our differences in a nonviolent manner, it occurred to me only gradually that "You like everybody" might have been a dig rather than a compliment.

And it wasn't until I'd almost reached Will that the other shoe dropped. I thought he was in the wrong place next to Travis. Then I remembered I was the drum captain at the end of the line now. And I realized that Angelica had said no to dating Will. My mission to get her back with him had been a complete failure. What if I was stuck as drum captain forever?

Just as I reached my place, DeMarcus must have made the motion to start practice. Will played the riff that the rest of the drum line echoed, snapping the band to attention.

I held my breath. I wasn't in trouble. But I felt like my body, not to mention my brain, was still rushing across the field.

"At ease," DeMarcus called.

As I exhaled and everyone relaxed, Will immediately whispered, "Sorry. I didn't mean to step on your toes, playing your riff like that."

"You didn't!" I exclaimed.

"You did that for me before and saved me from getting in trouble, so I thought I'd return the favor."

"I know!" I sighed, so frustrated in my first few hours of being drum captain that I could hardly stand it. "Look, this is going to be completely insufferable if we're tiptoeing around each other. Let's make a pact that whatever happens for the rest of the year, we will always have each other's backs."

"Deal," he said, sticking out his hand.

My palm touched his. We gripped hands. He slid his fingers down my arm. We touched elbows. "And then like this," I suggested, linking arms with him. It was a badass secret handshake if I did say so myself.

"And now we're flirting," he scolded me.

I wiped my hands on my shirt. "Ew, flirt germs."

I'd hardly gotten this out of my mouth when Will played the riff again. Ms. Nakamoto had finished giving us instructions, which obviously had been very interesting to me, and DeMarcus was calling us to attention to run through the show. This time I realized what was happening in time to echo the riff with the rest of the drums, just like I used to, but damn. This drum captain thing required a lot of concentration and did not agree with me.

It wasn't until we'd played through the entire halftime show, and my ears were ringing with the ending squeals of our trumpets, who really were awesome if you were listening to them rather than looking at them, that Will asked, "What did Angelica say?"

"She said no. But you have to challenge me for drum captain, because at least I tried," I burst out. I'd been worrying about how to say this through three numbers and a drum break. Clearly I'd needed more time to think it through.

"No way," he said. "You promised you would convince her to give me another chance."

"Blugh," I said, shaking out my arms. My shoulders were sore from wearing the drum harness so long without a break. I looked past Will down the line of drums. I was only one person higher in the line than I'd been yesterday, but from this perspective, the snares seemed to continue forever like they were reflected in two mirrors pointed toward each other.

"Don't give up so soon," he said in the tone of a basketball coach in an inspirational TV movie for preteens. "Tell you what. You and I will go out for a few days, just to make Angelica jealous. That will get her interested in me again."

I snorted, remembering how flatly she'd rejected his offer of reconciliation. "I don't think that's going to work."

He said, "It worked on you."

I felt my face flush red underneath my hat. He must have known how attracted I was to him, but I thought we had an unspoken rule that we wouldn't mention it. My soul seemed as bare to him as my body had been on my bed our first night together.

But he was right, wasn't he? Dating would make Angelica jealous if she felt anywhere as strongly about Will as I did. I'd sworn him off, promising myself our flirtation meant nothing and I didn't want him or anyone as a boyfriend. And one glance at him lying on the beach with his hand on Angelica had transformed me into a scheming freshman.

I jumped as Will played the riff, calling the band to attention again. This time I completely missed echoing him. If I kept this up, Ms. Nakamoto would kick me out of the

JENNIFER ECHOLS

drum captain position on my own lack of merit. But I had more pride than to leave that way. It was throw a challenge or nothing for me.

I was hopeless.

"Say yes," he whispered, standing stock still at attention and moving only the corner of his mouth as he spoke. "Get Angelica back for me, and I'll challenge you. Think how carefree you'll be as a civilian again."

"Don't talk at attention." I sounded so silly trying to throw my weight around like a drum captain that I almost laughed at myself.

But by the time we'd played through the show a second time and Ms. Nakamoto had sent the band to one end of the field to learn the drill for the pregame show, I'd made up my mind that Will was right. I was lucky there was nothing I could mess up today other than the call to attention. Sometime soon, Ms. Nakamoto was sure to send the drum line to the parking lot to rehearse on our own, and I would spend an hour ordering people around, convincing them to hate me, and generally inviting Armageddon.

"All right," I told Will calmly as we walked toward the goalpost together, though my stomach was turning flips.

"Great," he said just as evenly. Most of his face was hidden by his shades and hat. His cheeks and chin shone with sweat. He betrayed no emotion other than disgust at the heat. "But we're not confiding in anyone that we've engineered this. You can't tell Harper and Kaye. That's going to get back to Angelica. Kaye will hop over here wanting to know how the plan is going before she remembers she's not supposed to say that out loud."

True. Or I would leap to the sidelines, eager to update her on the same thing. Will was observant. I would just tell Kaye and Harper that Will and I were giving dating a trial run, which wasn't too far from the truth. I didn't like discussing bad news anyway. Pretending there *was* no "cockamamy scheme," as Harper had called my thwarted plan to throw the drum challenge, sounded like the perfect way to deal with my problems.

"Can you go out tonight?" he asked. "Might as well get it over with."

"No, I have to work late," I said. "I promised Bob and Roger that I'd train them on the inventory database I set up. I tried writing down the directions, but old people can follow instruction manuals fine until they involve computers, and suddenly their brains explode. I'm going to have to hold their hands and lead them through it."

Will nodded. "Wednesday night? Or are you busy then, too?" He sounded suspicious, like he was afraid I was making up an excuse about tonight and he expected one for tomorrow. I thought we knew each other pretty well, but obviously he didn't understand that I tried not to make excuses. If I hadn't wanted to fake-date him, I would have told him so.

"Tomorrow night," I agreed, "as soon as I get off work."

"Great," he said again, emotionlessly. "What kind of date would you like to go on? We can do anything you want, as long as we're likely to be seen so the news will get back to Angelica."

I imitated what he'd said our first night together. "I want you to take me to lunch, and then I can show you around town."

He turned so suddenly that his drum knocked into mine—a mistake I made all the time when I was talking to people on the field, but he did not. This time I could hear the hurt in his voice as he said quietly, "I want to do this, and help you out, but not if you're going to take stabs at me."

I put my hand on his back. His shirt was soaked with sweat. I kept my hand there. "Kidding. I didn't mean it ugly. I wanted to go on that date you invited me on last week. I just . . ." The band was loud around us, milling into place in two long lines for the football team to run through on game night, but the silence between Will and me was louder.

"I'll pick you up from the shop when you close," he finally

said. "I'll take you to dinner, and you can show me around town." He took my hand off his back and wiped it on his cargo shorts, which were dryer.

"More flirt germs," I commented.

He gave me my hand back hastily and looked around to see if Ms. Nakamoto had noticed him rubbing my palm close to his crotch. Sometimes our flirting was innocent like this: We weren't thinking dirty, and we realized how it looked to other people only after the fact.

Sometimes not.

He put the head of his drumstick on my drum and traced loud circles there, making the snares rattle. It was his way of touching me, I thought, without actually touching me and getting in trouble. As the circles he made got smaller, I started to wonder exactly what was going to happen on our fake date, and whether our facade would include feeling each other up like lusty pirates on shore leave. The heat was finally getting to me.

"One more thing, though," he said, ending his solo on my drum with a loud tap. "I heard you were with Sawyer all last weekend."

I countered, "I heard you and Angelica studied together at the library, and you licked her copy of *Fahrenheit 451*."

"That is a lie," he deadpanned. "The spine doesn't count."

He turned to me as if to look into my eyes, which had no effect when we were both wearing shades. "Seriously," he whispered, "even though we're only fake-dating, I don't want you with Sawyer. If you're dating him, we won't do this. If you're just fooling around, I want you to stay away from him. That's my one condition."

I thought through it. Sawyer would be difficult to corral. "Can I flirt with him while I'm dating you, even if it doesn't mean anything? A little tit for tat? No?"

Will lowered his chin so that I could see his blue eyes boring into me over the edge of his sunglasses.

"No!" I concluded. "Okay. Just let me dump my bike in the back of his truck after school and hitch a ride to work with him so I can explain."

For the rest of practice, Will and I talked but didn't really flirt. Suddenly we were acting reserved around each other, afraid to let ourselves go, like we were telling jokes at a funeral. I wasn't sure what he was thinking, but I for one had a lot of anxiety about our evening together tomorrow. I tried not to get my hopes up. What could happen? It would be, after all, a Wednesday. But when we'd played around in band before, nothing had mattered. Now I felt like we had a lot at stake, and not all of it had to do with the drum challenge and Angelica.

Finally we ran through the pregame show, DeMarcus intoned the announcements, and Ms. Nakamoto dismissed us. As the band walked off the field and Will and I neared the gate, I called out to Kaye, who glowered at me but dropped her pompons to wait for me. I told Will to go ahead while I talked to her. I hoped he understood that I was really asking him to wait to change his shirt until I arrived at his trunk, but I wasn't sure that message got across.

Then I walked right up to Kaye and eased my drum down onto the grass. Facing her with nothing between us, I wasn't sure what to tell her. I'd meant everything I'd said to her in the lunchroom. I thought she was a hypocrite for letting a boy take over her life, then scolding me for doing the same. I just hadn't meant to yell it.

She glared at me a moment more. Then she stuck out her bottom lip and opened her arms.

I walked into her embrace, slid my arms around her, and squeezed. We were going to argue about our issues again, obviously, but not today.

Softness enveloped me like a blanket. Sawyer had put his wings around both of us.

Kaye got the bad end of this deal. She was shorter than me and way shorter than Sawyer in his costume, so her head was down in a hot hole between us. Her voice sounded muffled as she called, "I love you, Tia, but for some mysterious reason, I find your friendship suffocating." Sawyer let us go, but he got very close to patting her on the butt with his wing.

On our way up the stairs, Chelsea asked Kaye and me if we wanted to go to a chick flick that night with her and a couple of other girls from calculus. Kaye said she was going out with Aidan. Remembering that he was waiting for her in the parking lot, she skipped ahead of us on the steps. Then I told Chelsea I couldn't go either, because of work. She asked if it would be better for me if we all went tomorrow night instead. "I would love to," I said, "but it's a school night, and I need to do my homework."

"Do you think I'm a stupid fool?" Chelsea asked. "Don't beat around the bush. Just go ahead and tell me, 'Chelsea, I think you're a stupid fool.'"

"Kidding!" I exclaimed. "Sarcasm! Tonight I have to work, and tomorrow I'm going out with Will."

She gazed up at him climbing the stairs with his drum. Then she raised one eyebrow at me. "I thought he was dating Angelica."

I grinned brilliantly. "That was yesterday."

"If you were *really* dating Will, of course you and I wouldn't hook up," Sawyer said, eyeing me from across the cab of his truck. He faced forward again as he drove past the HOME OF THE PELICANS sign and turned onto the road by the school. "We're philanderers, but we're not cheaters."

I wasn't sure of the difference. I resisted the urge to ask Sawyer to look up "philanderers" for me using the definition app on his phone, because he was driving. He aced standardized tests, but only the verbal part, never the math, and definitely not the logic.

He was doing a great impression of a logical person, though, backing me into a corner. "If you're only fake-dating Will," he reasoned, "why can't we still hook up?"

"He asked me not to," I said. "I understand where he's coming from. He's trying to make Angelica jealous. If he and I are supposed to be dating, but you and I have something on the side, it won't look like Will and I are serious."

"What if we were careful?" Sawyer said in the voice of a lecherous old man, sliding his hand under the leg of my shorts and up to the top of my thigh.

"I don't think so." Laughing, I tossed his hand away. "You are the opposite of careful."

"This sounds like the opposite of faking," he pointed out. "Will really cares what you and I are up to. You're genuinely concerned about what he thinks. There's nothing fake about that. Why don't you give in and date him?"

I shrugged to the live oaks passing by the window. "I don't want a boyfriend," I said for the millionth time in my teenage life. "But for once, somebody's come along who's making it hard to keep that promise to myself."

I turned to look at Sawyer, so handsome in an offbeat way. His white-blond hair, even when it was damp from his shower, was a color I'd only seen before on small children, and his preppie clothes looked like something his mom would have picked out for him in elementary school. But his strong hands lay on the wheel, his sinewy forearms tensed as he steered downtown, and something dark behind his eyes reminded me he was more experienced than he should have been at seventeen.

"You've never come across a girl like that?" I asked.

"Nope," he said like he didn't have to think about it.

Suddenly I burst out, "Sawyer, you can tell me if you're gay."

"Gay!" He gaped across the cab at me, then jerked the steering wheel to straighten the truck and avoid hitting the curb. "After what we did Sunday night?"

"Sunday night was good," I admitted sheepishly.

"I thought you enjoyed it," he said as though I hadn't spoken. Turning onto the main drag through town, he grumbled, "You've just got gay on the brain because you work for Bob and Roger."

"No." Well, maybe. "It was just an explanation for why you never commit, even to the point of asking the same girl out twice in a row."

He pulled the truck into a space near the antiques store, killed the engine, and looked over at me. "What's *your* excuse?"

He had me there. Backed against the door of his truck already, I had nowhere to go. I didn't want to talk about this. He knew it. And in his challenge, I heard all the regret I felt myself when I expected to hang with him at a party but he went home with another girl.

Seeming to realize he'd gone too far, he took a deep breath, popped his neck, and settled his shoulders back against the driver's seat. "I like somebody who would never fall for me," he admitted. Then he gave me his sternest glare. "A girl-type person."

"Is it me?" I asked.

He blinked. In that pause, I was afraid the answer was yes, and I was the one who'd gone too far. I wished I could take it back.

"No!" he exploded. "Are you insane?" He started laughing uncontrollably.

I talked over him. "That makes me feel like a million bucks, Sawyer."

Still grinning, he pulled himself together. "Look, Tia, I will just flat-out tell you. I really enjoy getting drunk with you. That's generally the highlight of my week, besides when you give me a hand job."

"I'm so glad." Yeah, I was beginning to regret Sunday night now.

"But you and me, together, we would be the death of each other. I'd be like, 'I know a guy who has some crack. Go with?' And you'd be like, 'Sure!' Somebody has to be the voice of reason in a relationship, Tia, and our voice of reason has had a tracheotomy. If we really dated, in half an hour we'd be facedown in a ditch on the south side of Tampa."

I glared across the truck at him. I wasn't sure whether he was making a reference to my mom doing drugs or not.

The next second, I decided he wasn't, at least not on purpose. He seemed to make the connection only afterward, and he looked sidelong at me with a guilty expression. By way of apology, he said, "I know I can tell you anything. If I wanted to come out, you would be the first person I would tell. I'm not gay. I honestly like this girl."

"Really?" *I honestly like this girl* was no statement of undying love. But I'd never heard Sawyer express even that lukewarm level of affection for anyone in his life, except me.

He nodded sadly. "It's not going to work out. There's nothing I can do. Talking about it won't change that."

"Are you sure?" I coaxed him. Despite all these confessions in the last fifteen minutes, Sawyer and I weren't the kind of friends to discuss our problems with each other at length. We both avoided saying anything serious if we could possibly help it. I was dying of curiosity about who this girl might be, though.

"This is weird," he said, "but I want to keep it private. I'm kind of enjoying, for once in my life, thinking something that doesn't immediately come out my mouth."

That made me laugh. "Let me know how it goes. I've never experienced that myself."

"I know." He extended his hand across the cab. "Come here."

With a glance around to make sure we weren't being watched by innocent tourists on the sidewalk, I scooted closer to him.

He kissed me on the mouth. Easily, languidly, like Sawyer and I had been kissing for the last two years.

He ended by tugging one of my braids, then backing away. Looking deep into my eyes, he said, "Good luck."

12

MY LESSON WITH BOB AND ROGER WENT ON forever. I desperately needed them to learn basic spreadsheet skills so they would stop relying on me, but teaching those two to use a computer for anything more than surfing the Web was like teaching Xavier Pilkington, Most Academic, to play a dance-competition video game. Bob and Roger took a certain amount of pride in not being able to do this, and they wasted my time bragging about how hopeless they were. I got frustrated with them and told them as much, and they folded their arms and told me I was being huffy. I hadn't run a practice as drum captain yet, but this was what it would be like.

The best part of my evening was getting text messages from Will. After we'd politely said good-bye in band and gone our separate ways, I hadn't expected him to check up on me. I definitely hadn't thought he would entertain me with texts like "Sorry you have to work. You should be here. This partay is off da HOOK!" with a photo of his mom scrubbing the ahffen.

I got home so late that my dad had already left for his shift. Then I stayed up later to do some calculus. Ms. Reynolds was totally on my ass about turning in my homework. She had threatened to petition the principal to *make* me join the math team if I didn't clean up my act. I was pretty sure this was unconstitutional.

"Tia," Will whispered in my ear. His warm breath tickled my earlobe.

"Mmmm," I said, enjoying this dream, even if doing my calculus homework on a date with Will *did* cast me in the part of Angelica.

"Time for school."

I sat straight up in bed. Morning light streamed through the window blind. Will jumped backward just in time to avoid my head smashing his.

I scowled at him. "Are you real?" He looked real. He was tall and taking up half my room, in the Vikings T-shirt he'd worn the night we first met.

JENNIFER ECHOLS

He sounded apologetic as he said, "Harper told me where the key was. You can't skip. She said you skipped a bunch of days last year, and then, when you got the flu, you had to come to school anyway or you would have flunked. She said whenever you haven't shown up at school by seven fifteen, everybody knows your dad stayed late at work and didn't come home to wake you. You don't wake up when people call your phone, apparently? Or when people bang on the front door."

"Mmph." I collapsed on my bed again. Something stuck me in the back of the neck. I pulled my calculus book out from under me and placed it on my tummy. "Why did she send *you*? She doesn't love me anymore?"

"She and Kaye said it's my turn. I hope you don't mind. I figured it would look like we're into each other if I came to get you." He wagged his eyebrows at me. "You know, for Angelica."

"Oh, we *are* into each other," I assured him. "You are seeing my sexy boudoir and sleeping ensemble. Take it all in, lovah." I flung my arms wide so he had a clear view of my tank top and plaid flannel pants. Then I held out my hand. After he helped me up, I brushed past him, whispering huskily, "Let me grab a shower."

He looked around the room for my nonexistent clock,

then pulled his phone from his pocket and glanced at it. "We don't have time."

I winced. "I smell, though. Do I smell?" I leaned down so he had access to the top of my head. "Sorry, I usually ask my dad, but you'll have to fill in."

He sniffed my hair. "Yes, but not unpleasantly."

"Aw, you're such a romantic." I yawned and shuffled toward the door. "Just let me brush my teeth, then."

"You're going to school in pajamas?"

"It won't be the first time. Or the last, probably, because production has picked up at the boat plant, and my dad will be taking a lot more shifts in the next few months." I stopped in the doorway and looked back toward the piles of clothes in my room. "I guess I could put on a bra."

"If you insist." He watched me like he was waiting for me to do this in front of him. Finally he said, "I'll leave you alone to do that."

He was clanking around in the kitchen as I slipped on a bra under my tank top. With weird green lace sewn around the edges of blue satin cups, it looked like something Violet might have bought at a discount store when she was twelve. I didn't know where half my clothes had come from or whether they were actually mine. I used to get in huge trouble for touching my sisters' stuff, but now that they were all gone, whatever they'd left behind had gotten absorbed into my wardrobe. The bra showed under my tank, but I didn't have time to paw through piles for another. While I was at it, I traded my pajama pants for gym shorts. I would have to dash home and change before work. On the other hand, if I showed up for my shift that afternoon looking like I'd just left the gym, maybe Bob and Roger would stop threatening to promote me.

I ducked into the bathroom to pee and wash my face and brush my teeth. When I opened the door, Will was standing there waiting for me with a plastic cup of orange juice in one hand and a Pop-Tart in the other. Toasted! I hadn't had a toasted Pop-Tart in years. "Dude! Where'd you find the Pop-Tarts? I lost them."

"Walk and talk," he said. As I grabbed my backpack and drumsticks and headed for the front door, he told me, "Kaye had some ideas for where they might be."

"Where'd you find the toaster?"

"It wasn't obvious." He held the door open. Locking it behind us and hiding the key, he said, "Kaye told me it was just you and your dad living here."

"It is." We headed up the street to the school fence.

"Why do you have two beds in your room, and someone's stuff that doesn't look like your stuff?" Will asked.

"Oh," I said, laughing at his reference to Violet's purple

taste. "My sister moved out last spring when she chased her boyfriend down south of town."

"And you hope she's coming back?"

"I hadn't thought about it," I said. "I mean, do I think her relationship with her boyfriend is dangerously unstable? Yes, but so were my other sisters' relationships, and they haven't moved back home. There's no room for Violet now, really, what with all the stuff in the way. Maybe that's why my dad keeps downsizing." I giggled because that was a funny thought, then stopped giggling because it might have been partly true. "Do I act like I hope she's coming back?"

"Most people who shared a room would take out the extra bed and dresser, or at least spread their own stuff around, when the other person moved out."

"I guess I never felt like I could do anything with Violet's stuff, because it's hers." Of course, Will had a point. Violet had been gone five months. She called me occasionally, but I hadn't seen her at all. If she'd wanted her stuff, she would have come to get it by now.

We'd reached the fence. He threw his flip-flops over first—bright boy—and then vaulted over easily. I tossed my flip-flops over, then handed my stuff to him on the other side. By the time I climbed down, he was peering at my phone.

"You *do* have an alarm on here, like everybody else," he

said. "You can make it louder so it will actually wake you up."

"Yeah, I know." I picked up my backpack and followed him across the parking lot, tapping my drumsticks on my hip. "But then it goes off on the weekends when I don't want to get up so early." Specifically, when I had been out late the night before.

"You can set it one way for weekdays and another for weekends," he said. "Look." He held out the phone.

I didn't even glance at it. "Too complicated."

He stopped so suddenly that I nearly ran into him. "Remember yesterday when you were complaining to me about how Bob and Roger won't take very easy steps to help themselves? You were getting really frustrated and wondering why they're such dorks?"

Grimacing, I secured my drumsticks under one arm and took my phone from him. "Point taken. And ambience ruined. I thought we'd had a nice sexy morning together, but you're basically calling me a pudgy old man."

His eyes softened, and he touched my bottom lip with his thumb and forefinger. He murmured, "Does this school have a rule about PDA in the parking lot?"

"I don't know," I whispered. "Let's find out."

He slid his hand down to my chin and held me there while he kissed me. His mouth was hot on mine. My whole body shivered in the humid morning.

"Hey!" somebody shouted from a passing car. "At least stand on a line while you're doing that. You're taking up a space."

Will broke the kiss but pulled me closer protectively. Squinting over my head and looking annoyed, he shot the car the bird.

"That's not going to help your popularity," I warned him.

"This is the Home of the Pelicans," he reminded me. "Shooting the bird is a sign of solidarity. Come on." He slid his arm around my shoulders, and we walked to calculus together, where I took my rightful place in the desk behind his.

In the shop that evening, exactly at closing time, I heard the antique cowbell jangle on the door. I was back in the shelves, cleaning pretty effectively because I was a little stressed out about my "date" with Will. And that was him!

Before I could even make it to the front counter, I heard him exclaim, "What a good dog!" But when I rounded the corner, I didn't see him. I peered over the counter. He was sprawled on the floor (*reserved Will Matthews was sprawled on the floor like a three-year-old*) and tangled up with the shop dog, which probably weighed almost as much as he did. He was scratching the dog behind the ears, but with his arms around the thing, he looked more like he was hugging it. The dog licked Will's cheek, flopped its tongue around in its mouth a few times like it was considering the taste, then lapped at Will's nose. Will laughed. "Good boy. Girl?" He peered up at me. "Whose dog?"

"I have no idea."

He cocked his head at me, perplexed, while the dog licked his temple. "Doesn't it belong to Bob and Roger?"

"No." I hollered toward the back of the long shop. "Bob, whose dog?"

His voice came faintly back. "I think she belongs to somebody on First Street. She's waiting for us when we open in the morning. She likes the air-conditioning."

"Makes sense to me," Will told the dog, who licked his eye. Standing, Will wiped at his eyelid, then brushed some of the dog hair off his T-shirt. "I've always wanted a dog. My mom says no because she doesn't want to clean up the hair, but I'm getting a dog the day I graduate from college."

"Most guys say that about a Porsche, like they could afford one on their starting salary."

Will shook his head. "Dog." He held out his hand to me. "Ready to show me the town?"

"What do you know about this?" It was getting late, and Will had told me he was taking me home. But in the darkness, he stopped the car in front of a white two-story house—a mansion, really, a stalwart survivor of countless hurricanes, built in 1910 in the Georgian style with a tropical twist.

I'd shown him all over our little town in the past few hours. I'd taken him to a seafood joint that was, frankly, way better than the Crab Lab if you were after food rather than free beer on the back porch. I'd taken him on a driving tour of the many beaches besides the one where we'd held the band party. He said he ran long distance on the weekends, so I showed him the trail that extended all the way through town and into the wetlands.

Best of all, we'd run into some basketball players I knew at the seafood joint, a trumpet with her family at the beach, and a sophomore cheerleader on the trail. All of them would alert the media that they'd seen Will and me together. In terms of Will's plan to make Angelica jealous, it was a triple word score.

But I doubted anybody I knew would be walking by on the dark, quiet street where we'd now parked. And this was the first time Will had suggested a stop on the tour.

I stared at the white mansion glowing in the moonlight, trying to puzzle out why Will had brought me here. "What do you mean, what do I know about it?"

"I want to major in architecture in college. My dad says no. He says I have to make sure I'm high up enough in a company that I never get transferred against my will. He wants me to major in business."

"I can't picture you as a business major," I said. "Public Will, the face you show people, yes. Private Will, no. I think you would go a little crazy."

"That's what I think too." He smiled at me in the near darkness. "Do you want to see my super-secret notebook that my parents can never find out about?"

"Sure!" I exclaimed, though I was frightened of what this secret could be. Maybe he was even more of a pirate than I'd imagined. God knew what Private Will had been hiding.

"Here." He reached in front of my knees and opened the glove compartment—not the first place I'd think of for keeping my own super-secret documents, but to each his and her own. He pulled out a spiral-bound artist's pad and placed it in my lap.

I opened the cover. On the first page was a careful drawing of an old building in a row of others, part of a historic downtown district like ours, but three stories instead of two. The drawing wasn't fully executed. Trees and bushes and a big dog on the sidewalk were only quick impressions from a pencil. A stylish wash of light strokes colored them in. But the drawing couldn't truly be called a sketch, either. The lines of the building itself were straight and true, measured and drawn with a ruler.

"Wow," I said reverently.

"I park in front of buildings and draw them," he explained.

I turned the page to reveal an even more detailed drawing of an exquisite old store. "Where is this one?"

"Duluth," he said, looking over my shoulder at the pad. "Most of them are in Duluth." As I turned the page to an elaborate cathedral, he said, "That's in St. Paul. I got grounded for that one, because I didn't tell my parents where I was going or why. They wouldn't have let me."

I turned the page.

"I'm probably going to get arrested eventually," he said. "Someone will think I'm casing the joint."

I turned another page. There was no end to these gorgeous drawings. Every one of them should have been copied a million times and framed and sold in a tourist shop here in town. They were that pretty.

"I have too much time on my hands, obviously," he said. "I should get a job."

I shook my head. "These are beautiful."

"Thanks." He said this matter-of-factly, proud of his work but confident enough that he didn't need my approval.

"You should major in art, not architecture."

He gave me a thumbs-up. "Great idea. My parents would lose their shit."

"Yeah." I turned the page to a grand house. "I can't even take this in, all the detail. I want to spend a couple of hours with these another day."

He laughed. "Okay."

"I'm not kidding, for once." I turned the page, and there was the house beside us, palm fronds softening the stark logic of the mansion's careful proportions.

"I think it's the coolest house ever," Will explained. "It's so much bigger and so different from everything else in this neighborhood. That's why I wanted to ask you about it. I wondered if it's a city landmark."

"Oh, I'll say!" I laughed. "I used to live there."

He gave me a funny look. "Are you serious?"

"Why would I make up something like that?" I heard my voice rise in anger. I wished it wouldn't, but I couldn't help it when I thought someone was assuming things about my family, and our income, and my dad.

Will's voice rose in turn. "Because I'm the Fucking New Guy, and everybody is giving me incorrect information about the school and the town because that's hilarious and I am a sitting duck."

By "everybody," I assumed he meant Sawyer. I wondered

what wild goose chase Sawyer had sent Will on just for spite. And I regretted that our happy talk about Will's cool drawings had unraveled into accusations. I said more quietly, "I really lived here. My dad used to buy run-down houses for cheap so he could fix them while we lived there. Then he sold them at a profit."

"Oh." Will's brows knitted, and he pointed to the FOR SALE sign in the yard. "You weren't able to sell it?"

"We did," I said. "It's been up for sale a couple of times since then. Folks probably buy it thinking they're going to finish fixing it up, and fail miserably, just like we did. I can see why they want it, though. You wouldn't believe the inside. High ceilings. Thick crown molding. An original chandelier in the foyer that makes the light look golden instead of white. And smack in the middle of the house there's an atrium with a fountain, all tiny glass tiles in a mosaic of stylized mermaids. That fountain and the chandelier just *look* 1910."

"That's so cool!" Will exclaimed. "Did the fountain work?"

I almost said yes without thinking. "No. In my mind it works, though. That's funny. I watch all these home improvement TV shows, and couples are always walking through a potential home and saying, 'Ew, we couldn't live here. The walls are blue.' Well, paint them, Sally Jane and Earl! I understand other people can't always see potential like my dad and I can." I paused. "In fact, there are a *lot* of things I can see in my imagination that don't actually happen."

"I know what you mean," Will said. "Me too." His tone told me all I needed to know about what he was thinking.

I grinned across the car at him, so relieved that we were back to normal. But when he didn't make a move on me, I looked toward the mansion again. It drew my eye. I couldn't ignore its white angles glowing in the night. "My dad is brilliant. He has a contractor's license, and he knows how to do everything in a restoration."

Will didn't say anything. As we continued to gaze at the house, I realized why.

I said, "You're thinking my dad is pretty bad at flipping houses, since we didn't finish it. After my mom left, he wanted something more stable. The real estate market was up and down. He had four girls to take care of on one income, and he needed a sure thing. He took a job at the boat factory, thinking he would use that money to supplement his real estate income. Then the factory job offered him extra shifts. He took them. He was never home to fix the house. And then our family shrank, and he realized we'd save money if we moved to a smaller house. That's why we've moved four times in the last seven years. When I leave, he'll probably move into a mailbox. A run-down one."

"Why does your family keep shrinking?" Will asked gently, like he suspected this was a touchy question.

It was. It was so touchy, in fact, that my family had been the subject of many rumors over the years, most of them true. I was surprised Will hadn't heard them all by now.

"I would say you don't have to tell me," he offered, "because obviously you don't want to, but I'd really like to know."

I shifted uncomfortably on the very comfortable black vinyl seat. "Well, I guess it started when I was nine, and my mom was in a car accident."

Out of the corner of my eye, I saw him flinch like he'd been hit. "Oh! Tia, I'm sorry."

"No, she's not dead or anything." I turned to smile at him, reassuring. "At least, we assume. I haven't heard from her in a while. What happened was, she hurt her back, and she got on pain pills, and she couldn't get off. I was so little that I didn't really know what was going on, except that something was wrong, and my sisters wouldn't tell me. Even now when I bring it up, they say they don't want to talk about it. But I gather that she made friends with the people who kept getting the pills for her, and she started a relationship with one of them."

Will took a long, slow breath, giving himself time to think of some way to respond to that. He exhaled without coming up with an answer. I knew how he felt.

"My parents had Izzy when they were seventeen," I explained, "and Sophia when they were nineteen, and they kept having kids. It's what my mom said she wanted. But I know it was hard on them both. The accident and the pills—it's unfortunate, but I think that opened the door to my mom's downfall. And she walked through it. She started sneaking out to be with the guy she met. She told my dad she was trying to get back something she'd missed out on when they were younger."

"And so you're not going to miss it," Will broke in.

I shrugged. I supposed there was a big contrast between my mom and me, but I'd never given it much thought. "Once when my mom went to see this guy, she forgot about me and left me home by myself. I was ten. I was fine by myself. I should have just stayed cool. But she hadn't told me she was leaving. I couldn't get her on the phone because she'd left it in her bedroom. I panicked and called my dad. He went to find her. And that was the end of their marriage."

I felt Will's hand on my bare leg. Then he mistakenly groped across his art pad and finally found my hand. He asked quietly, "Your dad didn't get her help or anything?"

"They had been talking about it," I said, "but after she

left me at home so she could cheat on him, no. Every once in a while, she'll go see one of my sisters and say she's going to clean up, but we've stopped believing it." I looked toward the house again. The front right bedroom on the second floor, the one with the window nearly obscured now by out-of-control palms, had been mine. All my own.

"So!" I turned to Will. "How did my family shrink? That got rid of one of us. Then my oldest sister—that's Izzy—got pregnant when she was—hey! our age. It wasn't exactly a shotgun wedding because my dad has a pistol. Ha ha ha, a little humor there for the boys who want to fake-date me."

"Ha ha," Will said uneasily.

"Izzy moved in with her new husband, and that marriage lasted all of six months. My dad felt more pressure to make money fixing up the house, but also to work more hours, so he could help her out. She was pregnant again by that time. She had to go to court to get her ex to pay child support. And when that finally calmed down, my sister Sophia married her boyfriend because he'd joined the navy and he was about to spend a tour on a submarine. Then she got pregnant. And then he cheated on her."

"On a submarine?" Will interjected.

"No, when he came back to town. And when that calmed down . . . say it."

"Your sister Jane got pregnant?"

"Her name is Violet, and see, that's what she thinks everybody assumes, so she goes out of her way to tell everybody she did *not* get pregnant out of wedlock. Her boyfriend moved south of town for a job. She dropped out of high school to go live with him because she missed him so much. She only had a couple of months left until graduation. That was one of the stupider moves my family members have made, though definitely not the stupidest. And that is how I got rid of my entire family in seven years, except for my dad, and why we have downsized to the point that the next thing smaller is a mailbox."

Will squeezed my hand. "And that's why you say you don't want a boyfriend."

I drew my hand away from his. He was probably right. But knowing where my heebie-jeebies came from didn't make them go away. Suddenly the heat of his skin was burning mine.

"It's not just a sex thing," I said quickly. "You can have a boyfriend without having sex. You can have sex without getting pregs. It's not sex that messes people up. It's love. You can have sex and protect yourself and still keep out of trouble. It's love that starts to tangle everything up, and makes you think that an army private who's been to juvie would make a great dad, and that seventeen is the perfect age to start a family. When my sisters and I used to talk about sex, it wasn't embarrassing as long as we were being honest. It's love that confuses things and makes you unable to explain later why you didn't use a condom. Love and pressure and the feeling that you're everything when you're with this guy, and when he leaves you, you're less than you were before. If you fall in love, you attach yourself to somebody, and you can't do what you want ever again." I examined his drawing of my house. With one finger I traced the outline of my bedroom.

I felt him watching me quietly from his side of the car.

"Sorry," I blurted. "You probably didn't do it with Beverly before you left, after all. You're a virgin, and I've just told you some things you weren't ready to hear."

He didn't say a word.

"Not that there's anything wrong with that," I said to fill the silence. "Some of my best friends are virgins."

Now his silence was making me uncomfortable. Normally I accepted that I was a talker and didn't beat myself up for my big mouth. But right now I felt like I was blathering on and couldn't stop. The only way to fix the blah blah blah was with more blathering, apparently. "You didn't do it with Angelica, did you?" I asked.

At least that got a rise out of him. "No!" he exclaimed. "I've only known her a week!"

That seemed like plenty of time to me, but whatever. "Beverly from Minnesota was your only one, then."

Because of his silence, I assumed that the answer was yes.

"There's your problem," I said. "*You* want to do it with someone you're in love with. Love gets you in trouble. If it were only sex, you could have been getting it on with Angelica by now. But you fell in love with Beverly, and you vowed to make it home to her as soon as you could. Now that she's cheated on you, you're caught between two worlds. You can't move back, and you can't move forward. You're stuck."

"I am," he agreed. "But so are you. You're afraid to make plans because they might get broken. What would having a boyfriend prevent you from doing? Seems to me you don't want to do anything at all."

I glared at him. "You're probably right about getting arrested. We'd better move on before the current owner of this house suspects we're casing the joint and chases us off with a chainsaw."

Will ignored that. Stubbornly he asked, "Why aren't you applying to college or . . . anything? Why won't you even try out for drum corps? You don't talk about any plans after high school, like your life is going to stop. But every one of your close friends is leaving town after graduation."

"Sawyer isn't." As soon as these words left my lips, I regretted them. Will wasn't saying anything that wasn't true, but the truth hurt, and lashing out was my natural response.

"I'll bet he does leave," Will said.

I wondered what he saw in Sawyer that made him think so. There was a lot more to Sawyer than most people knew. He seemed to grow deeper all the time. And since he'd convinced me yesterday that he was interested in someone . . . maybe Will was right. Sawyer would follow a girl elsewhere. I couldn't picture most of our class hanging around town. Not just anybody could get elected Mr. and Ms. Least Likely to Leave the Tampa/St. Petersburg Metropolitan Area.

Will reached over to me. I stiffened, expecting him to take my hand again. Instead, he tugged his art pad out from my hands and tucked it back into the glove compartment where it was safe. He didn't trust me with his work anymore.

He ran his fingers through the shorn back of his hair. "Remember when you told me that Izzy insulted you, and you haven't seen her since?"

I nodded.

"Does Izzy know you're mad at her?" he asked.

"I don't know." I really didn't care. "Why?"

"When you've got a beef with somebody," he said, "you don't act mad. Not right away. You avoid confrontation. It only comes out later, when you make cutting comments. Izzy's lived with you, so she understands that about you. But if you haven't been by her shop, she probably doesn't even know you're angry. She's busy with her job and her kids, but she's wondering why you've gone missing. She thinks you're just busy too."

Letting that hypothesis hang in the air, he started the car.

I was shocked into silence. It made me uncomfortable that he understood so much about me, so quickly. We were already driving through the town's main drag, past the shop where Izzy worked, before I managed to stammer, "I'm—I'm sorry, Will. I'm sorry about unloading all of that on you. I have a chip on my shoulder."

"What you have is not a chip," he said.

As he prepared to turn onto the street leading into my neighborhood, he looked right. His earring glinted under a streetlight. Feeling miserable, I wished I could take back the last half hour of spilling my guts. I tried to balance the evening a little by asking him a personal question, something I'd been curious about since our first night together. "Why did you pierce your ear? Is it a Minnesota thing?"

He huffed out the smallest laugh. "It's a drum line thing."

"Some kind of sick initiation for the Marching Wrath of God? I love it! We should totally do that to the damn freshmen."

"No," he said, "we won the state championship."

"*What?*" I exclaimed. I was impressed with his band, and frustrated all over again about everything our second-rate town was putting him through. Our band made great marks at contests, but we didn't *win*.

"A tattoo would have been better," he said, "but you can't get ink in Minnesota until you turn eighteen."

"You mean, everybody on the drum line got an ear pierced?" I couldn't imagine everybody on *our* drum line doing *anything*, especially not as an organized group.

"Yeah."

"What about the girls?"

"They both had their ears pierced already, but they got another piercing in one ear. Carol—" As the memory came back to him, he cracked up. "They loomed over her with the gun, and she passed out. The first thing she said when she came to was, 'Drum line forever!'" He laughed again, then looked sidelong at me. "I guess you had to be there."

"It sounds like you guys had a lot of fun together."

"We did." He smiled into space and fingered the stud in his ear.

And with a rush, I realized how much he'd lost when

he'd moved here. Not just the position of drum major, the office of student council president, the status of Most Academic, but a group of close friends. Like a second family.

Will put his hand down and glanced at me. "Is wearing a stud uncool in Florida? I thought I might quit wearing it, but then I would have a hole in my ear. Somehow that seems worse."

"I see what you're saying," I told him, because I really did. "And I have never met anyone who took his earlobe so seriously."

He cracked another smile. "I'm a serious guy."

A week and a half ago, I would have agreed with him wholeheartedly. Now I was beginning to wonder. I'd thought Sawyer was growing deeper the longer I knew him, but Will seemed fathomless.

I told him truthfully, "Your earring is the first thing I liked about you."

"For all the wrong reasons." He pulled to a stop in front of my house and looked across the car at me in the dim light. "You were completely wrong about me."

"I'm not sure," I said. "I may be the first person who's been absolutely right."

13

I FELT SO TERRIBLE ABOUT MY PITY PARTY Wednesday night that I was determined to make it up to Will when we went out Thursday. I'd been wrong when I'd made fun of him for thinking the Tampa area was a hockey mecca. There *was* a rink not far from town. I laced up skates and let him half teach me, half drag me around the oval. But I wished I could have sat there, without being a weirdo, and watched him skate. He made it look easy, even natural. The cold breeze ruffled his short hair as he sped around the rink without me. Best of all, it was cold as Minnesota in the building. While I shivered in a sweater, he grinned in his T-shirt and looked genuinely happy.

Friday we drove a few towns south to a tourist spot full of neon lights and corn dogs for their sunset celebration. The long pier was full of couples embracing each other, acting like they couldn't wait for the day to end and the dark to start their night of romance. More than once I caught Will glancing at girls and guys our age making out. Now that our relationship was fake-official, flirting wasn't as easy as it used to be. An awkwardness still hung between us after I'd gone all TMI Wednesday night.

Saturday was different. I could feel it when I woke up, and I heard it in his voice when he called me to ask about going out that night. We were both sick of these polite dates that ended with him giving me a peck on the cheek at my front door. I made sure that when I opened my front door on Saturday night, he had something to look at.

He gaped at me. Simply looked me up and down with his mouth open.

"You've never seen me quite so clean before." I bent toward him. "Smell me."

He obliged, taking a long whiff of my floral hair. "Great dress." He stared at my legs.

"Thanks."

He lifted my chin with two fingers. "Is that . . . mascara?"

"Yes!" I exclaimed, triumphant.

His eyes roved all over my face, making me feel like our senior class's Best Looking, a title I'd never wanted but that didn't sound too bad when Will was the one bestowing it on me. Finally he said, "Your hair's down."

"It unravels from the braids, sure enough."

"Indulge me for a minute." He tapped his phone, then held it out in front of us. "Selfie. Kiss me right here." He pointed to his cheek.

Taking this picture reminded me a bit too much of Beverly's treacherous selfie with Will's best friend back home. But I wasn't going to deny him this. I pursed my lips—with shiny gloss on them, even—and gave the phone a knowing glance. He snapped the photo.

As we looked down at the image, he slipped his arm around my back with more of that Minnesotan sleight of hand. He said ruefully, "I wanted to post it online to show my friends how cool I am. It's not going to work. You look gorgeous, but I look too exuberant standing beside you, like I can't quite believe it."

I laughed. He did look a little starstruck. Guys didn't get starstruck around me. "I think it's perfect."

Kaye was throwing the night's party in her big, beautiful historic home on a lagoon where the homeowners docked their massive sailboats and had access to the ocean. As we parked at the end of a long line of cars stretching along the grass near her house, I explained to Will that Kaye didn't have parties when her parents weren't home. Her mom actually helped her throw them. Consequently there was no alcohol, but the food was good enough that people came anyway. These gatherings had an innocent, fifties, sock-hop vibe. Frankly, I found them a refreshing change from sitting on the ground and trying to use an empty Coke can as a weed pipe. But guests really bluesing for a drink could always access a box of wine. One had only to determine whose truck bed it was in.

As we hiked up the lawn to her house, holding hands, Will asked the next logical question, knowing me. "Do you want a drink?"

I had a crazy answer: "Not if you're not. It's really hard to communicate with somebody when one of you is drinking and the other isn't."

He gave me a quizzical smile. Now that we were walking near the house, we were getting close to other couples making their way up the yard, so he lowered his voice. "That's an excuse. You don't want to drink every time you go to a party, but by now you have a reputation to uphold. You're glad I'm here, aren't you? You can blame me for all your good behavior."

This boy scared me sometimes, he was so right. I tried to throw him off balance by murmuring, "If I cut down on my drinking, I will still have plenty of bad reputation left. I'll show you later tonight."

He laughed out loud. He looked as pleased and aston-ished as he had when we took a picture a few minutes before.

"Aw, you're blushing!" I exclaimed, squeezing his hand. "You're cute."

Chelsea and DeMarcus were walking a few yards away— approximately fifteen, in my expert estimation from years of marching up and down a football field. Chelsea called, "I thought it was a robot, but it laughs!"

"It laughs only for me," I called back. I said more quietly to Will, "Seriously, I think that's where we went wrong the first night, why we were misreading each other. I was drunk and you were . . . new."

He winced. "It's terrible being new."

"Is it? Sometimes I fantasize about what it would be like to start over."

"You want to move to Minnesota?" He made it sound like a threat.

"No. I would freeze to death."

Keeping hold of my hand, he backed far enough away to get a good look at my gauzy dress. "You would," he agreed, "because I would want you to keep wearing stuff like that."

"And I think it's beautiful here."

He looked up at the live oaks arching over the house. "It is."

"But I fantasize . . . this is terrible."

He tugged me closer. "You've told me a *lot* of terrible things."

"Er, this is not sexy-terrible but actual-terrible," I said. "I wonder what it would be like to start over without sisters. Not that I want them dead, of course, but if they never existed, and it was just me. I wonder if I would be the same person, or if I would be like Angelica, fighting it out for valedictorian with Aidan and Kaye and DeMarcus and Xavier Pilkington."

Will gave me a dubious look. "You would never be anything like Angelica."

That hurt. After he'd been so nice tonight, though, I was pretty sure he hadn't meant to spray lighter fluid on my feelings and set them on fire. "I know," I said. "I'm sorry."

"I don't mean *that*!" he exclaimed. "It's just . . . Angelica tries really hard, but she's not that bright."

"Really!"

"Yes. Not to be mean. Just my opinion."

Why do you want to date her, then? I wondered. But we didn't all want a rocket scientist, did we? Girls didn't hang out at Xavier's locker. I tried to edit the bitterness out of my voice as I said, "That's my opinion too. I've never heard anyone else say it, but I've known this about Angelica since kindergarten."

He nodded. "She does well in school because she cares and she worries. Like me."

At the bottom of the grand stairs up to the covered front porch, I pulled him to a stop. "You're not like that. Angelica and Aidan care, and they worry, and it's part of their nature. You care and worry too, but it makes you tired." I reached up and rubbed my thumb across the worry line between his brows. "Do you feel tired?"

"Since I've been in Florida, I've been exhausted," he admitted.

I sighed. "Tonight will take care of itself. Angelica will be here. If she's going to get jealous seeing you and me together, we don't have to help that along. Let's forget about our nightly goals and have a good time. Okay?"

The worry line disappeared as he gave me his sexy sideways smile. "What kind of good time do you mean?"

Fifteen minutes later, we were facing off for a dance-competition video game throwdown. I had thought I would laughingly drag him into the space in front of the huge TV and he would flirtatiously back out again. But as soon as I suggested it, he was ready to go. A crowd gathered around us, bored with my antics but astonished that tight Will Matthews was really going to do this thing.

And then, while the game beeped an electronic count-down to begin and the people around us held their breath, he pointed at me, meaning I was dead meat—just like I'd pointed at him on the football field before the challenge for drum captain.

"Oooooh," the spectators moaned. I felt my face turn bright red. I had to win now.

But at the end of the song, Will had beaten me up and down Kaye's expensively appointed living room. *And* he'd drawn an even bigger crowd. Will Matthews could totally do the Dougie.

"That is not even fair!" I squealed after guys had stopped slapping him on the back and Chelsea had shooed us off the dance floor so she could have a turn. "There's no way I would have challenged you if I'd known you could actually *dance*! I should have made you sign some sort of disclaimer." I poked him in the chest.

He grabbed my hand, grinning. "Never underestimate me."

"I won't!"

"My sisters have that video game. Let's get in line and go again." He tapped me on the chest like I'd poked him. This placed his fingers in the bare V-neck of my dress, just above my cleavage and my heart. "You're mine."

Over the course of the party, he beat the stuffing out of me twice more, then beat Chelsea to become the undisputed champion. The rest of the time, we were mostly standing to one side while somebody else took a turn. His arm circled my waist and my head nestled under his chin in a way that absolutely turned me on, and not just physically. I felt my friends' eyes on us, overheard their whispered conversations about us, and I loved it. I began to understand, just a little bit, why couples latched on to each other and went off into a corner to watch the party instead of participating themselves. There was a certain high, a heady bonding experience, in seeing and being seen.

A bonding experience with Will was the *last* thing I needed when our alliance was only temporary, to drive Angelica to distraction. But I did think the party was good for both of us as individuals. As we moved from circle to circle, entering different conversations, *everyone* told me, "You look great!" I could have taken this to mean, "Normally you look like crap. I am pleasantly surprised that you can hang when the affection of a ridiculously cute guy is on the line!" But there was no point in taking offense about an observation that was true. I *felt* great.

And *everyone* said to Will, "Nice moves!" He colored and laughed when people told him this. He didn't offer his own thoughts on his dancing prowess or join the conversation, but he didn't look like he wanted to crawl away and die, either. Being crowned our unofficial Best Dancer had given him an identity besides Fucking New Guy or Cheating Dog, and his new title was one he seemed strangely comfortable with. I found myself looking up at him, his earring glinting in the lamplight, and experiencing a wash of pleasure that he was so adorable and, for the time being, mine.

But one thing nagged at me the whole night. When Will was in conversation with some football players about the Tampa Bay Lightning professional hockey team, a subject on which he was the authority and I was clueless to the point of not knowing the nouns from the verbs in this terminology, I took him aside and whispered in his ear. "Look without looking like you're looking. Who is Sawyer staring at so forlornly?"

I held still while Will gazed over my head. Sawyer stood against the wall. He talked to the many people who passed by him, but he wasn't organizing a practical joke or getting plastered on surreptitious boxed wine, like normal. He seemed quiet, for Sawyer—almost thoughtful. And I could have sworn he was staring at one girl in particular.

"Kaye?" Will asked in my ear.

That's what I'd been afraid of. Talk about a girl out of Sawyer's reach.

"Now he's headed for the door," Will reported.

I looked up at Will. "Don't say anything about this, okay? It's sensitive."

"Okay."

"I'm going to talk to him for a sec because I'm worried about him. I am not flirting with him."

"I trust you," Will said.

If he'd genuinely trusted me, he wouldn't have needed to say this.

I couldn't think about that right now. After squeezing his hand one last time, I crossed the crowded living room and slipped out the front door, hoping to catch Sawyer before he disappeared.

From the high porch, I should have been able to glimpse him descending the staircase or walking through the yard toward the street. I didn't see him until I caught a movement out of the corner of my eye. He was sitting by himself on the porch swing, one foot propped on his knee and the other on the floor, propelling himself gently back and forth. I slipped onto the bench next to him.

His arm had relaxed along the back of the seat, but now

he pulled it close. "Careful. Your boyfriend will get jealous."

I glanced at the house behind his shoulders. I didn't want anybody inside to overhear us. I was pretty sure the nearest window was the dining room rather than a place where the party was going on. Not taking any chances, I asked very quietly, "It's Kaye, isn't it?"

He gave me that half-crazed look he got when threatened—but this time his raised eyebrows made him look less dangerous and more desperate. "Am I being that obvious?"

"Definitely not," I assured him. "I only saw it because I was looking for it. Anybody else would be flabbergasted." I gazed at him, his blond hair bright in the dim light. He looked incredibly sad. Now that I saw this, I couldn't believe I hadn't noticed before. "How long?"

"Since I moved here," he murmured.

That was two years ago. By that time, Kaye had already been dating Aidan for a year and was locked into the habits of her life with him.

"It's worse lately," Sawyer said. "I used to think surely she would get tired of him telling her what to do and break up with him. That's when I would make my move. But the closer we get to graduation, the clearer it seems they're not breaking up. Being back at school with her makes it excru-ciating. The mascot travels with the cheerleaders to every school event, you know. I thought I wanted to be near her, but it turns out I'm just putting myself through hell."

I nodded. "I know what you mean." I remembered marching through the halftime show next to Will on Monday, so close to him physically, but so far away. My stomach turned over. And my heart went out to Sawyer. I couldn't imagine living with that pain for a couple of years.

"I'm blowing this joint," Sawyer said, easing up from the swing so it didn't shift and send me flying. He *could* be courteous, but Kaye would never believe it. "I'm sure I can find a better party."

"I hope you have a good night," I called as he headed for the stairs.

Descending into the darkness, he called back over his shoulder, "I hope you don't fall in love."

Walking back into the party, I tried to shake the uneasy feeling he'd given me. I'd had a great time with Will that night. Just like my very first night with Will, I counted it as one of the best experiences of my life. The key to enjoying myself with Will was making sure I didn't think too hard about it. I wanted that euphoria back again.

Will was exactly where I'd left him, talking hockey with the football team. He was even speaking as I approached. But his eyes cut to me and stayed on me. When I reached him, he encircled me with one arm and whispered, "Angelica watched you follow Sawyer out."

Tingles spread across my face as I whispered back, "Then you and I need to look like we're finally having that good time we talked about."

14

I TOOK HIS HAND AND TUGGED HIM FARTHER
into the living room. I'd thought we could claim a couch in the
corner or—if push came to shove—one overstuffed chair. But
the night was growing old, and the comfy furniture was occu-
pied by couples getting to know each other better. Will saw this
too. He walked through the stately arched doorway of the living
room and kept walking until we reached the kitchen table.

I stepped closer to him and spoke in his ear so he could
hear me over the video game music and the laughter. "We
can't flirt here. All the surfaces are hard."

He turned his head slowly. His eyes were wide and his
mouth was twisted to one side to keep from laughing while he
pretended to be outraged at me for uttering the word "hard."

"Damn it," I said, "you know what I mean." Surely he

did. Settling in for flirting (or more) at a party required plush seating.

"We'll make it work." He pulled out a chair for me from under the table. After I sprawled in it with a dispirited sigh, he sat in the chair next to mine. We might as well have been doing our calculus homework together, the turn-on nobody could deny.

And then he reached around my sides, grabbed the seat of my chair, and dragged me toward him until we were facing each other, knee to knee. "There," he said.

That did seem better for flirting. But all of a sudden, I felt shy around him. I found myself looking toward the cabinets—nothing more interesting there than a state-of-the-art microwave—and then the other way toward the crowd in the living room, where, on the couch, Brody and Grace had not gotten into it sufficiently to draw anybody's attention for real.

Will put two fingers on the side of my chin and pointed my face toward his again. "Hey. You're supposed to be flirting with me."

"Oh, suddenly this is *my* job? *You're* supposed to be flirting with *me*."

"I *did* flirt with you," he insisted. "I touched your chin just now."

"Oooh!" I said, raising my eyebrows and pursing my lips to show him exactly how impressed I was, which was *not*.

"I touched your *chair*," he said.

"If that counts for flirting, I'm going outside to touch the right rear fender of your car. That will count for getting to third base." I started to get up.

"No," he said, grabbing both my thighs just above the knee.

While the shock of his touch shot through me, I eased back down in my chair. He slowly took his hands away, a horrified expression on his face. He started to put his hands up in the air to show me he hadn't meant to touch me quite so high—and then realized this didn't look very flirtatious. He put his hands back on his own thighs.

After another silent thirty seconds of staring at the design on his T-shirt, I said, "I don't know why this is so hard."

Then I realized I'd said the *H*-word again. He gave me the fake-outraged look, which should have broken the ice but didn't. Nothing could. We sank into another excruciating silence. The more our flirting mattered, the worse we were at it.

The song on the video game changed, from an emo classic to a funky groove. Will relaxed as he always did when the beat was good, transforming from an uptight faux-boyfriend to my friend the drummer. His shoulders settled against the back of his chair, and his fingers tapped out the beat on his thigh, his right pointer finger on the snare downbeat and his left finger on the bass drum.

I relaxed too. My unease fell away, and all that was left was the usual desire to be around him, talk to him, joke with him, capture his attention, bask in his glow—coupled with the fun of sitting so close to him, our knees touching.

Slowly I reached across my thighs, across his, and put my fingers on top of his hands. I moved his hands from tapping on his thighs to tapping on mine.

Still drumming his beat, he glanced up at me, flashing those blue eyes, and gave me a sly smile.

I kept coaxing his hands up my thighs, so high that if Angelica had looked in, I might have gotten called a name.

Will was aware of this too, apparently. His lips parted like he couldn't believe I was so forward and he wanted out.

Now I wished I hadn't done it. I'd only been teasing him, frustrated that we were reduced to this awkward silence. I hadn't meant to chase him off and make things worse.

He turned and glanced into the living room. With his eyes still on the front door, he leaned toward me and said, "Angelica just left with Xavier Pilkington."

Inside, I burst into laughter. Of *course* Angelica was

finally going to get it on with Xavier Pilkington. They would be rocking his car with their synchronized typing as they spent the end of their Saturday night working on the English paper that wasn't due until two weeks from Tuesday.

But I died a little too. I was afraid of what this meant. Now that she was gone, especially with another guy, there was no reason for Will and me to continue this charade. Our heady night together was over.

"Tia," he said.

I nodded, bowing my head and bringing it closer to his. At least I could feel his breath in my ear one last time before we went our separate ways.

"When we arranged our deal to make Angelica jealous, I didn't say what I really meant, which was, please go out with me. I want to be with you. I don't want it to be fake, and I don't want it to end tonight."

Heart racing, I sat back in my chair. "So, you never really wanted to get Angelica back? That was just a ruse to get me to go out with you?"

He watched me carefully, like he was afraid I would bolt. "No, not exactly. I didn't think it all the way through. But you said you wanted to help me. This was a way you could help me. And in the back of my mind I was probably thinking, *Grab*." He slid his hand around my waist. "*Opportunity*."

JENNIFER ECHOLS

He circled my fingers with his. *"Grab."* Holding my hand, he met my gaze and waited for my answer.

I found the courage, but slowly. "Okay."

His fingers massaged mine as he leaned forward and whispered, "You left out a stop when you took me on a tour of town."

"What's that?" I asked, beaming in anticipation of what he would say.

"A place people go to be alone. Do you have one of those?"

"We do." It was Harper's grandfather's strip of beach. He could have sold it for a billion dollars and retired in a mansion, but he chose to continue living in his little bungalow on the same street as Sawyer's house and keep his fishing boat down at the city marina. Harper had given Kaye and me the code to open the gate at this private beach in case we ever needed it.

Now I did. Harper's boyfriend, Kennedy, seemed more interested in talking smack with his artsy guy friends after hours than going parking with her. Aidan and Kaye would stay here at her house until the end of her party. The beach belonged to Will and me tonight.

"Do you have a condom?" I asked.

We were driving in Will's throaty car toward the beach. The question hung so starkly in the air that I almost imag-

258

ined I could see it centered over the armrest between us, blinking as streetlights and the shadows of palm trees alternated overhead. Asking the question meant clarifying what we were about to do.

After a pause, he said, "Yes. I bought them on my way home from your house that first night."

I hooted laughter. "A little sure of yourself, weren't you?"

He grinned. "No. Just motivated."

"I'm on the pill, too," I said. "Due to my family history, I make sure I'm super safe."

He nodded, then swallowed with difficulty like his mouth was dry. "I want you to know something," he said. "When I got so mad on the first day of practice and threw my phone, and you said my girlfriend had taken advantage of me before I left . . ."

"I was so out of line," I said. "You were right when you said I hold stuff in and pretend I'm not mad, and it comes out later as a backhanded insult. I'm sorry."

He shook his head. "No, I mean, she didn't. Take advantage of me. We didn't do it. The whole time we were dating, she said she wasn't ready. And the night I left, she did it with my best friend. So she *was* ready, just not for me. I guess it doesn't matter. But I didn't want you to think that I was that . . ."

"Experienced?"

"Naïve," he said, "that I wouldn't know what was going on if she tried to trick me into, like, putting out or whatever." He glanced at me. "Or experienced."

I touched his hand on the gearshift, lifted my hand when he had to shift, and settled my hand on his again. "Are you sure you want to?"

"Yes," he said instantly. He wasn't smiling, exactly, but his whole face looked happy, starry eyed and breathless with the idea. Then he started laughing uncontrollably. "Yes!" he chuckled. "Good Lord. But you're not."

"Me!" I exclaimed. Then a rush of warmth flowed through me. It was relief that we wouldn't do this. Not tonight. And something more: a deep appreciation that he knew somehow what I'd been feeling without me having to tell him.

"If it didn't mean anything, you'd be willing," he said. "Now that it means something, you want to go slow."

I gazed at him across the car, his head and shoulders mostly in shadow. The moonlight burnished his short hair, turning it bronze, and kissed his long lashes and long nose, his expressive mouth. This time I knew better than to think he looked handsome only because of the moon. I had been a fool to push this guy away.

"Well," I said, "I don't know about *slow*."

He was laughing again as he pulled up to the gate. After

we were through and I'd locked it behind us, he drove underneath the palms. The trees were thick at first, then more sparse, until the grove opened onto the beach. The moonlight streaming toward us across the ocean was as brilliant as the sun.

"Wow," he breathed.

"I told you it was beautiful here."

He cut the engine. Instantly the sound of waves crashing on the beach rushed to fill that space. He turned to me. Now he would hand me one of his delightfully cheesy pickup lines. It *was* beautiful here, he would say, but he didn't mean the beach. He meant me.

He caught me completely off guard when he said instead, "I fell for you that first night we were together. And you can say it's because of what we were doing, or I was rebounding from Beverly, or I was stressed from the move, but I know how I feel. I love you."

We weren't touching anymore. I sat on my side of the car. He sat on his, watching me with a serious expression in his shadowed eyes, the worry line between his brows deeper than ever.

"I love you too," I breathed.

"You have got to be kidding me," he complained. "Now I'll *never* get laid."

I giggled as he tumbled his big frame over into my side

of the car and eased the seat back flat. Kissing me deeply, he unbuttoned the front of my dress, then reached around to unhook my bra. Then he bared my breasts and put his mouth on me.

"I like it when you do that."

His lips brushed my skin as he spoke, and his low voice sent chills through me. "Yeah, I remembered you like it when I do that."

A long time and endless explorations later, his warm hand moved into the front of my panties and rubbed me there. He knew what he was doing, and I figured he'd done this plenty of times before. Naïve he was not—not about this. I'd done it before too, but with him, it definitely felt different. Before long, sparkles like points of moonlight on the waves washed down my body. He kissed me deeply as it happened.

Then he placed sweet kisses on the corner of my mouth and chuckled to himself. "I'm the king of the world," he murmured.

In a sexy, satisfied tone that most chicks would use to reaffirm their love, I said, "You are the king of the dorks."

He closed his eyes and rubbed the tip of his nose back and forth against mine. He breathed into my mouth, "I'm the king of you."

"Yes, you are," I said softly, "but not for long." I slid my hand onto him. "Your turn."

15

THE ALARM ON MY CELL PHONE WOKE ME midmorning on Sunday, and I cursed Will within an inch of his existence. I was justified in doing that now that we were in love. He was the one who'd convinced me to start using an alarm to get myself up in the morning. Now, because I was responsible, the timer had gone awry. After staying up late with him last night, I was up bright and early, rather than sleeping until the last possible second before I had to go in to the antiques shop.

But when I glanced at the screen, I saw it wasn't the alarm. It was Violet calling. That meant she was in trouble.

Five minutes later I was on the phone with Will. "Can I borrow your car?"

"Yes," he yawned. "Why?"

"Don't ask," I said.

"I'm asking."

I let out a sigh that lasted for about seven seconds, one for every year my mom had been gone. "Violet wants to come home. She wants my dad to come get her right this moment before her boyfriend shows up, which means she feels threatened. And I can't wake my dad for this. He has to get a full night's sleep before he goes to work tonight, or it's a safety issue. He used to take off work all the time to get Izzy and Sophia out of trouble, and he racked up so many demerits that they were threatening to fire him. He can't take off work for that shit anymore. I'll go get her myself."

"I'll go with you," Will said.

"No!" I exploded. If I wasn't careful, I was going to wake up my dad with my hysterics. I said more quietly, "This is exactly why I shouldn't have called you, but I thought you would be furious if you found out I called Sawyer."

"Tia!" he barked right back. He must have been afraid his parents would overhear him, too, because he took a deep breath, then lowered his voice. "Sawyer wouldn't let you go alone either. No guy in his right mind would let you borrow his car to do something dangerous by yourself."

"It's not dangerous, exactly," I qualified. "Maybe not. Her boyfriend disappeared with his friends for three days and left her at their apartment with no car. The only reason it might be the slightest bit dangerous is that they have a bad habit of coming back."

"Who is *they*?"

"My sisters' boyfriends and fucked-up husbands," I explained. "And in all the times my dad has rescued my sisters, a gun has never come out, but I wouldn't be surprised. I keep up with the news. This is how people get shot."

"Then why are you going?" Will demanded.

"My dad can't," I said. "So I have to."

"Then so do I," Will said. "I'll be there in five." He hung up.

I cursed him again, not because he'd fallen down on the job this time, but the opposite. I did *not* want him witnessing the Cruz family's annual audition for a reality show. But he was right. I should have known there was no way to borrow a guy's car without the guy attached.

If he was coming with me, though, I was going to use him. After finding something to put on among the piles in my own room, I waded to the laundry room and searched there. When we'd first moved in, I'd been very careful about sorting the clean laundry from the dirty. I knew the clean shirt I wanted was under there somewhere. But we'd had way too much stuff to store in this tiny house, and over the months, the laundry room had become the place to stash things. I excavated the back wall like an archaeological dig. By the time Will knocked softly on the front door, I'd found it.

I pulled him inside the house. "Put this on," I said, handing him one of my dad's sleeveless T-shirts that he used to cut grass in, back when he cut the grass. "It's clean."

Will held it up and eyed the oil stains dubiously.

"Let me rephrase that," I said. "It's been washed. But you know what? You're right. You have a respectable tan now, and you could just take off your shirt when we get over there." I stretched the bottom of his T-shirt up above his waistband to make sure there wasn't a preppie flat front going on, like Aidan would wear. They were cargo shorts, which would do nicely. My eyes moved to his thick arms. Briefly I considered giving him a Sharpie tattoo on his biceps.

"You've got your shades?" I asked. "And a baseball cap you can turn around backward?" When he nodded, I said, "Let's go."

The apartment was worse than I'd pictured. I knew Violet and Ricky had moved three times in the five months they'd been together. They had a nasty habit of not paying their rent. I figured the apartment had gotten worse each time, but I wasn't prepared for this: brick buildings that didn't look so old but hadn't been taken care of at all, tagged with black graffiti—not even colorful, pretty graffiti—underneath a tangle of palm trees and dehydrated-looking water oaks, surrounded by long grass and trash, all practically underneath the interstate.

Will pulled his car into one of the empty spaces, between a rusted-out truck propped up on concrete blocks and a scary-looking van for plumbers or kidnappers. "Wow," he said, gazing at the building. "Really?"

"Yes," I said. "Honk the horn."

"That's rude," he said. "You'll get us shot."

"Not for that," I said. "They're used to it." Teenage high school dropouts had their own code. I was a little horrified that I knew it so well.

He hit the horn, two short beeps.

"No, really lay on it," I said.

Grimacing, he gave the horn a good long honk.

I watched the apartments. Violet opened a door and waved. I waved back so she'd know where we were, because Will's down-and-out 1970s Mustang blended in pretty well with the other vehicles in this lot. Will fit in himself with his aviators on, his hat backward, and his shirt off. I didn't mention this to him.

The next second, Ricky appeared beside her in the doorway. He grabbed her raised arm. She jerked away from him and vanished into the apartment. He shot us the bird before following her.

"Nice," Will said. "Shouldn't we go help her move her stuff? Because it looks like that asshole isn't going to."

"Nah, she won't have much." She hadn't left with much, and I doubted she'd had the money to buy anything while she'd been here. "But here's how you can help." I dug in my purse and handed him the cigarettes and lighter I'd bought when we'd stopped for gas. "Stand against the bumper, light a cigarette, and glare toward the apartment. Flex your guns if you can find an excuse."

He stared at the package in my hand. "I've never smoked."

Sighing impatiently—and then wishing I hadn't, because Will was doing me some very serious favors here— I unwrapped the cellophane and drew out a cigarette for him. "Light the tobacco end, with brown stuff in it. Suck on the filter end. Just inhale the smoke into your mouth, not your lungs, so you don't have a coughing fit."

Taking the cigarette and lighter, Will swore and slid out of the car, slamming the door behind him. He rounded to the front on the side nearest the apartments and leaned back against the hood, as instructed. Though the midday was oppressively hot and sunny and calm, like every August day in Florida that happened to be hurricane free, he cupped his hand around the cigarette while he lit it, as if he were standing in a high wind. Then he exhaled in one steady stream of smoke. He must have seen this on TV. From where I was sitting, I couldn't tell whether he was glaring at the apartment, but he'd followed my other instructions impeccably. He was probably following that one too.

Ricky watched him through the apartment window. If he'd toyed with the idea of convincing or forcing Violet to stay, in the face of my tough boyfriend who'd come to help rescue Violet, now he was thinking twice.

Ricky disappeared from the window. Violet backed out the door. Ricky came after her. I could see him yelling and hear the echo on a two-second delay. But he didn't follow her, just hung on to the doorjamb and hollered as she jogged down the stairs with a garbage bag slung over her shoulder.

"Show's over," I told Will. "Come inside." I was afraid that if he was going to get shot, now would be the time.

He bent toward my window and blew smoke at me. The sight surprised him, and he jumped a little. "Sorry," he said, exhaling more smoke at the same time. He coughed and turned whiter than normal. "What do I do with this?" Discreetly he held up the butt in front of his body, where Ricky wouldn't see what he was asking me.

"Throw it on the ground and step on it to put it out," I said carefully, like I was presenting Smoking 101 on *Sesame Street*.

"That's littering."

I gestured out the window. "They seem to like that here."

He couldn't argue with that. He threw down the cigarette to join the others on the asphalt, ground it out under his shoe, then rounded the car and slipped behind the wheel, reeking of smoke. "I think I might throw up."

"From the heat or the smoke?"

He closed his eyes and leaned back against the seat. "Both."

"Sorry," I said, patting his knee. "You did great."

"How many other sisters do you have, again?"

I watched Violet turn around in the parking lot and scream a parting shot at Ricky before running toward us. "Two," I said absently, "but they've already been through this, so maybe we're done." More likely, we *weren't* done, but Will and I would have moved on from each other by the time history repeated itself.

With a start, I realized that my usual way of thinking about Will was wrong. We were together. He would still be around the next time Violet did something stupid like this.

Or, now that I finally had a boyfriend, maybe it was *my* turn to do something stupid.

Stupid*er*.

I got out of the car and pushed my seat forward so Violet could collapse into the tiny back seat with her garbage bag containing all her worldly possessions—other than the ones littering my own bedroom floor. Will immediately cranked the car and backed out. I think all three of us tensed, watching the rearview mirror, until we made it up the ramp onto the interstate.

Violet let out a long sigh. "Where's Dad?"

"Asleep."

"On the weekend?"

"Yes, he's going in tonight. He's worked the last twenty-eight nights without time off."

"Jesus," Violet said. "Well, thanks for rescuing me, sis." She leaned over the seat to plant a kiss on my cheek. "And you." She kissed Will's cheek.

"Violet is like me but drunk," I explained to Will, "even when she's sober."

"Violet Cruz," she said, sticking one hand very close to Will's face.

Will reached back to shake her hand awkwardly without looking around at her. "Will Matthews."

"You talk funny," she said. "Are you from Russia?"

"Yes," he said.

"Are you a friend of Tia's, or . . ."

"I'm her boyfriend," he said self-righteously.

Violet gasped dramatically. "*You* have a *boyfriend*?" she squealed at me. "You said you would *never* have a boyfriend."

"Yes." My stomach turned upside down. Now I knew how Will felt. I might vomit, but not from the heat.

"Are you pregnant?" she asked me.

I whipped around in my seat. "Sit down and put your seat belt on." Waiting for her to do this, I said, "You look like shit." She really did. She used to put a lot of effort into her clothes and hair and makeup, drinking up anything Izzy could teach her. This morning she wore sweats pushed up to her knees and a tank top. She could have used her blue-and-green bra. She had dark circles under her eyes. At least her dirty hair was done up in a cute topknot like she hadn't completely lost touch with how teenagers dressed when they were trying to look like they didn't care but they actually did.

She smirked at me. "Thanks."

"You look like you dropped out of high school and spent the last five months smoking pot, getting screwed, and watching TV."

"The cable got cut off." She settled back against the seat and let out another long sigh. "Downtown Tampa is really beautiful."

I looked around at the skyscrapers surrounding us as the

interstate snaked through town. I supposed it was a pretty city. But then, when we crossed the bay, she said, "This bridge is really beautiful," and when we turned onto the coastal highway, she said, "This town is really beautiful," even though at that point we were passing a used car lot. I thought she was just glad to get away from Ricky.

"Oooh, boiled peanuts!" she exclaimed at a hand-lettered sign in front of a big boiler on the side of the road. "Stop stop stop! I haven't had breakfast."

Neither had I. Will might not have either, but it was all about Violet. He pulled the Mustang into a gas station parking lot and stopped. I climbed out of the car and pushed the seat forward to let Violet out. As she stood, she asked me, "Do you have three dollars?"

"Listen," I told her. When we were little, my sisters had screamed bloody murder at me when I so much as *touched* something of theirs. I wanted them to love me, though, so I let them take anything of mine that they wanted—until I figured out what was going on. I had really gone off on Izzy one day. It had been a week before any of them spoke to me again, much less laughed at my jokes, but they *did not take my stuff anymore.*

"O-*kay*," Violet said, digging in her own pocket for cash and stomping toward the guy ladling peanuts into plastic bags that looked, frankly, used.

I leaned against the car while she finished this important transaction. Will looked at me through the window. "You're not dealing well with this."

"Shut up," I snapped. I knew I should regret that, because Will was helping me out and I was supposed to love him, but all I felt was fed up.

Violet skipped back to the car and ducked inside. As I slammed the door and Will pulled back onto the road, she tried to hand me a peanut still in its shell. "Want one?"

"*Violet,*" I said.

"Jeez!" She exclaimed. "Will Matthews, do y'all eat boiled peanuts in Russia?"

He laughed nervously. "No."

And then, of course, she shelled the peanut and pressed the meat of the nut past his lips, into his mouth.

"Would you stop?" I whined, so annoyed by her manic mood swing. Any other day I might have thought she was halfway cute, but not while Will was there to see.

Will spit the nut into a napkin. "That is horrible! Nuts should not be mushy."

Violet giggled and retreated quietly into the back.

After a pause, Will held his hand out toward her over the seat. "Give me another."

He was so adorable. Handsome, strong, stoic. Vulnerable.

Willing to laugh at himself at every turn. A wave of love washed over me, a yearning to touch him and talk to him alone, chased closely by blind panic that this was exactly how Violet had felt at first about Ricky.

"Ahhhhhh!" Violet yelled, teasing Will. "I knew it." She shelled a peanut and put the meats in his palm.

They settled into a companionable silence. The car roared along the road. Alt-rock whispered on the radio. Violet cracked nuts and deposited some in Will's hand whenever he held it out. Only I was fuming in my bucket seat, knowing now that I would have to break up with him as soon as we got home.

16

HE WAS SO SURPRISED AT MY WORDS THAT
he stepped backward, crunching through the magnolia leaves
in the driveway. To give himself time to think, he reached
through the open window of his car, snagged his T-shirt, and
pulled it on.

He recovered quickly after that, walking forward to
tower over me again. "No," he said. "You're upset. It's been a
really stressful morning. Just have something to eat, a shower
might be nice, go to work. I'll come pick you up after your
shift at the shop, and we'll talk about it."

"See?" I spat. "This is how it starts. You convince me
of things. You get everything you want, and I forget what I
wanted in the first place."

I was serious, and he began to get it. His nostrils flared

as he said, "So you're breaking up with me after we've been together for . . ." He pulled out his phone and glanced at it. "Nope, it hasn't been quite twelve hours."

"That's a record for me," I said, "because I've never been with anybody at all."

"*I* don't think this is funny!" He half turned away from me and ran his hands up the back of his neck, where his long hair used to be. "When you said on the first day of band practice that Beverly tricked me . . . no. *You're* the one who did that. You wanted another hookup that didn't mean anything. Maybe you even wanted to see this look on my face again. Do you get off on making me feel like an idiot?"

"Listen," I seethed, then cringed at the volume of my voice. I would wake my dad over this stupid shit. Though my heart was racing, I managed to say calmly and reasonably, "I haven't been the person that you wanted. I've sent you mixed signals. I've also changed my mind. But I've never lied to you. What I've said and done is exactly what I was feeling at the moment, and—"

"*That's enough,*" he barked, putting his hand up to stop me. "I'm going to get in my car and drive away. You can't change your mind after this. Don't flirt with me. Don't cry. Don't stare at me and look jealous when I go out with somebody else. You've jerked me around enough, and now it's over."

"Fine." I shrugged and headed for the house. Behind me I could hear the Mustang backing out of the driveway and roaring down the street. In front of me, my vision collapsed into a tunnel, dark all around and clear only at the center. I opened the front door.

As I stumbled inside, I heard Harper say *Breathe* inside my head. I inhaled a long noseful of stale air, a house full of dust.

I left the front door open.

Violet was in my room—our room—lying on her bed, staring at the ceiling. The manic mood that took over her when she was stressed was fading away now. She and I were opposites in that regard. She was normally more serious and got silly under pressure, whereas I was silly and got serious when everything went to hell, like now.

She looked up at me. "I like what you've done with the place."

"I'm sorry. It's kind of a mess." Just as when Will came over, I was seeing the house through the eyes of someone who didn't wade through it daily.

"Don't be sorry," she said. "You're sweet to come get me in the first place. And the house was a mess when I left."

This was true, but I was pretty sure it was five months' worse now. Before, we'd been kicking things aside to make a path through the den to our bedroom, but I didn't remember that we'd been balancing piles on top of piles like now.

"Anyway," she said, gesturing to her bed, "I won't have trouble finding my stuff, because everything's exactly where I left it."

I took another long breath, shallower now. My body wanted the oxygen. When I was angry, I needed to remember to keep breathing. But now that I'd noticed the stale smell, I didn't want to inhale it. I said slowly, "I . . . am going to call in to work and ask for the afternoon off . . . and clean."

"Really!" she exclaimed as though this was a novel idea, like hanging festive streamers from the ceiling. She sat up and said, "I'll help you."

We stuffed a towel under the door of my dad's bedroom and set up an electric fan for white noise outside the doorway so we wouldn't wake him with our banging around. With both of us working, it didn't take us long to pick up, sort through, and stash away everything in our tiny bedroom, and vacuum and dust the whole thing. She moved on to the bathroom. I tackled the laundry room. The den was going to take longer. By that time, some of my adrenaline from my fight with Will was draining away, but I wasn't ready to think about him yet. As I folded blankets into boxes and found a place for books on shelves, I listened to Violet talk about Ricky, and what had gone wrong.

"You know, I never liked school, and I wasn't doing too well. The whole thing seemed pointless. The only time I felt great was when I was with Ricky. Then he decided to drop out of school and get a job. I wouldn't see him any-more. He asked me to go with him. And I felt so unexpect-edly great thinking about that possibility, like the doors of heaven had opened. I'd thought I was saddled with high school and more school and living here for another few years, but instead of that, I could become an adult *right then*."

I gazed at a history report that I was supposed to turn in last May but had gotten lost under the cushions of the sofa, apparently. I didn't understand what she meant, not really. I didn't see what was so awful about living here, or how a life with Ricky could seem better.

But I did understand how she felt good about herself when she was with Ricky. That's how Will made me feel.

And I understood her view that a different life was within her grasp, a better life, like a magic door opening. I felt that way every time Will wanted us to get more seri-ous. The thing was, Violet thought this was a magic portal. I thought it was a painting of a magic portal, like on the cover of one of Sophia's fantasy novels. If you tried to step into it, you would realize it was only 2-D.

"I don't know what to do now," Violet murmured, wiping off a photo of Dad and Izzy and setting it on a shelf.

"Sure you do," I said with all the fake cheerfulness that went with pathological cleaning. "You'll get a job." I snapped my fingers. "Actually, I have a good fit for you. You always loved helping Dad restore the woodwork and the fountain in the white house, right?"

"Aw, the white house!" She sounded as sad as I was about the loss of our mansion. We'd never talked about it, because moving out of that house had been tangled up with Mom leaving.

"I might be able to hire you at the antiques shop if you wanted," I said.

"I love that place," she said. "How's Bob?"

"Better," I said. Man, hiring Violet for the shop was the best idea I'd had in years. She would get a steady job that paid okay. With her working there too, I could wean Bob and Roger off relying on me to the point of making me feel trapped. I would have been impressed with myself if I hadn't been panicking about Will underneath.

"You get a job there," I told Violet, "live here, and go to school. Look for one of those programs where you study for your GED and take college classes at the same time."

"School!" she said. "I couldn't do that. I was never smart like you."

"Like me!" I snorted.

"Of *course* like you. Are you crazy? We're all proud of you for getting in that special class for smart kids, and for doing so well on the drums."

I almost laughed when she put the gifted class and band together in the same sentence, as if they were related. But I probably sounded just as nonsensical to Izzy when I talked about hair color.

"Dad always said you'd be the first person in the family to go to college," Violet went on.

"Well, of course he would say that now. You and Sophia and Izzy haven't been to college."

"He said that when you were a baby. You picked up on everything so quickly. Mom said Izzy didn't talk until she was three, but she didn't have another baby to compare her with. She said if she'd had you first, she would have put Izzy in an institution."

I laughed. That was the funny yet slightly wrong sort of comment I remembered my mom making. "News to me," I said. "I thought you only kept me around for comic relief. That's all anybody ever seemed to think I was good for."

"Well, sure," Violet said, "back when you were in third grade. But now you're grown up."

That, too, was news to me. My heart started pounding again. It knew what I had done to Will. My brain didn't want to deal with it yet. But as Violet pointed out how old I was, my fear of having a boyfriend seemed immature. It might have worked for me in ninth grade.

Not now.

"This didn't take as long as I thought," Violet said, rescuing the last pair of panties from the sofa and twirling them around on one finger. "If we could get the kitchen counters and the stove cleared off, I could run to the store for groceries."

I inhaled as if the house already smelled like Puerto Rican food instead of dust. "We could make carne guisada," I said.

Her dark eyes flew wide open. "And pasteles? And—"

"Amarillos!" we both said at the same time with all the reverence of two hungry girls who hadn't eaten fried plantains in months. If we made them, maybe Dad still wouldn't eat them. I didn't care anymore. *I* would eat them.

"Divide and conquer," she said. "Kitchen or store?"

"Kitchen." If cleaning would make me feel better about breaking up with Will, I still had a whole town to polish.

After the kitchen was in reasonable order, I went outside.

As we'd cleaned, we'd thrown mounds of trash into the yard, which probably frightened the neighbors. I bagged it up and stacked it neatly by the curb. Then I raked the magnolia leaves. I was pleasantly surprised to see that grass was living underneath. With some rain in September, the yard might start to look like a yard again.

I crossed the street with my rake and looked at our house from a distance, really *looked* at it like a potential buyer would have viewed it if Dad had followed his original plan of flipping it. A previous owner had painted it an unfortunate dark brown, but it had good bones for someone who didn't mind a funky 1950s bungalow with retro lines.

My heart thumped painfully again as I realized I was viewing this house as if I was Will, parked in his Mustang on the street, capturing the proportions with a pencil and a ruler.

"Uh-oh, what's the matter?" Harper said beside me.

I jumped. I'd been so absorbed in my thoughts that I hadn't heard her roll up on the sidewalk. She and Kaye straddled their bikes, watching me with worried eyes.

"We came to ask what was up with you and Will last night," Kaye explained. "But your yard looks beautiful. Obviously something has gone horribly wrong."

That's when I broke down.

*   *   *

"I have a theory," Harper said.

My crying jag was over, but she kept her arm around my shoulders, even though this must have practically dislocated her arm because I was seven inches taller than her. We sat on a handmade bench my dad had brought home and set under the magnolia tree, then lost under the leaves. Cleared of plant rubbish, it was a nice place to sit—or would have been, if the heat hadn't been so oppressive.

Kaye stopped sweeping the sidewalk to circle her finger in the air, telling Harper to cut to the chase. In spite of my despair, I almost laughed at this interaction I'd seen play out between them countless times since third grade.

"Your sisters missed your mother," Harper told me, "and they felt like your family wasn't whole. Starting their own families was their way of getting back what they'd lost. The problem was, they were so young that it didn't work. I mean, I get carried away buying art supplies and run out of lunch money. You"—she poked me—"can't get up in the morning. Could you imagine one of us being the primary caretaker for somebody else?"

"No," I said. Izzy seemed stable now, but I had seriously worried about her children at first. I still worried about Sophia's baby.

"And the boys your sisters hooked up with are even

worse," Harper said. "They bailed on their girlfriends and their babies. Seems to me Izzy is doing a pretty good job putting her life back together, though."

"*Now* she is," I acknowledged. Two years ago was a different story.

"You've watched your sisters make mistakes. You're younger, so you may have seen your mother leaving very differently from the way they saw it. You miss your mom, but instead of trying to fix your life by filling her shoes, you avoid further complications by sidestepping responsibility when you can. You have an allergic reaction when you do get put in charge. You stay out of any relationship at all."

"But that's a good thing," I defended myself. "I'm a lot better off than my sisters."

"But what if you don't change?" Kaye asked. "At some point when you're older, you're going to look around and see that everybody is in a relationship while you're alone. And pretty much everybody in your high school classes will have gone off to college."

"*I'm* going to college," I declared. "I'll be a National Merit Scholar."

Kaye raised her eyebrows skeptically. "Not if you don't get your grades up and convince some teacher to vouch for you. I worry that you're going to stay right here because you couldn't be bothered to take the next step."

"At least the house will be clean," I said.

"True," Harper said. "And maybe there will be other boys you can mess around with. But most people want a relationship sooner or later. Even those boys will move on while you stay put. And as for your relationship with Will . . ."

I held my breath, waiting, hoping, praying for Harper to give me some insight into how to fix this.

"I wouldn't have paired you two up in a million years," she said. "But now that I've seen you together, I get why you're so compatible. You're different from each other, but you each understand what makes the other tick. It would be a shame for you to let your knee-jerk reaction rule your life, and let him go."

I shrugged. "Our time together was all a misunderstanding to begin with," I said. "He misread me as girlfriend material. I misread him as a player. By the time we found out we were wrong about each other, it was too late."

Kaye nodded sadly. "You'd already fallen in love with each other."

"Well, I don't know about *him*. That's what he said, yeah. But I . . ." The full meaning of her words hit me. "Yeah, I'd already fallen . . . Oh, God." I put my hands over my face, horrified that I was crying in front of them yet again.

Harper drew me closer on the bench. Kaye called, "Group hug!" and wrapped her arms around both of us. This was a little much in the heat, but I relaxed into their embrace and tried to stop panicking about Will.

Kaye knocked her booty against mine so I'd scoot over to make room on the bench. After I'd crushed Harper sufficiently, Kaye sat down, then stroked a lock of hair out of my eyes with her middle finger. "Teen hygiene tip. If you try to get Will back today, bathe first. Guys love that."

"Yeah, okay," I grumbled.

"I agree with Harper," she said. "After seeing you and Will together, I think you may be meant for each other. It's obvious that he loves you. It would be a shame for your fear to be the only reason you let him go."

We all turned as the front door opened. I hadn't realized how late it had gotten—time for my dad to wake up. He called across the yard, "*Lucita!* What happened to the top four layers of the stuff in the house?"

Kaye and Harper left when Violet arrived in Dad's truck with enough groceries for a feast. An hour later, she and Dad and I sat down to our first family dinner since we'd moved in, because we had cleared off the table.

"*Lucita,*" he mumbled between bites. "So good."

"Thanks." I wondered why he was into this meal now when he'd never wanted what I'd cooked before. Maybe the table made the difference. Or Violet. Or the fact that the meal was not offered with an air of desperate sacrifice.

"Violet," he said. "Delicious. And—" He put his hand over hers on the table. In Spanish he told her that he was very glad she'd come home. He said he'd always thought she would return eventually. He'd wanted her to figure that out for herself. Love was a complicated thing, but that boy she had picked out would not be his choice for her. Then there was a series of epithets that involved Ricky's private parts.

"I know, Dad." Violet took a bite. "This house doesn't seem like home, though, with Sophia and Izzy missing. I haven't seen Izzy and the kids in months. Maybe I could cook again one day this week, and we could have them over, now that the house isn't a death trap for the children and we've found all the chairs. I could drive up to get Sophia and the baby one weekend." She gazed around the den/dining room/kitchen. "It would be kind of small in here for all of us, though."

"The white house is for sale again," I said casually.

Dad's eyebrows shot up. Suddenly he looked more awake than I'd seen him in years. "Really?" The eager look settled into wistfulness. "I loved that house. I think about it a lot."

"Me too," Violet said.

"Me too," I said.

"I looked forward to tackling that fountain," he said. "Remember, in the atrium, with the mermaids?"

"I'll bet it would be cheaper than it was before," I said. "It's been on the market a few times. Why don't we buy it back?"

He laughed. "I wish. I work too much, *lucita*."

"Yeah, you do," I said. "Why? Izzy is stable now. Sophia is stable-ish."

"Ish," Violet echoed with a laugh.

"Violet will get there," I said.

Violet snorted.

"And you don't have to worry about me," I told him. "I'll get college paid for."

"College!" he exclaimed. "I always said you would be the first one to go to college, but you've been hemming and hawing."

"I decided I'm going," I said.

"When did you decide this?"

"Today. I'm getting online and registering to take the SAT in a minute." I had no doubt I could score high enough on the SAT to get a full ride to college, provided I could get really stressed out with responsibilities before test time. The way things with band and work and Will had been going, that shouldn't be too hard.

"In the meantime, I would help you with the house," I said.

"I would too," Violet chimed in.

"I'll only be here for a year before I leave for college," I said, "but we could get a lot done."

Dad put down his fork and nodded, staring into space. "I was about to sign up for another month of weekends at work. I didn't know how to break it to you, *lucita*, but I was going to miss all your band performances at the ball games. It's funny how you work so much that you don't even have time to think about how much you're working, or what you're working for."

"Yeah," said Violet. "Sometimes when you're in the thick of something, you lose perspective."

I put my fist to my mouth and squeezed a sob back in. Talk about being in the thick of things. I'd been so caught up in my own childish way of dealing with my fears that I'd driven off my favorite pirate, maybe forever. But before that possibility settled into fact, I had to try to get him back.

I stood to take my plate to the sink. On my way, I stopped and kissed my dad on the cheek. "Please consider it. We'd rather have you home."

* * *

I'd never been inside Will's house, but he'd pointed it out to me on our tour of town last Wednesday. I rode my bike into his neighborhood, a newer development where the trees were small, the houses all looked the same, and there weren't any unique architectural details for Will to draw. I felt a little sick as I laid my bike carefully on the lawn and walked up to the door. I put out a finger to ring the doorbell and noticed my hand was trembling.

Will's mom was as tall as me, with Will's worry line between her brows. She wore a tank top and shorts. Those clothes would have made sense if she was walking at the beach or working in the yard, but I was surprised she wasn't freezing when she had the air-conditioning in the house set below zero. It seeped out, surrounding me and making me shiver as she said in her own clipped Minnesota accent, "Oh, hello. Will's talked about you a lot. I'm afraid he's asleep right now, though. He said he was feeling sick."

"Sick?" I repeated. "Is he okay?"

His mom nodded. "I think he's just homesick."

I nodded too, because that seemed to be the thing to do. "Homesick."

"There's no cure for that but time," she said sadly. "But thanks for coming by, Tammy. I'll tell him you were here." She backed me out of her house and onto her porch. She shut the door, sealing out my voice, before I could tell her my name wasn't Tammy.

I stood there for a moment in the quiet night, listening to the breeze rattle the palm fronds. It was an evening for staying inside, where it was cool, and wishing you were back in Minnesota, away from me.

I walked down the sidewalk and picked up my bike. What else could I do? Yes, Will and I had argued, and we'd been genuinely mad at each other, with reason. But in the back of my mind, I suppose I'd assumed that we could fix it. We hadn't flirted like we used to since the trouble began—it all started with that stupid title—but I'd thought we would get back there.

And now I knew we wouldn't. I was such a poor replacement for his friends that I made him sick.

I got back on my bike and rode. The Sunday night was bustling with traffic. Folks were driving inland after a day at our beaches, one last weekend before Labor Day. Families had eaten one last meal out on the main drag and were packing into their cars to go home and prepare for work and school. I was riding the wrong way, heading downtown. I steered into the alley and propped my bike against the railing of the Crab Lab.

Employees kept the lights out on the restaurant's back

porch so they could do what they wanted without being seen from the alley. I was all the way up the steps before I could make out Sawyer's shape in the darkness. When he saw me, he put down his beer. I walked into his open arms.

"Things didn't work out with Will?" he asked, his breath warm in my ear. "You wouldn't be hugging me otherwise."

I sighed as I collapsed on the bench beside him. "I broke up with him."

"Why?" Sawyer asked.

"Violet finally decided to come home, and we went to get her, and . . . I don't know. I guess I started comparing Will and Ricky."

"Will is not a shit like Ricky," Sawyer said. "*I* am a shit like Ricky."

This seemed like a new low of self-deprecation, even for Sawyer. I nodded toward his beer. "Starting early, aren't you? How many of those have you had?"

He didn't respond to my question but asked, "What happened then?"

"I cleaned my entire house."

"Oh, poor baby," he cooed. "You *are* upset. I've got something for you." He pulled a joint from his pocket. I watched him light it, closing his eyes against the smoke. He took a long toke and handed it to me.

I held it between my fingers and looked at it. This was what I needed: to forget a problem that couldn't be solved. But my brain was stressed, which put my body in organization mode. It did not want this weed. I needed to take my hit so Sawyer's pot didn't burn down and go to waste, but every atom inside me screamed to hand the joint back.

Sawyer snatched it from me. When I looked at him in surprise, he was staring past me. I turned. Will was on the top step.

"That's exactly what I thought," Will said. He jogged down the stairs again.

"Go." Sawyer nodded at Will, urging me to follow him. "Go, go, go."

I ran after Will, leaping down the last two stairs in my effort to catch him before he reached his car at the end of the alley. Sweating in the hot night, I grabbed his elbow.

He stopped short and whirled to face me. "Don't. I told you that I was done with you. You're just like Beverly. When my mom said you came by, I thought maybe my instincts were wrong, but now I see I was right about you the whole time. I left town for five minutes and she was cheating on me. You and I have one little fight—"

"Little?" I broke in. "I put a lot of effort into that fight."

He raised his voice for some reason. "—and you just

move on like nothing happened, and go back to doing drugs and God knows what else with Sawyer De Luca."

"I was *not*," I said emphatically. "I was in the process of politely refusing a joint. Even if I had taken a hit, calling that 'doing drugs' makes it sound like I was shooting up heroin."

"It's the same," he said. "You and Beverly are the same. I don't want you back now that I know what you're like." He stalked to the driver's seat of his car, slammed the door, and roared out of the alley.

I was left standing in a cloud of the Mustang's exhaust, the smell of frying food, and an utterly empty late summer night.

17

"DON'T YOU LOOK NICE," MS. NAKAMOTO said as I sat down in the chair facing her desk. She closed the door on the noise of people dragging their instruments out of the storage room for practice.

I supposed I *did* look nice. I'd set my alarm for school so I had time to iron my dress this morning. I'd fixed my hair and put on makeup. Violet had cooked me a balanced breakfast. I'd gotten my calculus homework finished during class since I wasn't flirting with Will or even sitting near him. I'd taken great notes in history. I'd generally felt like I was about to lose my grip on my sanity.

And didn't Ms. Nakamoto *sound* nice? She'd never spoken so pleasantly to me before, possibly because she was usually yelling at me across a football field to stop screwing around.

"Thank you," I said politely, as though I was pleased with her comment and my brain had been eaten by zombies.

"That usually means something's gone wrong in your life," she said. "Is there a problem you want to tell me about?"

"There is a problem," I affirmed, "but I don't want to tell you about it."

"All right, then," she said, because she was used to this kind of thing from me. "My news probably isn't going to help. I called you in to let you know that Will Matthews has challenged you for drum captain."

"Really!" I crowed. Will was fulfilling his promise. He still cared about me!

Wait a minute. He just wanted his drum captain position back. I amended my previous statement: "Really."

"It's not going to happen," Ms. Nakamoto said. "I told him no."

"But that's the rule," I protested.

"All rules are at my discretion," she said firmly. "We have four contests coming up this season. We're not going to ruin the cohesiveness of the drum line by switching leadership every week."

"I don't want to be drum captain," I whined. "I challenged Will, but it was a mistake."

"Correction: You *meant* to throw it, like every other

challenge, but you made a mistake and played a perfect exercise."

I was afraid I would get in worse trouble if I copped to this. But I didn't want to lie to her either, so I sat there blinking.

"You're crafty, I'll admit," Ms. Nakamoto said. "I didn't get wise to you until Señorita Higgenbotham told me you made a C in her class even though you're bilingual. And now there's talk that you've scored high enough to be a National Merit Scholar. A faculty member would have to write you a letter of recommendation, and we're not sure we can do that in good conscience. Why do you sabotage yourself, Tia?"

I uncrossed and recrossed my legs, because that's what respectable women did when they were in a meeting and wearing a dress. I had seen this on TV. "I don't want to be in charge and ruin everything."

"How have you ruined the drum line in the past week? You haven't."

Damn it. "Will would be better."

"I have no reason to think so," she said. "I was happy you were drum captain, and I wasn't looking for anyone to replace you when he showed up. You know when you impressed me?"

"No, I have no idea," I said honestly, refraining from laughing at the thought.

"When Will cursed and threw his phone across the field on the first day of camp. I was going to kick him out of the position right then, but you handled him and you handled *me*. You saved drum captain for him, at least until you challenged him." She stood as if the conversation was over.

"No, wait a minute, nuh-uh," I told her, keeping my seat. "I'm an underachiever. You don't seriously *want* me in charge!"

"Sometimes we put underachievers in positions of responsibility and they rise to the occasion. You are one of those people. You're a sharp young lady and a fine percussionist, Tia. You *are* the drum captain. Why not enjoy it? You only get one senior year in high school." She opened the door for me, letting in the bustle of band, and nodded toward it, since I wasn't budging. "Now I'm running late. Please tell DeMarcus to get practice started without me."

Grumbling under my breath, I trudged across the parking lot to Will's car, where he'd left my drum propped against a tire. I was guessing that I was evicted again. I pulled my harness over my shoulders and carefully descended the stadium stairs.

From this height, the band formation looked beautiful. The circles and curlicues weren't squashed anymore. They were as precise as if Will had drawn them.

He stood in his place in the drums, close to Travis, leaving an empty space for me. And—wonder of wonders—today he was *talking* to Travis. As I watched, he threw back his head and laughed.

He glimpsed me on the stairs. His smile faded. He turned back to Travis.

This was how it was going to be from now on. He must have been furious that he couldn't get his drum captain position back. He'd already been furious with me at school all day. But *furious* on Will was the silent treatment. He simply didn't interact with me. He stayed away from me. The only time he'd acknowledged I existed was in English when a couple of basketball players hit on me. He'd gone out of his way to walk slowly down the row where we were standing, and he'd shouldered each of them in turn, saying "Excuse me" as if he simply wanted to get by. They'd watched him wide eyed and told me they would catch me later. They'd gotten the message.

I should have been angry. Will didn't want me back. Where did he get off elbowing basketball players away from me? Apparently I had a better chance of hooking up with someone new now that I was stressed out and practicing good grooming habits. I had tried to lay out my room and bathroom so that when this stress reaction inevitably faded, I would still be organized enough to look decent in the morning. I'd enjoyed the attention I'd gotten at school all day, along the lines of Ms. Nakamoto's *Don't you look like you've bathed this year!* Too bad the one guy I'd really craved that comment from no longer wanted to take a selfie with me.

When I reached the sidelines, I gave Ms. Nakamoto's message to DeMarcus. He glanced down at his watch, then up the stairs at the stragglers. We had a little time left before practice began. Rather than spend it in a shroud of silent treatment beside Will, I dumped my drum and sat down on a bench, next to Sawyer. I'd never seen him sit down in his costume. He immediately leaned over until his huge pelican head lay in my lap. I stroked his feathers absently.

"Being in love totally sucks when they don't love you back," I said.

He felt for my hand and held it in his feather-covered pelican glove.

Kaye looked over at me from a cheerleader huddle and stuck out her bottom lip in sympathy. She and Harper had taken one look at me when I got to school and had known my talk with Will hadn't gone well.

DeMarcus climbed to the top of his podium. He was about to start practice. I needed to be in the drum section when that happened, ready to play my riff. "Sawyer," I said, "I have to go."

He didn't budge.

"Sawyer," I complained, "not funny. You're going to get me in trouble. You know I'm stressed out, so I actually care about that shit today."

He was incredibly heavy in my lap.

"Now you're worrying me," I said. "You're making me think you've passed out in there. Come on, Sawyer. Joke's over."

DeMarcus made his move and Will played the riff, which the rest of the drum line repeated. The boom of drums echoed around the stadium, followed by silence, just as I pulled Sawyer's pelican head off.

Sawyer's soaked blond head and broad shoulders lay limp across me. He really had passed out.

"Will!" I shrieked.

DeMarcus turned around on his podium. The cheer-leaders off to the side of the band rushed over. "No, no, no," I yelled as they gathered around, "Don't crowd us. I need Will."

And then he was there, towering over the girls. "Back up," he told them. They all stared at him with wide, heav-ily made-up eyes and took two steps back. He shouted to DeMarcus, "Call 911." He told me, "Hold him," and when

I put my arms around Sawyer, Will pulled off the rest of his costume. Sawyer wore only a pair of gym shorts. His muscular body flopped like a rag doll. That's when I really got scared.

Will knelt down under Sawyer, then stood so Sawyer's whole body draped over one shoulder. "Come on," he told me. "Get them out of my way."

I jumped up. "Move," I barked to the cheerleaders and majorettes gawking at us. They parted, clearing a path to the gate. I stepped aside to let Will pass, then closed the gate behind me, glaring at the girls and daring them to cross me. I turned and jogged up the stairs behind Will, who was making great time up the incline despite carrying a hundred and fifty pounds.

At the top of the stairs, he grunted, "Help me." I reached up to ease Sawyer onto the ground, in the shade underneath the bleachers. Will nodded toward a hose coiled next to the concession stand. "Turn that on."

I dragged the hose over and let the water gush over Sawyer's legs, then his torso—soaking his gym shorts, which I would have made a joke about any other time—then his arms and his neck, keeping the flow away from his face so I didn't drown him.

"No, get his head." Will turned Sawyer on his side.

I wet Sawyer's hair, then looked to Will for guidance.

"Keep doing it," Will said. "We just need to cool him down." He pressed his thumb over Sawyer's wrist to feel his pulse.

"How do you know this?" I asked, moving the hose down to Sawyer's chest again.

"I googled 'heatstroke' because I've spent the last two weeks thinking I was going to have one." Will glanced up. "You must have known, or you wouldn't have called to me for help."

"I called to you for help because you're you. I knew you would keep your shit together in a crisis."

I sighed with relief as sirens approached. And then Sawyer blinked his eyes open and tried to sit up. "Stay cool, man," Will said softly, pressing one hand on Sawyer's chest. He told me, "One of us should go with him to the hospital."

I wanted desperately to go. More than that, I wanted what was best for Sawyer. "You go, because you'll be more helpful."

"I'll go," Will agreed, "because you have to work after school." He looked up at me. "Kaye and Harper told me you took off work and cleaned your house yesterday. Are you okay?"

I nodded.

Sawyer tried to sit up again, struggling against Will's

hand. "What the fuck," he said weakly. "Get the fuck off me."

Will glanced at me. "He'll be okay."

All at once, the parking lot was bursting with sirens, louder and louder until Will and I put our hands over our ears. An ambulance arrived, plus an overkill pumper truck from the fire department, a couple of police cars that had come to see what all the excitement was about, and Ms. Nakamoto, followed by the principal, who was really booking it across the asphalt. I'd never seen an old lady run that fast, especially in heels. I was impressed.

With all those folks crowding around, there wasn't anything left for me to do but turn off and coil up the hose and watch the paramedics argue with Sawyer, who insisted he was fine, and promptly threw up. I shared one last look with Will before the paramedics closed him and Sawyer inside the ambulance. As it retreated across the parking lot, I heaved a long sigh and realized for the first time how tense my shoulders had been.

I wandered back down the stairs to the stadium. The band was running through the halftime show. While I watched, four people tripped over Will's drum, which nobody had the foresight to remove from the middle of the field where he'd dropped it. Before I retrieved my own drum from the bench, I took Kaye aside from the rest of the cheerleaders.

"When class is over," I whispered, "could you hang out around the boys' locker room and ask someone to get Sawyer's stuff for you? I have to work."

Kaye frowned. "You want me to take it to him? His homework can wait until tomorrow."

"No, he needs his wallet with his insurance card," I insisted. "He needs his phone to call people because he won't remember anybody's number off the top of his head, and he needs his keys to get inside his house in case he's actually released from the hospital today."

"What about his dad?"

"His dad is up in Panama City, selling blown-glass figurines on the pier. They have a bigger Labor Day crowd than we do."

The resistance on her face melted into sympathy. "What about his brother?"

"You can't count on his brother for anything."

I snagged my drum and made my way through the band to my place. As the rest of the period crawled by, I decided it was too bad I couldn't take the SAT on demand. Right this second I would have made a perfect score.

Violet was in a job interview with Bob and Roger in the back office, and I was manning the front counter, when the antique cowbell rang. Will came through the door, his big body blocking so much sun that he made the room turn dark.

"How's Sawyer?" I asked. I hoped he hadn't come by to give me bad news personally.

"He's fine," Will said. "He's dehydrated. He's getting an IV." He touched the back of his hand with two fingers, which I assumed was where the IV went. "A bunch of people from school are there with him now. He wants you to come by after work."

I nodded.

Will looked uncomfortably around the shop, as if he didn't want to meet my gaze, then pointed at the floor. "I'm going to borrow this dog."

"Okay," I said, like that was not weird.

"Come on," he said. Even though his voice hadn't changed and the dog wasn't looking at him, she jumped up when he spoke to her. They disappeared out the door.

I stared through the window and into the street, which looked like it always did, as though the boy I loved most in the world hadn't just bopped in to steal the shop dog. If it wasn't for the antique bell still swinging on its ribbon and chiming gently, I would have suspected it hadn't happened at all.

I slid down from my stool, emerged from behind the counter, and leaned out the door, peering down the street. Far away, past all the shops, in the tree-shaded park next to the marina, the dog was chasing Will. Will stopped suddenly and reached for the dog, who bent her body just out of his reach and scampered away. Now Will chased the dog. The dog spun to face him. They both crouched in the stance of a dog at the ready, each daring the other to jump first. Will made a grab and the dog dashed away.

I knew Will was still missing a lot of what he'd had back home. But at least he'd taken this first step toward finding what he needed here in town. I watched him and the dog for a while, playing together in the long shadows of the trees.

By the time I made it to the hospital that night, everybody else had cleared out. Sawyer was alone in a room for two patients. The other guy must have died. Sawyer was curled into the fetal position with an IV tube snaking to his hand. He faced away from the door, and his hospital gown fell open to reveal his butt crack, because Sawyer did not care.

"Nice ass," I said from the doorway.

"Thanks," he said without moving.

I walked to the other side of the bed. "Are you hungry at all? I thought you might be, since you lost your lunch. I brought you something." I peeled the aluminum foil off the plate of amarillos, beans, and an empanada. "Violet made it vegan for you."

He sat up, took the plate and fork I handed him, and shoveled in a mouthful. He swallowed and rolled his eyes. "Oh. My. God. They don't do vegan at this hospital. I was starving. This is so good." After a few more bites, he held the plate out to me, offering me some.

"I ate already," I said.

"Good, because I didn't really want to give you any." He ate another mouthful. "Violet should be cooking at the Crab Lab."

"Nah. She'd rather explain to two old men where their antiques are."

He swallowed. "It's been forever since I had Puerto Rican food. I forget y'all are half Puerto Rican."

"Me too," I said. "Can I get you a drink?"

"Yeah, a Sprite. My eleventh Sprite. Down the hall in the fridge."

Wandering back in with the can, I asked him, "When are they letting you out?"

"They would have let me out already, but someone is supposed to watch me. They need somebody to release me to. My dad isn't coming home, and my brother won't get off work until after visiting hours are over. He said he'll come buy me out tomorrow morning."

I flopped down in the chair beside the bed. "Will they release you to me?"

"No. I took the liberty of asking, but when I said your name, the nurse looked all outraged and hollered, 'That girl who—' Well, never mind what she said."

I knew which nurse he was talking about. I'd seen DeMarcus's mom on my way in. DeMarcus had thrown a big Halloween party in seventh grade, and his mom had walked in on me teaching him to French kiss. I guess I didn't have a reputation for being nursing material.

"I can get somebody down here to spring you," I said. "Harper's mom, or—you know who would be perfect? Kaye's mom." She was the president of a bank and looked it. Nobody messed with her.

"I don't want to do that to anybody who isn't you," Sawyer said.

"Aw. Hugs." I stood up and wrapped my arms around him, careful to keep my dress out of the amarillos.

"I'm swearing it all off," he said into my hair. "Alcohol and weed. All mind-altering substances."

I sat back down, shocked. "You are?"

"Yes."

"Working in a bar?"

"Yes."

"Well, you're a vegan working in a restaurant that serves primarily seafood and meat," I said. "If anybody could swear off alcohol working in a bar, it would be you. And I think that would be great. It's not good for you, or me either. But if you're doing it because you had heatstroke . . . I do think being dehydrated the day after drinking didn't help you, but you had heatstroke because you were dressed up in a pelican costume at two p.m. on the hottest day of the year in Florida."

"I know."

"Does it have something to do with your mystery girl?"

"I'm never getting Kaye," he said. "And I wouldn't change my life for her. I've learned that from you. I'm not changing for somebody else, because that person could disappear. The only person to change for is yourself."

I was astounded. I'd thought I had him figured out. It never occurred to me that *he* had *me* figured out in return. And when he took my thoughts and put them in his own words, I sounded halfway noble.

"But like you said," he went on, "alcohol was a contributing factor to my mortifying collapse. I shouldn't be giving in to contributing factors when I already have an asshole brother and a jailbird dad. You know, for the first time in my life, I feel like I'm really good at something. I was a mediocre athlete. I'm an indifferent student. But I'm an excellent pelican. I support the school and I make people laugh."

"You do. You're a great symbol for the school."

"Being an excellent pelican is pretty sad, as career skills go. It isn't everything. But it's not nothing." He set his clean plate on the bedside table. "What I feel worst about is Minnesota coming around the corner after I'd handed you that joint. I mean, nice guy. I heard he hauled me up the stairs at the stadium."

"He did," I said.

"And he stayed with me here until Harper and Kaye and DeMarcus and everybody showed up. He was as nice as he could be after all the shit I've given him during the past couple of weeks. I ruined everything between you two."

"You didn't," I said sadly. "I did that all by myself."

"Obviously not, or he wouldn't have come looking for you last night."

I stayed with Sawyer, even doing my English homework there while he made fun of me and called me a sellout. When visiting hours were over, DeMarcus's mom kicked me out of the room. But all the while, in the back of my mind, I was formulating a plan for how I could put my stress-induced organizational skills to good use.

The next day, at the beginning of band, I waited until Ms. Nakamoto turned on her microphone and started explaining what we would do that period. Then I set my drum on the grass—Will watched me curiously but didn't ask what I was doing—and I walked through the band and up the stadium steps. Ms. Nakamoto didn't seem to notice Harper walking down the steps in another part of the stadium. She'd gotten out of last period to take pictures and document the coming event for the yearbook.

Ms. Nakamoto kept talking to the band until I stopped right beside her. "Yes, Ms. Cruz?" she asked.

"May I borrow that?" I asked, reaching for the microphone. "Just for a sec."

Surprised, she handed it to me.

I cleared my throat and read from my notes. "We—" My voice boomed around the stadium. The band yelped a protest, and the cheerleaders slapped their hands over their ears. I backed the microphone away from my mouth. "Sorry. We the students present to you, Ms. Nakamoto, the Sawyer De Luca/Will Matthews Heat Relief Proposal. We understand that dress codes are necessary for schools to function in what the faculty thinks is an appropriate manner. However, our school, in allowing students to disrobe partially during summer practices on school grounds, has already acknowledged that its dress code is not always comfortable for its students, or even safe. We would like that exception to be extended to practices outdoors year-round. We would like you, Ms. Nakamoto, to be our advocate in presenting this proposal to Principal Chen. In the interim, while the proposal is being considered, we respectfully request that you stop enforcing the dress code during afternoon practices on the field." I pulled off my shirt.

That was the cue. With a prolonged whoop, all the cheerleaders and the entire band took off their shirts—the girls were wearing bikini tops underneath—and threw the shirts up in the air. The cheerleaders unfurled a long paper banner they'd made like their spirit signs for football games. It said REMEMBER THE FALLEN PELICAN.

When the rainstorm of shirts cleared, Harper still stood on one of the benches along the sidelines, snapping pictures. Besides her, only Will was still fully dressed, because he was left out of Kaye's student council call tree. He looked around at the half-naked band, bewildered.

Ms. Nakamoto glared at my bikini top, then at me. "I told you I wanted you to take on more responsibility, and this is your first foray?"

I put the microphone down where it wouldn't pick up what I said. "Yes ma'am," I told her. "You weren't here when Sawyer fainted yesterday."

She nodded and seemed to search my face for a moment. "Okay," she finally said.

JENNIFER ECHOLS

I put the microphone to my lips again. "Mr. Matthews," I said in Ms. Nakamoto's voice, "you may take off your shirt."

The band whooped again, the cheerleaders clapped, and the drums yelled "Take it off!" through cupped hands. Will shrugged off his harness, slowly and sexily pulled off his shirt, balled it up, and hurled it toward the goalpost, just like he'd thrown his phone on the first day of practice.

Ms. Nakamoto was glaring at me again. Hastily I handed her the microphone, dashed down the stairs and across the field, and loaded my drum harness onto my shoulders.

As she resumed her announcements, Will leaned over. "Did you do this for me?"

"I felt really bad about Sunday," I whispered. "I shouldn't have broken up with you that way." I looked into his eyes, as best as I could guess through both our sunglasses. "I shouldn't have broken up with you at all. And I honestly wasn't doing what you thought I was doing with Sawyer. But as you said about putting your hand on Angelica at the beach, you and I aren't together, so it doesn't matter whether you believe me or not. I just wish you did."

He put his drumstick on my drum and circled it slowly. "What if we went back to hooking up, like you wanted at first? We tried it my way, and now we'll do it your way. You can be with other people, and I won't get jealous."

316

I raised my eyebrows at him.

"Okay, I will," he acknowledged, "but I won't make a stink. I feel like we're meant to be together. We just haven't figured out how. And I would really like to get in trouble for touching you right now."

I crossed my hand over his to place my drumstick on his drum. "What if we tried it your way again? I'll give it more than twelve hours this time."

He grinned. "What are we talking? Eighteen? Twenty-four?"

"Three days," I suggested. "Until the first football game, and then we can decide whether we want to renew our contract."

"Why don't we wait until *after* the first football game to talk about it?" he suggested. "At whatever party we go to. Or at the beach, in my car." Ever so slowly, watching Ms. Nakamoto, he edged toward me. His earring glinted in the light. He turned and kissed the corner of my mouth while I giggled.

Ms. Nakamoto called through the microphone, "Mr. Matthews, get off Ms. Cruz. I'm starting to sound like a broken record."

Down the line of snare drums, Jimmy tapped his watch and said, "Seven minutes."

ACKNOWLEDGMENTS

Heartfelt thanks to my brilliant editor, Annette Pollert; my tireless agent, Laura Bradford; my hilarious critique partner, Victoria Dahl; and the readers who have enjoyed my books, told a friend about them, and made my dream career a reality. I appreciate you.

Don't miss Jennifer Echols's

the superlatives

perfect couple

FAMOUS PHOTOGRAPHS WALLPAPERED MR. Oakley's journalism classroom. Behind his desk, Martin Luther King Jr. waved to thousands who'd crowded the National Mall to hear his "I Have a Dream" speech, with the Washington Monument towering in the distance. Over by the windows, a lone man stood defiant in front of four Chinese tanks in protest of the Tiananmen Square massacre. On the wall directly above my computer screen, a World War II sailor impulsively kissed a nurse in Times Square on the day Japan surrendered.

Mr. Oakley had told us a picture was worth a thousand words, and these posters were his proof. He was right. Descriptions in my history textbook read like old news, but these photos made me want to stand up for people, like Dr. King did, and protest injustice, like Tank Man did.

And be swept away by romance, like that nurse.

My gaze fell from the poster to my computer display,

which was full of my pictures of Brody Larson. A couple of weeks ago, on the first day of school, our senior class had elected the Superlatives—like Most Academic, Most Courteous, and Least Likely to Leave the Tampa/St. Petersburg Metropolitan Area. Brody and I had been voted Perfect Couple That Never Was. Brody had dated Grace Swearingen the whole summer, and I'd been with the yearbook editor, Kennedy Glass, for a little over a month. Being named part of a perfect couple when Brody and I were dating other people was embarrassing. Disorienting. Anything but perfect.

And *me* being named one half of a perfect couple with *Brody* made as much sense as predicting Labor Day snow for next Monday in our beachside town. He was the popular, impulsive quarterback for our football team. Sure, through twelve years of school, I'd liked him. He was friendly and *so* handsome. He also scared the hell out of me. I couldn't date someone who'd nearly lost his license speeding, was forever in the principal's office for playing pranks, and had a daily drama with one girl or another on a long list of exes. And he would never fall for law-abiding, curfew-obeying, glasses-wearing me.

So I hadn't gone after him as my friend Tia had urged me to. I only found excuses to snap photos of him for the yearbook. For the football section, I'd taken a shot of him at practice in his helmet and pads. Exasperated with his teammates, he'd held up his hands like he needed help from heaven.

For the candid section, I planned to use a picture from my friend Kaye's party last Saturday. Brody grinned devilishly as he leaned into his truck cab to grab something. I'd cropped out the beer.

For the full-color opening page, I'd taken a close-up of him yesterday in study hall. His brown hair fell long across his forehead. He wore a green T-shirt that made his green eyes seem to glow. Girls all over school would thank me for this when they received their yearbooks next May. In fact, Brody had implied as much when I snapped the picture. He made me promise I wouldn't sell it to "a porn site for ladies," which was why he was grinning.

In short, he was the sailor in the poster: the kind of guy to come home from overseas, celebrate the end of the war in Times Square, and sweep a strange girl off her feet.

I only wished I was that girl.

"Harper, you've been staring at Brody for a quarter of an hour." Kennedy rolled his chair down the row of computers to knock against mine. I spun for a few feet before I caught the desktop and stopped myself.

Busted!

"You're not taking that Perfect Couple vote seriously, are you?" he asked. "I'll bet a lot of people decided to prank you."

"Of course I'm not taking it seriously," I said, and should

have left it there. I couldn't. "Why do you think we're so mismatched? Because he's popular and I'm not?"

"No."

"Because he's a local celebrity and I'm not?"

"No, because he broke his leg in sixth grade, trying to jump a palmetto grove in his go-cart."

"I see your point."

"Besides, *we're* the perfect couple."

Right. I smiled. And I waited for him to put his arm around me, backing up his words with a touch. But our relationship had never been very physical. I expected a caress now because that's what I imagined Brody would do in this situation. I was hopeless.

I said brightly, "If I was staring at Brody, I was zoning out." I nodded to the Times Square poster. "I get lost in that image sometimes."

Kennedy squinted at the kiss. "Why? That picture is hackneyed. You can buy it anywhere. It's on coffee mugs and shower curtains. It's as common in the dentist's office as a fake Monet or a print of dogs playing poker."

Yes, because people loved it—for a reason. I didn't voice my opinion, though. I was just relieved I'd distracted Kennedy from my lame obsession with Brody.

When Kennedy had bumped my chair, he'd stopped himself squarely in front of my computer. Now he closed my screen *without asking*. I'd saved my changes to Brody's photos, but the idea of losing my digital touch-ups made me cringe. What if Kennedy had closed my files before I saved them? I took a deep breath through my nose, calming myself, as he scrolled through the list of his own files, looking for the one he wanted. I was tense for no good reason.

I'd known Kennedy from school forever. We'd talked a little last spring when Mr. Oakley selected him as the new editor for the yearbook and I won the photographer position. Back then, I'd been sort-of dating my friend Noah Allen, which made me technically off limits. I'd viewed Kennedy as a tall guy who looked older than seventeen because of his long, blond ponytail and darker goatee, his T-shirts for punk bands and indie films I'd never heard of, and his pierced eyebrow.

Sawyer De Luca, who'd been elected Most Likely to Go to Jail, had taunted Kennedy mercilessly about the eyebrow piercing. But Sawyer taunted everyone about everything. I'd had enough trouble screwing up the courage to get my ears pierced a few years ago. I admired Kennedy's edgy bravery. I'd thought it put him out of my league.

We hadn't dated until five weeks ago, when we ran into each other at a film festival in downtown Tampa that we'd both attended alone. That's when we realized we were perfect for each other. I honestly still believed that.

I crushed on Brody only because of the Perfect Couple

title, like a sixth grader who heard a boy was interested and suddenly became interested herself. Except, as a senior, I was supposed to be above this sort of thing. Plus, Brody *wasn't* interested. Our class *thought* he should be, but Brody wasn't known for doing what he was told.

"Here it is." Kennedy opened his design for one of the Superlatives pages, with BIGGEST FLIRTS printed at the top.

"Oooh, I like it," I said, even though I didn't like it at all.

One of my jobs was to photograph all the Superlatives winners for the yearbook. The Biggest Flirts picture of my friend Tia and her boyfriend, Will, was a great shot. I would include it in my portfolio for admission to college art departments. I'd managed to capture a mixture of playfulness and shock on their faces as they stepped close together for a kiss.

Kennedy had taken away the impact by setting the photo at a thirty-degree angle.

"I have the urge to straighten it," I admitted, tilting my head. This hurt my neck.

"All the design manuals and websites suggest angling some photos for variety," he said. "Not every picture in the yearbook can be straight up and down. Think outside the box."

I nodded thoughtfully, hiding how much his words hurt. I *did* think outside the box, and all my projects were about visual design. I sewed my own dresses, picking funky materials and making sure the bodices fit just right. The trouble

I went to blew a lot of people's minds, but sewing hadn't been difficult once I'd mastered the old machine I'd inherited from Grandmom. To go with my outfit of the day, I chose from my three pairs of retro eyeglasses. The frames were worth the investment since I always wore them, ever since I got a prescription in middle school. They made me look less plain. If it hadn't been for my glasses and the way I dressed, everyone would have forgotten I was there.

As it was, my outside-the-box look and the creative photos I'd been taking for the yearbook made me memorable. That's why Kennedy had been drawn to me, just as I'd been intrigued by his eyebrow piercing and his philosophy of cinematography. At least, that's what I'd thought.

I wanted to tell him, *If this design is so great, tilt the photos of the chess club thirty degrees, not my photos of the Superlatives.* Instead I said carefully, "This layout looks a little dated. It reminds me of a yearbook from the nineties, with fake paint splatters across the pages."

"I don't think so." Turning back to the screen, he moved the cursor to *save* and communicated how deeply I'd offended him with a hard click on the mouse.

I kept smiling, but my stomach twisted. Kennedy would give me the silent treatment if I didn't find a way to defuse this fight between now and the end of journalism class. Tonight was the first football game of the season, and I'd be busy snapping shots of our team. I was the only student with a press pass that would get me onto the sidelines. Kennedy would likely be in the stands with my other sort-of ex-boyfriend, Quinn Townsend, and our friends from journalism class. They'd all be telling erudite jokes under their breath that made fun of the football team, the entire game of football, and spectator sports in general. After the game, though, Kennedy and I would both meet our friends at the Crab Lab grill. And he would act like we weren't even together.

"It's just the way the picture is tilted," I ventured. "The rest of it is cool—the background and the font."

In answer, he opened the next page, labeled MOST LIKELY TO SUCCEED. I hadn't yet taken the photo of my friend Kaye and her boyfriend, Aidan, but Kennedy already had a place for it. He selected the empty space and tilted that, too, telling me, *So there.*

"When are you going to turn in the rest of these photos?" he asked me. "The deadline to send this section to the printer is two weeks from today."

"Yeah," I said doubtfully. "It's been harder than I thought. I mean, taking the pictures isn't hard," I clarified quickly, before he reassigned some of my responsibilities. "We've had so many tests. It's tricky to get out of class. And convincing some of our classmates to show up at a scheduled time is like herding cats."

"Harper!" he exclaimed. "This is important. You've got to get organized."

I opened my lips, but nothing came out. I was stunned. I prided myself on my organizational skills. Kennedy should have seen the schedule on my laptop. My arrangements for these photo shoots were difficult but, in the end, impeccable. If the people who were supposed to pose for my pictures didn't meet me, how was that *my* fault? I couldn't drag them out of physics class by the ears.

"I need these shots on a rolling basis so I can design the pages," Kennedy said. "You can't throw them all at me on the last day. If you make us miss the deadline, the class might not get our yearbooks before graduation. Then the yearbooks would be *mailed* to us and we wouldn't get to *sign* them."

My cheeks flamed hot. What had seemed like a fun project at first had quickly turned into a burden. I'd been trying to schedule these appointments during school, around my classes. At home, I selected the best photos and touched them up on my computer. But I also had other responsibilities. I'd signed on to photograph a 5K race at the town's Labor Day festival on Monday. And of course I had to help Mom. She ran a bed and breakfast. I was required to contribute to the breakfast end of it. I didn't see how I could produce these finished pictures for Kennedy any faster.

"Is everything okay here?" Mr. Oakley had walked up behind Kennedy.

"Of course," Kennedy said. From his position, Mr. Oakley

couldn't see Kennedy narrow his eyes, warning me not to complain. Mr. Oakley had said at the beginning of school that he wanted the yearbook to run like a business, meaning we students reported to each other like employees to bosses, rather than crying to him about every minor problem. That meant Kennedy had a lot more power than a yearbook editor at a school where the advisor made the decisions.

For better or for worse.

Mr. Oakley looked straight at me. "Can you work this out yourselves?"

"Yes, sir." My voice was drowned out by the bell ending the period.

As Mr. Oakley moved away and students gathered their books, Kennedy rolled his chair closer to mine and said in my ear, "Don't raise your voice to me."

Raise my voice? *He* was the one who'd raised his voice and caught Mr. Oakley's attention.

The bell went silent.

Kennedy straightened. In his normal tone he said, "Tell Ms. Patel I'll miss most of study hall. I'm going to stay here and get a head start on the other Superlatives pages, now that I know we're in trouble."

"Okay." The argument hadn't ended like I'd wanted, but at least he didn't seem angry anymore.

I retrieved my book bag and smiled when I saw Quinn waiting for me just inside the doorway. His big grin made his dyed-black Goth hair and the metal stud jutting from his bottom lip look less threatening. Most people in school didn't know what I knew: that Quinn was a sweetheart. We wound our way through the crowded halls toward Ms. Patel's classroom.

"I overheard your talk with Kennedy," Quinn said.

"Did you see his designs?" I asked. "I understand why he'd want to angle some photos for variety *if* the pictures themselves were boring. Mine aren't."

"He'll change his mind when he sees your masterpieces," Quinn assured me. "Speaking of the Superlatives, Noah said Brody's been talking about you."

I suspected where this was going. Noah and I hadn't been as tight this school year, since I'd started dating Kennedy. In fact, if I hadn't checked his calculus homework every day in study hall, we might not have talked at all. But last spring when we'd gone out, he'd told me what great friends he and Brody were. Brody's dad had been their first football coach for the rec league in third grade. They'd played side by side ever since. Now Noah's position on the team was right guard. His responsibility was to protect Brody from getting sacked before he could throw the ball. Friends that close definitely shared their opinions of the girl one of them had been teamed with as Perfect Couple.

ABOUT THE AUTHOR

Jennifer Echols has written many romantic novels for teens and adults. She grew up in a small town on a beautiful lake in Alabama, where her high school senior class voted her Most Academic and Most Likely to Succeed. Please visit her at www.jennifer-echols.com.